A SHOT AT NORMAL

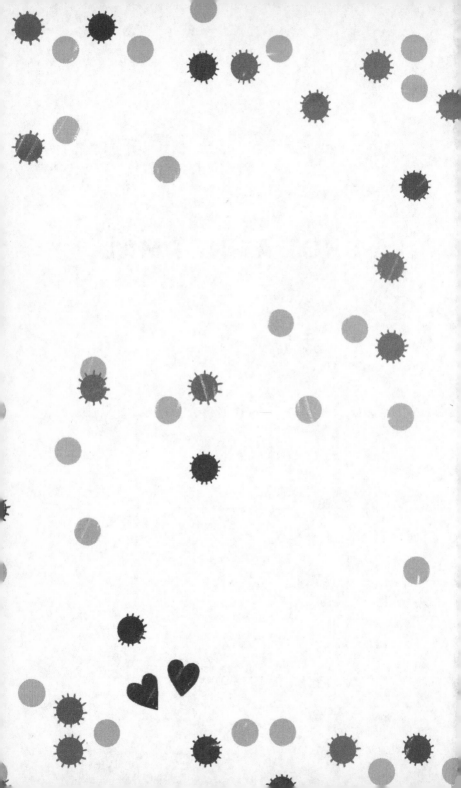

A SHOT at NORMAL

MARISA REICHARDT

Farrar Straus Giroux
New York

Farrar Straus Giroux Books for Young Readers
An imprint of Macmillan Publishing Group, LLC
120 Broadway, New York, NY 10271

Printed in the United States of America
Designed by Aurora Parlagreco
First edition, 2021
10 9 8 7 6 5 4 3 2 1

fiercereads.com

Library of Congress Cataloging-in-Publication Data
Names: Reichardt, Marisa, author.
Title: A shot at normal / Marisa Reichardt.
Description: First edition. | New York: Farrar Straus Giroux Books
    for Young Readers, 2021. | Audience: Ages 12–18. | Audience:
    Grades 10–12.
Identifiers: LCCN 2020006160 | ISBN 9780374380953 (hardcover)
Subjects: CYAC: After contracting measles with devastating
    consequences, sixteen-year-old Juniper Jade sues her anti-
    vaccination parents, hoping she can have a more normal life. |
    Anti-vaccination movement—Fiction. | Vaccination—Fiction. |
    Home schooling—Fiction. | Family life—California—Fiction. |
    California—Fiction.
Classification: LCC PZ7.1.R45 Sho 2021 | DDC [Fic]—dc23
LC record available at https://lccn.loc.gov/2020006160

Our books may be purchased in bulk for promotional, educational,
or business use. Please contact your local bookseller or the Macmillan
Corporate and Premium Sales Department at (800) 221-7945 ext. 5442
or by email at MacmillanSpecialMarkets@macmillan.com

For Kai—
May you always remain inquisitive.
May you always seek your truth.
And no matter how far you roam, may you always
know where home is.

A SHOT AT NORMAL

ONE

Poppy and Sequoia are already sitting at the kitchen table when I walk in. Books out. Pencils sharpened. Writing pads open. There are three essay prompts on the chalkboard my dad sets up on school days. One for a second grader, one for a sixth grader, and one for me. All the questions are designed to get at what we did this summer and what we learned and how we're now better people because of it.

I ignore the assignment and pull a plate from the cupboard. I pile the last two oatmeal-blueberry pancakes onto it and top them with a dollop of freshly whipped cream. The cream is unsweetened because my parents are my parents.

"A tardy on the first day isn't a good way to start off the school year, Juniper," my dad says.

"It's two minutes."

"Late is late. You should've already eaten and been

in your chair, ready to work, at eight o'clock on the dot, like your brother and sister."

Still, my dad scoots his own chair away from the table to fill his coffee cup, so I guess the rules don't apply to him. I grab a mug for myself from the rack by the sink and hold it out. His eyebrows rise. He replaces the steaming pot on the warmer. "You're sixteen. No."

"It's coffee."

"It's for adults."

"People my age practically live at Starbucks. It's their starter home."

"Addicts."

"They're drinking Frappuccinos, not shooting up heroin."

"Either way, it's a travesty."

"Then why are *you* drinking coffee?"

"I drink my coffee black. Only one cup a day." He holds his drink up proudly, takes a sip, and makes a smug *ahh* sound. "Black coffee is full of antioxidants and reduces the risk of Alzheimer's and Parkinson's diseases. Kids fill their coffee with cream and sugar and syrups and all the things that negate the benefits."

I add another dollop of whipped cream to my pancakes.

"Have orange juice," Poppy says, smiling, and all I notice is how her four front teeth look too big for her eleven-year-old face. "I made it this morning for extra credit."

"Of course you did." Only Poppy would be looking for extra credit on the first day of the Jade Family Homeschool. Kiss-up sisters are the worst. "Where's Mom?"

"Backyard," Sequoia says as he balances a pencil in the space between his upper lip and the bottom of his freckled nose.

"Farmers market day, remember?" Poppy says.

"I'd rather not."

I can't exactly wax nostalgic about the way my mom spends every Monday morning tying up just-plucked sprigs of rosemary and thyme and whatever else with twine so she can sell them in bunches along with essential oils on the parking lot by the beach. I had to stand in that parking lot every Monday afternoon this past summer, baking on the asphalt as sweat slid down my spine. The cool ocean waves would wink at me from a few feet away. *Come here*, they'd whisper as I eyed groups of people my age with more exciting lives than mine. They had surfboards and board shorts and bikinis and beach bags and would arrange their towels in a circle, like a sunburst, so they could all have their heads in the center to talk and laugh and be sixteen.

Sure, I could've gone to the beach if I wanted—my parents insist we learn more outdoors than indoors—but I couldn't exactly plop my towel down in the middle of a bunch of strangers on a California beach. We weren't friends. They didn't know me. I was new here, and the friends I would've set up towels with lived six hours away.

When we lived in NorCal, my mom and dad hung out with other parents who also taught their kids at home, and we'd do field trips together every once in a while. Museums. Aquariums. The theater. Through it all, I had Sasha. And it was a relief to be able to ditch the freak show that was a dozen homeschool kids watching Shakespeare in the Park while our parents swapped turmeric recipes. Having the same eleven p.m. curfew meant Sasha and I could hang out on weekends, too. In the daytime, we'd kayak and hike or swim at the local pool. At night, we'd go to the bookstore in town or skateboard in an empty parking lot by the beach. Our friendship was easy. Convenient. She was there. I was there. But Sasha never understood me the way I'd hoped a best friend would. For one, she actually liked being homeschooled. She didn't constantly beg to go to public school like I did. She never felt like she was missing out on something.

Since cell phones were forbidden to me for reasons ranging from cancer to tendonitis, Sasha and I resorted to snail mail to communicate after I moved away. All of April and all of May, I stalked our mailbox like the anxious wife of a World War II soldier as I awaited a letter handwritten in glitter gel pen. Unfortunately, teenagers aren't very good at keeping in touch without a cell phone, so by summer my letters from Sasha dwindled from once a week to never. I don't fault her for it. She has to live her life. But I miss knowing someone who would be brave enough to walk up to that group of strangers sprawled out on their beach towels and ask them some random question that would make us look normal and cool enough to befriend.

Now that the new school year has started and my parents have reached out to other local homeschoolers to plan field trips, I'm hoping I'll make some new friends.

Until then, I'll remain on the outside looking in.

Like this morning, in my room, where I spent from seven forty-five to eight a.m. watching through the window as bright yellow buses pulled up to the curb in front of Playa Bonita High School. The bus doors opened and students spilled onto the sidewalk. Others rode up on bikes and skateboards. The older ones, the juniors and seniors, arrived in cars crammed with passengers, two in the front seat and three in the back. Everyone wore shorts or sundresses, because it's still the last week of August and the heat of summer hasn't let go of this town yet.

I could feel that heat in my armpits and the sweat marks collecting along the edges of my tank top when I woke up. I slathered on deodorant from the half-empty mason jar on my dresser like I do every morning. It's sticky and lumpy and leaves behind a white, oily residue that stains my shirts. I've asked my mom for real deodorant. Or at least something from the natural health section at Whole Foods.

"Tapioca starch and coconut oil take care of things fine," she says. I'm sure that's not true, because if I notice the stink of my mom's BO, then surely I have it, too.

The girls at PBHS probably smell like strawberries and freedom. I bet they spent all morning soaking themselves in those scented body washes from that store at the mall that always smells like a fruit stand. I also bet my mom can recite the exact paraben levels in each bottle. Because that store, like the mall itself, is not a place my parents would ever let me spend money.

That's why those girls across the street are there and I'm here. The chemicals and the toxins and the mercury levels and the melting ozone layer made my parents take a big step back from the real world. Everything from our deodorant to our food to our cleaning products to our furniture is organic. Important things, I know. But there's such a thing as too much. My parents are rabid in their beliefs.

"Organic isn't what's new. It's what's old," my mom says proudly. "We're original."

She operates in a rose-colored version of history, which is also why my sister, my brother, and I don't get vaccinated. This makes us ineligible to enroll in schools in California. Not that I haven't tried. When we moved, I thought maybe this was finally it. The public high school was right across the street. I'd practically still be at home. I begged to go. But couple the strict California vaccination requirements with the fact that my parents think homeschooling creates lifelong learners as opposed to kids who simply regurgitate multiple-choice information for state tests, and it was easy for them to say no. "We decide what goes into our children's bodies *and* minds," they said. So here I sit at the kitchen table, digging into my putrid pancakes, trying to figure out if selling baled herbs and essential oils this summer made me a better person.

My guess is no.

To be fair, I did other things, too. There was the hike through Yosemite with a backpack that weighed as much as Poppy.

And the eight-hour train ride I took alone to visit Mimi and Bumpa—the nickname that stuck when I first tried to say the word *grandpa* as a toddler—for three whole weeks in Sacramento earlier this month. It was the first time I'd made the trip by myself, and it was so glorious that I'd do it again tomorrow if I could. But that would mean Mimi having hip surgery again, which I wouldn't want.

Mostly, I spent the summer dreaming about a boy finally kissing me, and I don't exactly want to write about that for my dad to critique and grade. So instead I eye the clock and count down the minutes from now until noon, during which time we'll cram in a full day of studies of multiple subjects in our kitchen. But once those four hours are up, the day is mine again. That's when my dad will say something corny like, "Fly away, my young birds!" and we'll all scatter, because my parents are very into the idea of free-range parenting as long as it's about where we travel in our bodies as opposed to what we put into them. This schedule also gives my dad the afternoons to finish up his freelance work from home.

Poppy rarely goes anywhere other than into the world of whatever book she's reading. And Sequoia retreats to the backyard to slay imaginary dragons, because he's seven.

But me?

I can't leave fast enough. To go wherever I want.

I ride my skateboard to the library to gorge on celebrity magazines and read *Teen Vogue* online, which is how I keep track of what's going on in the world. Or I skate to the beach and jump into the ocean.

The first bell rings across the street at eight fifteen a.m. It echoes through our too-warm kitchen, bouncing off the countertops and the rickety chalkboard of our makeshift classroom, reminding me how different here is from over there.

The classrooms across the street are probably air-conditioned.

And the students don't have their little sister and brother for classmates.

And their first-period teacher isn't their dad. With his

8

man bun and his beard and his second-wave Woodstock agenda.

There were two Woodstocks: the real one and the one my parents went to. The big festival, the one the whole world pictures when they think of Woodstock, was in 1969. It was the Summer of Love and Jimi Hendrix riffing on "The Star-Spangled Banner" and the warning not to eat the brown acid. But then there was the other Woodstock. In 1994. Where there was rain and mud and Green Day and an impromptu Slip 'N Slide. My parents went to that. My parents went to the Wannabe Woodstock. And now they insist on telling their children the best music is their music, so we know pretty much all of it.

They got married a few years after, because they were in love and had decided that as two only children they understood each other in a way nobody else ever had before. Instead of my mom taking my dad's last name and giving in to social norms, they picked out a whole new last name to share. *Jade.* Based on the simple fact that my dad proposed with a jade stone instead of a diamond.

I appreciate my mom and dad and all their quirks. I do. But sometimes I want to be like everyone else. I wish I could write about that, but my dad would get annoyed. He says I need to learn to not only appreciate what I have, but what I don't have.

Poppy and Sequoia keep their heads down, hard

at work writing about their summers, when my mom comes in. Her dirty hands hold a ratty cardboard box full of herbs. She slides it onto the counter so she can pull up the bottom of her flowy flowered shirt to dab at the sweat on her face.

"Happy first day of school," she says when we can see her mouth again.

My dad gives her a look. One that says he's in teacher mode and she's interrupting. I shrug and give my mom a different look. One that says this might not seem like real school but it supposedly is.

"How's the herbage?" I ask, and my dad gives me the same frustrated stare he gave my mom.

"Be quiet," Poppy says. "I'm concentrating."

My mom grabs the box and flicks her head of wavy dark hair streaked with gray—because she read some-where that hair dye causes cancer—toward the living room to let me know I should join her.

My dad sighs. He is very serious about our sched-ule because he needs to work, too. "She has school, Melinda."

"Oh, hush," my mom says, giving him a playful pinch on the arm.

"Seriously," Poppy says. "Hush, everyone."

I slide the final bite of my pancakes through the last peak of whipped cream, get up chewing, and follow my mom into the living room. My gaze catches on the open window, where the dingy curtains blow blissfully in the breeze. When my other grandma—my mom's mom—died and we inherited the house my mom had grown up in, my dad was able to swap his full-time copyediting job for freelance and split homeschooling duties with my mom. The corners of our house could use a more thorough cleaning, and the shelves could stand to be cleared of the outdated knickknacks, but my parents are thankful to trade in renting for a place they own outright, so they can grow food and sell herbs and teach math to their kids in the kitchen.

Through the window, across the street, the school buses have pulled away from the curb. All the students have gone inside to sit in rows and rows of desks to talk about their summers in ways that I can't. They'll scroll through their phones and make plans for Labor Day weekend, even though it's five whole days away.

"You're helping me today, right? At the market?" my mom says.

I pull my gaze away from the school to look at her. I'd helped her out in June and July. But then I went to Sacramento. And today school started. "I thought that was only a summer thing."

"No. It's a job thing."

"It's not a real job."

"It's a perfectly fine job."

She delicately untangles bunches of herbs from her cardboard box and separates them into bundles across the top of the newspaper-covered coffee table.

"It's not the kind of job I want." Ever since becoming old enough to work, I've wanted a job that teenagers do with other teenagers. Like ringing up cups of frozen yogurt covered in fructose-heavy toppings at Yogurtorium downtown. Or handing out fluffy striped towels at the pool of the fancy hotel where famous people sometimes stay. Or renting bikes and surfboards to sunburned families of tourists by the beach. "It's bad enough I can't go to real school, but can't I at least go to real work?"

"Honestly, June. Why are you always complaining?"

"Wanting a normal job with people my age isn't exactly complaining. It's having a life. Lots of teenagers work. I might actually meet people if I had a job."

"Slow down. And sit. I need you to help me bundle."

I plop onto the worn green velour cushions of the couch, grab the twine and scissors from the box, and start cutting.

TWO

The farmers market is a happy commingling of Playa Bonita's hippies and the upper crust. We've been here an hour and I'm already burning up under the hot afternoon sun, because my mom forgot the pop-up canopy for our booth. There's a sheen of sweat collecting along my hairline, and I discreetly wipe it away with the back of my hand as I make change for a customer who purchased a bundle of rosemary. The heat must be making my brain fuzzy, because it takes me three times to count out the right amount.

My mom hands me a ten from her apron when I'm done. "Do me a favor? Go grab tomatoes from the Central Farms booth for tonight's spaghetti sauce."

I scramble up quickly, untying my apron and shoving the cash into the front pocket of my shorts. As I weave my way through the crowd, I bump into strollers and push past lines of people waiting to make purchases.

The hand-painted banner of the Central Farms booth is easy to spot among the professionally printed signs of the other booths. Mary is working today. I'm glad. She gossips more than her husband, who wears his hair in a long, stringy gray ponytail and always talks about how he spent two years following the Grateful Dead around the country in the seventies, but I'll take her gossip over those concert stories any day. Mary and her husband are old-school hippies. Peasant skirts. Birkenstocks. Fringed macramé vests. No Wannabe Woodstock for them. They're the real deal. Which is probably why my mom was instantly drawn to Mary from the moment we set up shop. Thankfully, Mary was friendly, taking my mom under her wing and making sure she felt welcome.

"Juniper Jade!" Mary says. "Whatcha looking for today, sweetheart? Strawberries? Avocados?" She leans in conspiratorially. Nudges my elbow. "Something more exotic?"

"I'm always looking for something more exotic than this." I toss a look over my shoulder at the crowd. "But today I'm stuck with tomatoes. For Mom's spaghetti."

"Healthiest spaghetti in town."

"So I'm told." My mom makes her noodles out of zucchini spirals.

"Well, get to it. You know what to do."

I sort through the tomato bin, squeezing one plump fruit after the other to find the right amount of ripe while Mary handles the next customer, a woman with a baby tucked tight against her chest in a pale yellow sling with ladybugs on it.

"She's here!" Mary says, clapping her hands together and twisting her body across a bin of peaches to get a better look.

I glance over and see the baby's squishy pink face. She has a little white bow in her nonexistent hair. It looks vaguely ridiculous, and I feel bad that she's too tiny and brand-new to have a say.

The woman bends forward so Mary can peek inside the sling. "Four weeks today."

"Bless," Mary says. "And look at you out and about. Supermom!"

"It's our first adventure. My husband went back to work this week, and the cabin fever was getting to me."

I quietly bag my tomatoes so I won't disturb the schmoozing Mary's up to with this mom and her baby.

Another woman walks up. She stands out in stark contrast to the rest of the crowd because she's wearing a way-too-professional navy-blue business suit. When Mary greets her, the woman offers a strained smile, like she's physically incapable of banal niceties when she has important phone calls to make and big meetings to take. But I scrap that assessment when she heads to the bin of peaches and I see she's wearing flip-flops. A suit and flip-flops. I like her. She buys one peach, bites into it immediately, and walks away.

I swipe at my forehead. I'm still sweating in the shade.

It's collecting on my upper lip and behind my ears. I twist my hair into a knot on top of my head, but the fresh air against my neck doesn't cool me off like I want. And I don't have anything to keep my hair in place, so it falls back down immediately. I notice Mary isn't sweating like me because her stand has shade.

The woman with the baby looks at me. Smiles.

I hold up my bag of tomatoes and hand Mary my money.

"This here is Juniper Jade," Mary says, counting out my change. "You might want to take down her info if you're ever looking for a babysitter. She's got littles in her own family, and I gotta say she's a natural."

Poppy and Sequoia aren't exactly littles anymore, but whatever Mary might be able to do to help me get a normal job makes me happy, so I nod enthusiastically.

"Oh, thanks," the woman says to me. "I'm not looking quite yet. New mommy nerves and all. But how do I find you when we're ready?"

"I'm over there at the herb bundles booth every Monday."

"Oh! I love that booth."

I smile as I shove the change into my pocket. "Thanks. That's good to hear." The baby stirs, lets out a tiny whimper. "What's her name?"

"Katherine. Kat with a *K* for short. When she stretches, she looks like a kitty in the sun, so the nickname has already stuck." She smiles down at her baby. "Isn't that right?"

"She's really cute."

Kat fusses, and her whimpers grow to a full-fledged angry-faced cry in five seconds.

"Oh, shoot." The woman does that same sway my mom always did with Sequoia. He needed to be held 24/7 due to my mom's attachment-parenting philosophy. "I think I have to feed her." Her eyes dart around the market in a panic. It's a parking lot. No benches. No tables.

"There will be no hungry babies on my watch. Have a seat," Mary says, pointing to the folding chair in the shady corner of her booth.

The woman blows her bangs from her face. "Oh, thank you, Mary. I'm still getting the hang of this."

She spins around in a flustered circle, trying to juggle all her bags and untangle a screaming baby from her sling all at the same time. I jump in to help, grabbing the woman's diaper bag and a canvas sack filled with fruit as she sits down. Once she's settled, I bend down to set the bags by the chair. The baby reaches out, and before I know it, she has a tangle of my curly brown hair in her tiny fist.

"Oh no," the woman says. "Whoops!"

"It's okay." I push the baby's fingers free, but she grabs hold of my index finger in the process. She has a fierce grip for a newborn. I let her give me one last tug before I pull myself free, and she instantly shoves her fist into her mouth. "It was nice to meet you. And when you're ready for a babysitter, don't forget the herb bundle booth. Every Monday."

"Thanks. I'm sure I'll be in touch." She has sunk into the chair now, prepping herself to nurse. Her eyes fill with the relief of having a calmer baby.

"You say hi to your mom for me," Mary calls out before I'm lost to the crowd.

"Will do!"

I get back to our booth, plop the tomatoes by my mom's reusable BPA-free water bottle, and put my apron back on.

My mom looks at me. Touches my cheek with the back of her hand. "You okay? You don't look well. You're all flushed. And warm."

"It's from the sun," I say. "It's hot today."

I don't mention the tickle in my throat. I'm probably just thirsty.

THREE

When we get home at five o'clock, Sequoia barrels into me, arms spread wide for a hug, as I get out of the van my dad rigged to run on vegetable oil and named Bessie. Thankfully, my reflexes are quick and I'm able to pull the bag of tomatoes up over my head before he smashes them against my chest.

"Watch it. Jeez."

"Ew. You're all sweaty," he says, pulling away.

"It was hot and we forgot the canopy. Be thankful you got to stay here with the shade and the lemonade."

"Phew." He wipes his brow in relief as he trudges into the house in front of my mom and me.

"Where's Poppy?" my mom says.

"Out back. Science stuff."

"And Daddy?"

"He finished work early, so he's reading another mystery. *Dun dun dun.*"

Our dad taught us that. He always says, "I'm off to read a mystery. *Dun dun dun.*" And we're all supposed to laugh like we're hearing the joke for the first time.

My mom pats my brother's messy head of hair. "Well, then it looks like you get to help me make spaghetti sauce."

"Yes!" Sequoia says, pumping his fist in the air.

I let out a hacking cough, and my mom turns to look at me again. She crinkles her eyebrows tight, making her forehead crease deep in the middle, then swipes her hand across my forehead. It comes back smeared with sweat. "You're getting sick, June. Why don't you go lie down, and Poppy'll bring you some tea with honey when she's done with her project."

"Fine." I don't want to be sick, but it's probably time to admit I don't feel completely well. Maybe all I need is a nap.

In my room, I draw the shades because the bright sun is making my eyes water. The school day is over, so there's nothing left to see across the street now anyway. I flip on the ceiling fan, kick off my sandals, and flop on the bed. My room is dark without the light from the window, but the breeze of the fan chills my too-hot skin, so I burrow under the covers. When I close my eyes, I realize how much my body aches. Every inch of me feels bruised, every muscle tender. I sink into the bed, hugged by the quilt my mom made for me two

Christmases ago. I drift into the comfort of home and await fuzzy dreams.

Dreams of boys and beaches and sunshine.

Summer music.

The slap of waves . . .

I jolt awake to Poppy hovering above me like an ax murderer. She has turned on the light and made my room too bright again.

"Tea," she says, heaving up a mug so heavy it takes two hands to hold it. "With orange blossom honey from Fresh Hive."

"Thanks." I prop myself up on my pillows and reach for the mug. The first sip feels good going down my scratchy throat.

"Your eyes are red," she says.

"No kidding, Nancy Drew. I'm sick."

"No. *Red* red. Creepy red. And gooey." She shudders.

"Okay. You can go now."

"Mom said to tell you dinner's in an hour."

I start to say thanks, but my body is suddenly overcome by a coughing fit. Hot tea splashes out over the sides of my mug, leaving teardrop stains on my shirt. Poppy grabs the mug from me and sets it on the nightstand before I spill it all.

"That sounds bad," she says. "Are you possessed or something?"

"Can you go now? I just want to sleep."

It's a miracle, but Poppy finally shuts off the light and

leaves. I turn to my side, pulling my knees up and my arms in because I'm cold again.

And soggy.

A lump.

Something's not right, but I'm too exhausted to care.

FOUR

I stare at one red dot.

It glares at me in the mirror as I use the edge of the sink to hold myself up. It's Friday. I've been sick four days. My mom figured it was the flu and that it simply had to run its course. She's kept track of my fever, plied me with herbal tonics, and insisted I needed sleep and liquids. I've barely found the energy to make it from my bed to the bathroom, but I had to pee bad enough to make my way here.

The dot is on my hairline above my left eyebrow. I assume it's a pimple at first. But then I notice another one by my right ear. Two more above that. I tug down my shirt. See more at the neckline, where my collar has been hiding them.

"Mom!"

Poppy cruises past the partially shut door of the bathroom, doubles back, and pushes it open all the way.

"Whoa," she says, looking at my face.

"Where's Mom?"

"Kitchen."

"Go get her."

Poppy races down the hallway and down the stairs. I can hear the hurried thump of her feet as she goes. I'm impressed she actually listened to me. And then my mom is standing in the bathroom, looking at the same reflection in the mirror as I am.

"Does it itch?" she asks. "Or burn?"

"Maybe? I don't know."

She presses her index finger to a red spot. The skin fades to white, then springs back to red when she pulls it away.

"It's probably only a rash. You've been pretty sick." She lifts up my shirt to look at my back. "You have a few more right here." She traces along the waistband of my pajama pants where they hit my lower back.

"It looks weird."

"Maybe I can get someone to see you today." My mom hasn't found a local doctor who will take Poppy, Sequoia, and me. Many doctors refuse to see unvaccinated patients. "There's always urgent care. But right now, let's wait and see. Maybe they'll clear up on their own."

There are more spots a few hours later.

They've spread along my hairline. Around my ears. Down my face and into my shirt. They keep running and forming all the way to my feet, smearing together, turning me red.

"I've never seen anything like it," my dad says, studying my back.

"Me either," my mom says. "Do you think it's an allergic reaction?"

"I'd buy that if she hadn't been so sick. You haven't eaten anything store-bought or processed, have you, Junebug?"

I shake my head.

My mom forces me into a baking-soda bath and rubs a creamy oatmeal concoction all over me when I get out. None of it helps, and by five o'clock I'm one big red welt.

"I need to take her to see someone," my mom says. "I can treat her better if I know what it is."

"Probably a good idea," my dad says.

So an hour later, my mom and I climb into Bessie—me still wearing pajama pants and a sweatshirt because I don't have the energy to put on real clothes—and drive to an urgent care clinic by the big grocery store in town.

The parking lot is crowded, so we have to park in the back. The walk seems too far, and I have to lean on my mom for support.

"Hang in there," she says.

The waiting room is filled with a few stuffy-nosed kids and their parents, a thirtysomething woman who coughs in fits, and a twentysomething guy in a soccer uniform holding an ice pack over his knee.

My mom checks me in, hands over my insurance

card, and pays cash for the visit while I slump down in a chair with my hood pulled up over my head.

"You doing okay?" my mom asks when she sits down next to me.

All I can manage is a grunt and a shrug.

"We'll get to the bottom of it."

An elderly woman checks in after us and takes the seat on the other side of me. I recognize her as someone I've seen buying produce and flowers at the farmers market. I've noticed her because she kind of reminds me of my grandma Mimi, perfectly put together. But her look is more severe, her hair pulled back into a bun so tight it looks like it hurts. She glances my way. Flinches. Looks again. Studies me. I pull the drawstrings on my hoodie tighter to cover my face and keep the light from burning my eyes.

By the time I'm called in to see the doctor, I can barely stand. My mom and I pass through the waiting room door that leads us into a hallway lined with additional doors to five different exam rooms. A nurse takes my vitals at a station in the hallway, clucks at my high fever, then leads me to an exam room about the size of my closet. I take off my hoodie, knowing the doctor will need to be able to see my rash, but I'm glad I remembered to wear a short sleeve T-shirt underneath. When I see the doctor walk by as he heads down the hallway, I decide he should be playing a doctor on one of Mimi's soap operas instead of seeing patients here.

He's young, with slick black hair and cheekbones too sharp to be a real doctor.

When he finally comes to my exam room, he looks at me for half a second and says, "Uh-uh. No. You have the measles. Up. Out. I can't have you in here."

"What?" My mom's voice is shocked. High. "It's a rash. She couldn't have measles."

"It's the measles."

"How? Nobody gets the measles anymore."

"Not true," he says. "Has she been immunized for the measles? An MMR shot?"

"Well." She tangles the thick strap of her recycled fabric purse in her hands. "Not exactly."

"What does that mean?"

"She hasn't been vaccinated."

"For anything?"

"That's correct."

"Why? Does she have a special medical condition?"

"I don't have to explain to you why I haven't had my child vaccinated."

"Well, explain it to her," he says, tipping his clipboard at me. "Because she's the one sitting here with a case of the measles. You need to make sure you get her proper medical attention, but I'm not equipped to give it to you here."

"But, but—" My mom's flustered in a way I've never seen before.

The doctor turns to me. "You have to go. I can't have

you shedding measles in my office. I have babies with compromised immune systems coming in. Chemo patients arriving with complications. It's not safe for them."

"What are we supposed to do?" my mom shouts loud enough for the people in the waiting room to hear. "You're a medical professional! We are here for treatment. You can't refuse us service!"

"I can if it puts everyone else in my office at risk. You need to go somewhere with a more structured protocol in place. I can let the hospital ER know you're on the way."

"Let's go, Mom." I grab my hoodie. I'm so cold. I pull it over my head as the doctor keeps lecturing my mom. He's saying all kinds of things about why she didn't recognize the measles and how we've exposed everyone at this clinic. I cringe as I listen.

"You have some nerve," my mom says.

I pull on her sleeve like a three-year-old, but she wiggles free. My hands fall back to my sides and I drag my feet out of the exam room, down the hallway, and back through the waiting room. In the fog of my fevered mind, I can still hear her arguing with the doctor.

Come on, Mom.

He wants us to leave.

He thinks I should be vaccinated.

He says I'm highly contagious.

People swarm in a hazy cloud in my head. My brother. My sister. Mary at her fruit and veggie stand. Everyone I sold herbs and oils to on Monday. Was I sick then? Like contagious sick? Because I touched a lot of money that I handed back to other people. And I touched almost every tomato in Mary's bin. And now I've breathed and coughed and sneezed all over every person in this waiting room. I push through the door to the outside air. I don't know if it's the fever that makes me want to crawl out of my skin or the thought of exposing someone else to this. I keep hearing the doctor's words. *It's not safe for them.* Meaning *I'm* not safe.

A guy my dad's age, wearing a neck brace, comes to the door. He holds it open for me, thinking I'm going in. I stand there. And then I hear the nurse.

"I regret to inform all of you that you have been exposed to the measles virus," she says. "If any of you haven't been immunized or have never had the measles, I need you to let me know immediately."

The elderly woman who had been studying me earlier stands up. Points at me. "I knew it!" she shouts.

Inside, the room becomes a flurry of activity. Chatter erupts. Voices rise. Yes, people have been vaccinated, but they're wondering if they're totally immune as the nurse does her best to calm them. The man in the neck brace turns right around and walks back down the sidewalk.

I make a move to go inside again. I want to apologize. But then I don't. They already know it's me. That's bad enough.

FIVE

By ten p.m. I'm in a hospital bed with a quarantine sign on the door to my room because on top of the measles, my fever has spiked to 103.6. The doctor says I have pneumonia, a common complication of the measles, apparently. I've never had pneumonia. I heard the doctor tell my mom how serious it is. All I know is it's hard to breathe, and I legitimately might throw up from all the coughing and the mucus.

My mom is here, but my dad is home with Poppy and Sequoia. The thought of my sister and brother getting sick like this makes me feel even worse.

Guilty.

I lay on the bed like a scoop of mashed potatoes. I don't even have the energy to turn on the TV. We don't have one at home because my dad thinks TV is a "box full of garbage," so I usually gorge on anything and everything whenever I end up in a room with one. Like this past summer when Mimi and I cruised through five seasons of her favorite reality show over the three weeks I visited. Sometimes Bumpa brought us artisanal dough-nuts, which are seemingly all the rage in places that aren't my kitchen. The irony isn't lost on me that most of my knowledge of pop culture comes from my dad's sixty-nine-year-old parents. But then again, Mimi and Bumpa are nothing like my dad. For one, they think homeschooling is "hogwash." And two, they believe their son's time could be better spent moving up the cor-porate ladder in some high-rise building with a corner office. This is probably exactly why my dad is the way he is. Kids never want to be like their parents. Because they're so different, my mom and dad were wary of letting me visit Mimi and Bumpa alone, but Mimi's hip surgery meant they needed the extra help I could provide, preparing meals and walking their Maltipoo, Duke. And even though I was finally away from my par-ents, I didn't have a ton of freedom, since Mimi needed my round-the-clock help.

My mom's voice is distant and garbled as she talks to the doctor. The words are swimming. Not loud and clear like the ones Dr. Soap Opera said to her at the urgent care clinic.

"There's a reason you didn't know what the mea-sles looked like when you saw them," he told her. "It's because you grew up in a generation when parents got their kids vaccinated, because they did know. They knew the dangers. But now we have people like you, thinking your kids are protected because every other parent out there does it for you. But that's not how it works. Not everyone is protected. Not everyone can actually have the vaccine. By not vaccinating, you don't just put your own child at risk, you put people you don't even know at risk."

"Well, I'm concerned about my child and my child only," my mom said.

"Of course you are," said Dr. Soap Opera sarcastically.

The doctors and nurses at the hospital are nicer than the doctor at the urgent care clinic, even though they wear gloves and masks whenever they come into my room. Their protective gear only drives home how serious this is and how contagious I am.

They come in a lot. Taking my temperature. Checking my pulse. Listening to my lungs. And peeking at the monitors.

I try to sleep in between the visits.

The next morning, my dad shows up, and I have a new doctor with gray hair and gray eyes. He talks to my dad about all the immunizations I don't have and makes earnest pleas to try to convince him to consider getting them for my siblings and me. He throws out words, saying they can be complications from the measles. Words like encephalitis. Blindness. Deafness.

None of it matters to my dad. "I'm looking at her

getting better right in front of me. She's going to be fine. Maybe we should talk about the possible complications from vaccines instead."

"We're certainly willing to help you work through your concerns," the doctor says. "There are immunization makeup schedules."

"I'm not pumping a bunch of carcinogens into my kids' bodies. No, thank you. Aluminum. Formaldehyde. Thimerosal, better known as mercury." He ticks them off on his fingers like he's making a grocery list for the ingredients of Death Soup. "Not to mention links to autism, as I'm sure you know but don't divulge."

"First of all, the MMR vaccine doesn't actually contain thimerosal. Secondly, the autism link is a fallacy," the doctor says firmly. "And the risks of not having vaccines far outweigh the very small chance of a reaction. To be clear, the American Academy of Pediatrics recommends—"

"Don't give me your Big Pharma bullshit. All you doctors have some kind of agreement with them, I just know it. It's a conspiracy so you can all make money. I've done my research."

I get the feeling the doctor wants to shake some sense into my dad, that he wants to point at me in the bed as exhibit A, but he stays calm. My dad eventually leaves. The doctor tries all over again with my mom when she shows up with clean underwear for me.

I see a flicker in her when he mentions Poppy and Sequoia and how it's basically inevitable that they'll get sick, too. Will they get as sick as me? Sicker? What if they develop encephalitis and long-term complications?

My parents are most likely immune because they had the measles shot in the mid-1970s, but the doctor warns my mom that immunity can fade over time. There's a blood test they can do to be sure. And there's always a booster shot.

"If those shots aren't good enough for my kids, they're not good enough for me," she says, and ends it at that.

Easy for her to say when her chance of getting the measles is relatively low.

In the afternoon, someone from the Centers for Disease Control visits. She sits down with my mom and me to trace my movements, taking note of everywhere I've been over the last few weeks. She tells us the CDC is trying to figure out where I might've gotten the measles in the first place and who else I could've exposed.

"Because there are reported cases up and down the state, our best bet is that you came into contact with the virus on the train coming home from Sacramento."

"How many cases have there been?" I ask.

"We know of five so far. But it's early days. It's important we get the word out because the measles is highly contagious, which is why we need your family to self-quarantine for at least twenty-one days," she explains. "A nonimmune individual has a ninety percent chance of contracting the virus if they come into contact with it. Plus, it can live for up to two hours on surfaces and in an airspace where an infected person coughed or sneezed." She writes down a note. "We'll put out public notifications on the local news and in the newspapers, so anyone at risk will be able to determine whether or not they were in the same places as you."

"Does the whole town really have to know this?" my mom asks. "It seems like a violation of our privacy."

"It's a public safety issue, so yes. But don't worry. The name of the patient is never identified."

My mom crosses her arms. "Yeah, well, people have a way of finding out such things when they're determined. Our town isn't exactly a metropolis. It's only a matter of time before they know who we are. And what happens then?"

"We'll do everything we can to keep you anonymous. Your safety and protection are priorities for us."

My mom doesn't seem convinced.

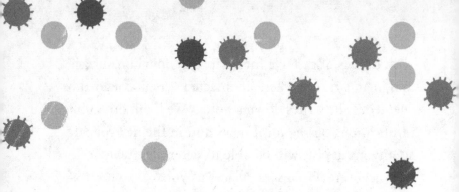

SIX

Two days later, I'm home from the hospital. Poppy comes down with a fever at dinnertime a few days later. It hits Sequoia the day after. I'm still too weak to get out of bed. I feel only slightly guilty that I can't help more. Not because I owe it to my parents, but because I know how awful my sister and brother are feeling. It's my fault they're sick. They got this from me. I'm the worst big sister ever.

My mom and dad have managed to convince themselves my siblings won't get as sick as I did, because they know what they're dealing with this time. My mom douses them in essential oils, while my dad keeps them on a steady diet of shiitake mushrooms and elderberry tea and whatever else he found in his natural healing book.

I bet that makes them feel like barfing, I want to say. *You don't know anything*. But I keep my mouth shut.

While my parents go back and forth, up and down the stairs, I try to read a novel my dad assigned for school, but the pages blur and I forget the words by the time I get to the end of each paragraph. I want a TV. Or a laptop. I bet when the kids at the high school across the street get sick, they get to eat Popsicles and watch frothy movies about people going to prom and falling in love.

Sigh.

I close my eyes to make up my own movie in my head. It's been playing on an endless loop for weeks, actually. It's about this past summer and the boy who lived next door to Mimi and Bumpa. His name was Noah, and even though I never met him officially, I felt like I knew him. He was tall and tan and graceful, with a tattoo on his arm that I'd see when he was mowing the lawn with his shirt off. I wanted to run my fingers across that tattoo, and I'd think about it when I passed him whenever I was out walking Duke. Mimi told me Noah's whole story because I asked her. He was home from his first year of college and had an internship at some financial office downtown. His job sounded like a total snoozefest, but he wore a button-down shirt and tie to go there, which I liked because I knew he had that tattoo hidden underneath it all.

I finally dredge up enough energy to go downstairs for a glass of water and settle in the living room for a change of scenery.

There's a dusty bookshelf in the corner. It's filled with

my grandparents' books. There are classics and westerns and a whole encyclopedia collection from 1989, two years before my mom graduated from high school. I'm sure she used these for research in the days before the internet. Even though I know the information will be outdated, I pull volume Ma–Me from the shelf and thumb past *Maps* and *Maui* until I land on *Measles*. There are photos of rashes and vivid descriptions of symptoms and risk factors. There are details of death. And then a lifesaving vaccine introduced in 1963.

I put that volume back. Grab volume Po–Pu. I flip to the section about polio. There are pictures of little kids in leg braces. People trapped in iron lungs that look like space-age torture devices. Death rate statistics. And then a lifesaving vaccine introduced in 1955.

I pick at my arm. At the peeling spots of red.

The measles could've killed me.

Polio still can.

I'd never thought about it before because I'd never gotten sick. But after this, if it were up to me, I'd choose the shot.

Why can't it be up to me?

I'm sixteen. I'm the one who has to live in this body for the rest of my life. Why do my parents get to decide what happens to it?

I hear Poppy calling from upstairs. "Mom!" Her voice is ragged and hoarse. "It hurts to touch my skin."

And then Sequoia: "Mom! My throat!" His words get swallowed by a coughing fit.

They sound miserable and they want my mom to comfort them, even though, when you really think about it, it's kind of her fault all her kids got sick in the first place.

SEVEN

The first two weeks of my twenty-one-day quarantine pass, and I feel better each day. Poppy and Sequoia still have at least two weeks to go. On Saturday, I venture from my room to the kitchen for breakfast, where my mom and dad sit at the table, passing sections of the newspaper back and forth. They don't read news online like everyone else. And they pat themselves on the back for supporting small businesses by subscribing to the local paper. In addition to national news, it has sports coverage of all the nearby high school teams and PTA fundraisers and monthly photos from Coffee with a Cop meetings at Java Jim's by the pier. We live in a town where nothing much happens, so you have to go to the front page for the important stuff.

I sit at the table, take a sip of my orange juice, and riffle through the newspaper sections to find the front page. As soon as I get ahold of it, my dad tries to pull it away from me. We wrestle back and forth across the table, and the thin pages almost rip in half.

My mom grips my wrist. Tries to get me to let go.

"Nothing you need to see, June," my dad says.

"Don't bubble-wrap me. I already know bad things happen in the world," I tell him.

My mom watches us, nervously biting her bottom lip. "Maybe not today," she says.

"Why? Is it going to be different tomorrow? Whatever happened, *happened*. Me not reading it won't make it go away."

I give the paper one more yank and look down at the front page, and my stomach instantly drops. The sip of orange juice I swallowed makes its way back up my throat. There, splattered in black ink, is the cover story about a local baby, six weeks old, who has died from complications from the measles. Her name was Katherine St. Pierre.

Mouth agape, I look at my parents. I turn back to the paper. Study the baby in the photo more closely. The white bow attached to her bald head. The pull quote from her mother: *I've gone back over every step I took, every doorknob I touched, every ounce of air she breathed. She was a newborn, so we were cautious about leaving the house.*

I drop the paper. My heart pummels against my rib cage. I know her.

"I killed this baby."

41

"Junebug," my dad says.

"Let's not jump to conclusions," says my mom.

"Mom, who else could it be? Seriously. That's why you didn't want me to see this."

"We didn't want to upset you." My mom grips her coffee mug. "We didn't want you to worry the same thing could happen to Poppy and Sequoia. They're recovering fine, as you can see. Same as you did."

"I wouldn't exactly call my recovery fine. I ended up in the hospital with pneumonia. You're lucky the same thing didn't happen to Poppy and Sequoia."

"But you're better now. Look at you!" It's like she's trying to convince herself. To tell herself the measles isn't much worse than the common cold. Stay home. Rest. Drink lots of fluids. You'll be fine.

But it wasn't like that for Baby Kat.

"Well, good for me. And good for Poppy and Sequoia, too. Because we all could've ended up like this baby. You do realize that, don't you? We could've died."

"It's very sad, but this baby was six weeks old," my dad says. "We don't know anything about her health. There could be circumstances that led to complications. Immunity disorders. Other things. For all we know, she got you sick, not the other way around."

"Her mother shouldn't have had a baby that new out in the first place," my mom mutters.

"Her complication was that she was six weeks old and too young to be vaccinated." I point at the photo.

"And you're talking about her like she doesn't even matter. This baby was named Katherine. Her parents called her Kat with a *K* as a nickname because she reminded them of a cat when she stretched. I met this baby. I helped her mom with her farmers market bags. That baby grabbed my hair and I touched her hand to get her to let go. I was sick then. Contagious. I gave her the measles. Not the other way around." I suck in a breath. I remember that baby's mom and how nervous she was to be outside. She wrapped her baby in a sling, kept her close to her heart, doing everything she could to protect her from people like me. She didn't deserve to get sick. "This baby was innocent. Don't I have to go turn myself in to the police or something? I should be punished."

"It's not like that," my dad says.

My mom talks on top of his words. "Maybe you're confusing her with another baby."

"I'm not confused." I pound my fist on the table. "Come on, Mom, it's the measles. People aren't walking around with it all over the place. It's rare because people are vaccinated. And that right there"—I point at the paper again—"is the reason why. Because babies like Katherine St. Pierre can't defend themselves. They're counting on people like me and Poppy and Sequoia to protect them. They're counting on parents like you and Dad to know better."

"Well"—my mom tsks—"if anyone should've known better, it's that baby's mother. She should've known you don't bring a newborn out like that. You keep infants safe and healthy by staying at home and letting them naturally build up their immunities through breastfeeding before taking them out in public."

"She just went to the farmers market. It's not like she flew across the country with her." I choke on a sob. "She was so little. She didn't deserve this," I say again.

My dad sighs like he's exhausted. "June—"

"The reality is that you guys are as dependent as the parents of newborns, because you have to rely on other people being vaccinated to keep your kids from getting sick. Except you had a choice and the parents of newborns don't have a choice. Still, you knew it was almost impossible for us to get the measles because hardly anybody makes the choice you made. Do you know how selfish that is? How privileged? What makes us so special? What makes us better than any other kid? What makes us better than Katherine St. Pierre?"

"Call it what you want, but my responsibility is to my own children, not anyone else's. I refuse to live in a police state. Every parent should have the right to make the choice that feels best for them," my dad says.

I cross my arms over my chest. "Best for them meaning the parent, not the kid. Of course, you've never asked me how I feel. Or Poppy or Sequoia."

"Poppy and Sequoia are too young. They don't know."

"How can they not know? They had the measles just like me. Because of that, we should all have a say."

"Juniper," my mom says calmly, "we understand your frustration."

"This isn't frustration. This is . . ." Tears fall down my cheeks. "A baby died! Don't you care at all?"

"Yes, we care," my mom says, her eyes misting. "It's tragic."

"I want to send flowers. I want to tell her mom I'm sorry."

"That's not a good idea," my dad says. "It's better if they don't know who you are."

"Why?"

"It's just safer for everyone," my mom says.

"Oh, now you care about safety?" I let out a sarcastic snort. "Maybe you should've worried more about safety when you chose not to vaccinate your kids. I can't believe the way you walk around here like you can survive anything with some herbs and some hippie-dippie remedy. You can't. And thinking you can makes you look stupid."

"June!" my dad yells. "That is enough."

But I will not stop.

"You know I'm right! And you can't stand that I'm right. And you know what? I would've gotten the shot if I'd had the choice. But you took that choice away from me."

My mom stands up, pushes her chair back with so much force it falls to the floor. "We're done. Go to your room."

I push my own chair back. Make it fall, too. I grab the newspaper, then stomp out of the kitchen and up the stairs. I slam my door shut and collapse on my unmade bed. I punch at the pillows.

My parents are fools.

Selfish.

Idiots.

I hate them.

Katherine St. Pierre is there on the front page, reminding me how short her time was and how she'll never get to do or be anything. She was a baby and her parents loved her, and the whole story of her life was ahead of her until she met me and I made her sick.

I curl up on my bed, clutching my pillow and sobbing into it. The sadness is a physical pain. It stabs at my chest and makes my bones ache. How do Baby Kat's parents even function in their grief? How do they wake up in the morning, face the world, and live? She was their first baby. Their only baby.

Their house must feel empty.

"I'm sorry," I whisper to Baby Kat. "I'm so sorry."

EIGHT

By Sunday, a week later, my rash has faded. My headache and congestion and fever are gone. But the empty
ache in my chest is still there. I study Katherine St.
Pierre's photo one last time, then fold up the newspaper
and shove it into my nightstand drawer. It doesn't feel
like something I can put in the recycle bin. I have to hold
on to it.

Yesterday, my mom paused, clasping my hand when
she saw the newspaper on my bed. Her eyes welled up
like mine.

"It's so sad."

"You don't seem sad."

"Well, I am. Dad, too. We're not monsters."

I pulled my hand free. "Whatever."

After a midafternoon shower, I smear clumpy homemade deodorant under my arms and look at the school
across the street. I wish I could fly out my bedroom

window, over the power lines, through the doors, and down the hallways filled with lockers tomorrow morning. I'd float, my T-shirt billowing like a hot-air balloon, until I quietly settled into a desk in a classroom full of people my age. Kitchen School has been on hold, and I don't miss my classmates. I want Poppy and Sequoia to get better, but not because I want to study with them.

I don't want to gather around the kitchen table where Sequoia will burp and Poppy will tell him he's gross and they'll argue for a full five minutes in the middle of a lesson.

When I float in across the street, nobody will even look at me. They'll sit at their desks like it's no big deal that I'm there.

Oh, her? She floats in every once in a while.

She just wants to be normal.

We let her stay.

I go to the bathroom to rinse the greasy deodorant residue from my fingers, then poke my head into Poppy's room. She's propped up in bed, her hands gripping a hardcover of *The Hunger Games* for her billionth reading. The cutouts of butterflies flutter across the headboard behind her when they catch the draft from an open window. Poppy spent a whole weekend on those butterflies when we moved in, her tongue sticking out of her mouth in concentration as she cut, folded, and painted craft paper to look like real butterflies. Then she threaded a thin wire through the paper and positioned the wire around the metal slats of her headboard, leaving a trail of butterflies across the top. She's way more artistic than I am. I'm almost jealous.

"Need anything?" I ask.

"Yeah. For this quarantine to be done."

I cross over to her bed and move her favorite sketchbook to the nightstand. When she's not reading, she's making art. "Scoot over."

She pulls *The Hunger Games* to her chest and drags herself farther into the center of the bed, leaving the cooler outer sheets for me, which I appreciate. She dogears the page, and I shudder.

"What?"

"So disrespectful to Katniss. Don't you have a bookmark?"

"Sure. Somewhere." She places her book between us, then throws her hands over her head and lets out a dramatic sigh that blows her blond bangs up from her forehead.

"What's wrong?"

"I'm bored." She says the word all long and drawn out. *Borrrrred.* "I want to go outside."

"Wanting to go outside means you're getting better."

She rolls her eyes. "I seriously can't stand this house anymore. It's like a prison."

I laugh. "Tell me about it."

"I don't mean it in the same whiny way you do."

"Hey!" I jab my elbow into her ribs.

She twists away, rubbing at the tender spot. "I'm not trying to insult you."

"You're doing a pretty good job of it for not trying."

"I'm just saying, I don't feel stuck like I want to go to school across the street and drink fancy coffee and all that stuff you're always fighting with Mom and Dad about." She eyes me warily. "I heard you and Mom talking about that baby, by the way. And how she got the measles from you. Can I see the newspaper article you kept?"

She should see it. She should know what our parents have caused. "I'll give it to you later."

"Okay." She kicks off her covers. Jiggles her legs. "I'm so antsy."

"You'll be better soon enough. See?" I hold my arm out, let her examine my healing skin. "You're only about a week behind me."

She moves her hand like a puppet mouth. "Blah blah blah."

I pull at a loose thread on the quilt my mom made her. "You really don't want any of the things I want? No fancy coffee, fine. But do you actually want Dad to be your teacher forever?"

I was around Poppy's age when I started wanting something else. When I started realizing my family was different. I played AYSO soccer to fulfill my homeschool PE credit, and one day at practice, all the girls on my team were talking and laughing about something that had happened in the cafeteria that day at lunch. When I realized I was the only one on the team who didn't know what they were talking about, I felt profoundly left out. That night at dinner, I asked my parents if I could go to real school so I could eat in the cafeteria with my soccer friends, and they laughed like it was a silly little thing I'd forget by morning. But I didn't. I never stopped wanting it. I keep waiting for Poppy to make that same shift.

"I dunno," she says. "Ask me in another few years when I'm your age. I'm sure you'll have figured out if it was worth fighting for by then."

"You're such a smart-ass. Usually more smart than ass, but not today." I push off the bed. "Need anything?"

"Mom's lemonade?"

"Glug, glug."

She giggles and it makes her cough. "Lots of ice," she manages to sputter.

I hand her a box of tissues. "Okay."

I peek in on Sequoia to see if he wants some too, but he's passed out, asleep. I pull his door shut as quietly as I can and tiptoe away.

NINE

When I get to the kitchen, I can see my parents through the window above the sink. They're underneath the pergola in the corner of our backyard. My mom is talking with her hands, which means she's trying really hard to make a point.

I put off getting Poppy's lemonade and head out to see what's going on.

"—but what if they find out?" my mom says, her tone worried. "What if they sue?"

"For god's sake, Melinda, it's not our fault."

"I doubt the mother of that baby would think June wasn't responsible if she knew."

"Excuse me, what?" I say, and my parents whirl around to look at me. "So you really do think I killed that baby. Just like I told you."

"I do not," my dad says, throwing his arms up in

exasperation. He looks at my mom. "See? Is this what you want? Really?"

My mom reaches out for my hand, eager to soothe. "June, honey, do you want to talk? Can we?"

"How can we help?" my dad says. The sun shoots through the slats of the pergola, crisscrossing us with light.

"You can't. Nobody can bring Baby Kat back."

My dad puts his hand on my shoulder to anchor me. "We've been over this. You did nothing wrong."

"Right. Maybe it's your fault, not mine. Maybe you should feel guilty. Maybe you should be crying yourself to sleep every night."

"You don't know that I'm not."

"I'd never know because you don't talk about the baby at all. You don't say anything."

He opens his mouth. Shuts it. Looks at me seriously. "It's my job as your parent to be strong for you. I understand that you hurt. I hurt, too. But if I'm breaking down over that baby every time you see me, how am I helping you? What happened is awful, but I didn't meet her. I didn't know her. I know you. I love you. Your pain is my pain, and that is my priority."

"It's selfish not to care about anyone's kids but your own. But I guess that's exactly why you can validate how you feel about vaccinations."

"That is patently false," my dad says.

My mom fidgets her fingers around each other. "Let's sit down. Please." She motions to the picnic table in the middle of the yard.

I shake my head. "No. I need to go. Now."

I'm like Poppy, my feet itching to be outside. Away. Free. I pull out from underneath my dad's anchor.

"Where do you think you're going?" he says.

My mom reaches out to me but only gets a handful of shirt. She calls my name behind me as I grab my skateboard and bolt through the back gate.

"Juniper Jade, you get back here right now!" my dad shouts.

"Russ. Let her go. Let her clear her head," my mom says. "She needs it."

I slam my board down and take off down the sidewalk, angrily pumping my leg to go faster. Too fast. I skid at the bottom of the hill at the end of our block and the deck wobbles under my feet, threatening to throw me. If I hit a pebble, it'll be game over. *Juniper Jade: survived the measles, died on a skateboard.* I slow down and continue rolling through suburbia. I'm literally shaking with frustration over my parents. I want to scream. I want to punch something. I hate that I have no say. Like no matter how much I talk, they won't listen. They think they're right and I'm wrong, and that'll never change.

I breathe steadily. Try to conjure some calm as the oxygen settles in my lungs. Tomorrow is the first day of autumn, but the warm air feels more like summer than it does in early July. Tendrils of backyard barbecue smoke creep into the sky. Over the fence. Into my nostrils. Smelling like meat fat.

I don't like it.

It reminds me of death.

I have to go.

I push away, turn the corner, and fly over the curb into the wide-open street. I pump faster, off and away, toward somewhere I can make my own choices.

TEN

I skate for at least an hour to clear my head, then arrive at the urgent care clinic at five o'clock. The sign on the door tells me they're open for another few hours. That should be enough time. I pull the bottom of my shirt up to wipe the sweat from my forehead and go to the front desk, not exactly sure what to do. My insurance card is in my mom's wallet. And I don't have any money.

The door to the hallway where the nurse took my vitals a few weeks ago is over my left shoulder, but the L-shaped check-in counter has one half in the waiting room and one half in the hallway. I can see the shut doors of exam rooms inside the hallway, which means those rooms are full and I might have to wait a while.

"I need to talk to someone," I say.

A guy looks up from his computer and pushes the clipboard on the counter toward me. "Sign-in sheet's right there."

"Can I get shots here?"

"A flu shot?"

"Shots. Plural. All of them."

He squints at me. "What do you mean? Are you traveling out of the country?"

"Nope. But I've never had any vaccinations, and I want all of them. How do I do that?" He looks at me like I'm kidding. "I'm serious."

He finally pulls away from his keyboard and really looks at me. "Are you eighteen?"

"I'm sixteen."

"Do you have a parent or guardian here with you?"

"They'll say no. I need to take care of this by myself."

He puts his elbows up on the desk. Leans forward. "No vaccinations ever? MMR? Tetanus? Chicken pox?"

"None of them."

He leans back in his chair, hands behind his head like a cradle. "Wow."

I'm a freak. An anomaly to someone in the medical field.

Coming up on the right, Juniper Jade, nocturnal and not vaccinated. Don't feed the bears. Don't vaccinate the children.

A patient and a doctor exit an exam room and walk up to the hallway counter. It's him. Dr. Soap Opera. With the cheekbones and the judgment. He's exactly who I need to talk to. I wait as he sends his patient's prescription into the pharmacy electronically and prom-ises she'll be feeling better soon.

"Hey," I say, leaning over the counter. "It's me. Do you remember?" I groan to sound sick and help his recall.

He looks up, and I can see the recognition dawn on him. "Measles?"

"Yep."

"Fully recovered?"

"I am."

"Good. What was your name again?"

"Juniper. What's yours?"

He sticks his hand out. "Dr. Villapando." We shake hands.

"Look, the measles was awful, and I never want to go through something like that again. I'm here because I want every other shot I should have. I was reading up on polio. I need that one first. Then what else? Mumps. Rubella." I count on my fingers. "I'm trying to remember them all."

He puts up his hand to stop me. "You're a minor. I wouldn't feel comfortable vaccinating you without at least one of your parents present."

"You met my mom. Do you think she's going to do that?"

"Have you tried discussing it with her?"

"I have."

He leans across the counter to check out the waiting room full of patients expecting to be seen next. Still, he motions for me to come through the door and into the hallway where he's standing. "Two minutes."

Two minutes doesn't seem like enough time for a dozen shots, but if that's how it has to be, at least it'll be over quickly. I'll close my eyes and visualize myself in the ocean to get through it.

I twist the door handle to the hallway, and a woman in the waiting room lets out an annoyed sigh as I go in before her. Whatever. I follow Dr. Soap Opera into the empty exam room the last patient was in. I prop my skateboard up against the wall, and sit on the paper-covered table with my arm out. He slides over to me on a stool with wheels on it.

"Talk to me," he says.

Damn. No shots. Only chatting. I let out a nervous laugh. It's hitting me now. Saying the words out loud to him makes this real. I'm defying my mom and dad. I'm taking care of myself.

"I think I'm smarter than my parents. I know they think they're making the best choices, but messing around with the measles is no joke."

"No, it's not."

"I did some reading," I say. "It scared me."

"Rightly so."

"I could've died."

"True. But you didn't."

"I didn't. And Poppy and Sequoia didn't." He looks at me quizzically. "My siblings."

"Ah."

"But a baby died."

He sits up straight. "What baby?"

"A baby in town. Her name was Katherine St. Pierre. I was around her when I didn't know I was contagious."

His eyebrows draw in. "Are you sure?"

"Yes." I look back at him just as seriously. "She died because of me."

"That is . . ." He shakes his head. "That's terrible." His eyes focus on mine. Soft. Sympathetic. "I'm sorry. Are you okay?"

"Not really."

He nods. "I can see how you think it's your fault, but you didn't know you were sick when you were around her."

"That's what my parents keep saying." I shift, and the paper cover on the exam table crinkles underneath my legs.

"Knowing that doesn't make it any easier, does it?"

I shake my head. A tear falls down my cheek. He scoots his stool over, grabs a box of tissues from the counter, and angles it to me so I can grab a few.

"Thanks," I mumble.

"I wish I could make it all go away. I think the hardest part about being a doctor is not being able to make everything better every time."

"I bet."

"Look"—he rubs at the stubble on his chin—"as

much as I'd like to help, you can't simply walk in here and get all your vaccinations, for a number of reasons. Parental permission being one of them. But also, I'm not even sure what the exact vaccination schedule would be, because I've never dealt with this. I'd have to do some research." He shakes his head at me, smiling. "I do admire your gumption, but can I give you a piece of advice?"

"That's why I'm here, isn't it?"

"Wait until you're eighteen. It's not that far off. And then you'll be in charge of making your own medical decisions."

I want to stomp my foot like Sequoia when he doesn't get his way, but my feet can't touch the ground when I'm sitting on this exam table. "I don't want to wait. Why should my parents be able to make choices for me when their choices could've killed me? It's irresponsible. You said it yourself."

"I get it. I really do. But they're your parents, and that's how the world and the law are going to see it. They'll say that their choice not to vaccinate you wasn't done to deliberately endanger you. That they thought they were acting in your best interest." He furrows his brow. "It's frustrating. I'm frustrated, too. I do find it irresponsible. But I'm also saying you're making a headache for yourself. You had the measles. You got better."

"That baby didn't get better."

"Please don't misunderstand me. What happened

with the baby you met is tragic and awful, but the likelihood of you, Juniper, contracting another rare disease is extremely unlikely. It's okay to wait another what? Two years?"

"One year, nine months."

"See? Not even a whole two years. I know that might seem like an eternity to you, but to an old guy like me, it's not that long."

"But it isn't only that. I want to go to a real high school. My dad homeschools us in the kitchen." I shudder just thinking about it. "If I wait until I'm eighteen, it'll be too late." I don't even get into the fact that convincing my parents to allow me to attend public school is a battle that will go way beyond my vaccinations, but fulfilling a school's vaccination requirement would be a starting point.

"You're talking outside my area of expertise now. While I'm sympathetic to your situation, I don't have any say in what school you go to, vaccines or no vaccines."

"What if I want to get a job? Do they check this stuff, too?"

"Not vaccines, necessarily. But some food service jobs could require a TB test."

"Would you want me to have parental permission for a TB test?"

He sighs. "Yes."

"How do I get around this?"

"Hire a good attorney," he snorts. He stands, and his stool glides across the floor and lands near the wall. "And for the record, I understand your concern with polio, but I'd push for a meningitis vaccination. Tetanus. Whooping cough. Honestly, those are more likely threats than polio."

"Great. That's good to know. Maybe I'll go step on a rusty nail so my parents will have to get me a tetanus shot so I don't die."

"I'd advise against that, obviously."

"I'm not going to do it. Obviously."

"Listen, I need to get to these other patients. They've been waiting. But I wish you the best of luck, Juniper." He puts his hand into the front pocket of his lab coat. "Here's my card. You can contact me if you have more questions." I take his card and study it.

"Okay."

I grab my skateboard, and it bangs against my hip as I hurry through the waiting room and out into the street.

ELEVEN

There's a Starbucks on the next block, and I go inside just to smell it. As the door whooshes shut behind me, I pat my pockets, hoping money will magically appear. It doesn't. Only Dr. Villapando's card. I left my backyard in a rush, taking nothing but my skateboard, which now dangles against the side of my leg, all awkward and dirty.

I scan the café for an empty table. Maybe I can hang out for a little while even though I'm not buying anything. I can pretend I'm here to meet someone. Like a cute boy with golden hair and an ironic T-shirt. Or maybe I can make new friends.

There's actually a group of high schoolers doing homework at a long table by the window. Their laptops and phones are out. Their books are cracked open. Sugary half-drained Frappuccinos sweat condensation into rings by their elbows. If I sat down next to them, would they look at me funny? Would they tell me they're saving the empty chair for someone better and make me leave?

I take a few steps toward the studying students until my eye catches two trays filled with tiny paper sample cups. One has thumbnail-size squares of some kind of cake, the other, a frothy drink with a dollop of whipped cream and a crisscross of caramel drizzle on top. I stroll to the counter and ask the girl with the purple hair at the register what they are.

"That's iced lemon pound cake and our Ultra Caramel Frappuccino," she says with a peppy smile. "Help yourself."

Frappuccinos and cake? It's everything my dad hates, so I scoop them up eagerly. "Thanks."

I tip the square of lemon cake into my mouth. It's too sweet and too tangy, with a chemical aftertaste. I wince and smack my tongue. Honestly, my mom's lemon cake is way better, but I take another sample anyway. I wash it down with the Frappuccino. The creamy caramel clashes with the sour of the lemon, but I swallow them together like it's the most delicious combination I've ever tasted.

The girl with the purple hair says, "Good, right? Do you want to order one?"

I shake my head no. "My dad says these are toxic." I grab another drink. Toss it back.

"Oh, um . . . okay."

"Don't worry. That won't stop me. But I'll order

when my boyfriend does. He's always running late, so if I order now I'll end up finishing before he gets here." I shrug as if to say, *Boyfriends. Aren't they annoying but also the best?*

I grab another square of cake and a drink. Purple Hair holds her index finger up as if she's going to say something—probably that there's a one-sample-per-customer limit and I need to slow my roll—but I walk away before she gets to it.

Once again I ponder sitting with the group of students at the long table. If they become my new friends, we could go to the beach and the movies and thrifting at the secondhand shops downtown with the money I make from my allowance and the farmers market. But they look too serious right now, all wrapped up in writing essays and doing math. I don't want to interrupt and annoy them like Sequoia does to me when we're studying in the kitchen, so I slide into the chair of a table in the back instead. I scan Starbucks. There's a woman in a business suit at a table by the door. She's typing away on her laptop, and I smile when she recrosses her legs and I catch a glimpse of her feet. It's the flip-flop lady from the farmers market.

One of the students from the long table glances my way. Instead of smiling and being cool, I nervously look away. My table is near the restroom, and I can hear the toilet flush through the door. Gross. A guy walks out, patting his wet hands against the front of his jeans to dry them. Gross again.

I decide to feign interest in the flyers on the corkboard above my head while I wait for my fake boyfriend. They're mostly local ads for fundraisers and lost pets fringed with tear-off phone numbers along the bottom.

But then another flyer catches my eye.

Candlelight Vigil at the Pier for Katherine St. Pierre

There's a picture of Baby Kat in the center of the page. The same photo from the newspaper. That bow in her hair. The date for the vigil is tonight at seven o'clock.

I glance over my shoulder at everyone here. Nobody's looking at me. Not even that student who made eye contact with me before. Nobody knows anything. But even though my photo is nowhere on that flyer, the idea of it might as well be a police sketch of me. A spotlight shining. *This is the girl who gave that baby the measles.* Are these flyers up all over town? I want to make them disappear. *I* want to disappear. Every time I turn around, I'm reminded, and the ache in my chest hurts all over again.

Please join us for a community gathering
to honor Katherine St. Pierre. Rev. Charles from
St. Mary's By-the-Sea will lead attendees in prayer.
Candles will be provided.

I rip the flyer down with so much force that the thumbtack holding it in place rockets toward me. I scramble across the floor and pick the pin up before someone steps on it. Because what if they're like me and they've never had a tetanus shot? After I push the tack back into the corkboard, I fold the flyer into fourths and shove it in my pocket along with Dr. Villapando's card. Then I stand up and grab my skateboard.

My parents will be worried. It's getting dark. If they'd let me have a phone like a normal person, I could text them. I could tell them how I have to go to the pier. I don't know why. I don't know if it's that I need to pay respects or apologize or tell someone who I am.

But I have to go to that vigil.

TWELVE

I stayed in Starbucks long enough for the smell of coffee to cling to my sweatshirt and my hair. The salty ocean air by the beach doesn't do anything to tame the scent as the wind whips around me.

I hop off my board and study the crowd gathered around a small pop-up stage at the mouth of the pier. It's the same stage the mayor stood on to sing the national anthem before the Fourth of July fireworks. The same stage local first responders stood on in May, a month after we moved here, to talk about earthquake safety. It's a stage made up of about six planks that snap together, small enough to set up and disassemble easily.

There are mostly grown-ups here. Or parents with little kids. A few elderly folks. Nobody seems to be my age. And I worry that makes me stand out more.

A little girl in a blue dress offers me a gap-toothed smile and an unlit candle, with a doily attached at the base, from the handful she's carrying like a bouquet of flowers. I take it, not sure what to do, since I don't have anything to light it with and neither does she.

As I wander closer to the stage, I notice people are quietly tipping their lit candles to the wick of the person standing next to them. And so on. I take my place in a row near the back and wait for the flame to get to me.

Did everyone here know Katherine St. Pierre? Has an overwhelming hurt taken over their guts and their bones? Or is that only me? I tuck myself in. Hide in the crowd. The sun has set. A late September harvest moon is out. It's big and bold and bright orange, like it's meant to glow for Baby Kat along with all these candles.

Eventually, as my candlelight flickers, a woman in a clergy robe stands up to talk. She says things into a microphone about how a parent's heart knows love instantly, and that even though Katherine St. Pierre wasn't here for long, the pain of her loss is undeniably enormous. She calls on the community at this time. To ask us to love and support not only the St. Pierre family, but anyone around us who might be hurting. She encourages us to reach out to our neighbors and friends. And then there's a prayer. And some songs sung by a kindergarten class from Playa Bonita Elementary School.

They open the mic to anyone who wants to come up and say something, and a few people step forward.

There's not a lot to say. Katherine St. Pierre was only six weeks old. Nobody can talk about her favorite songs or the things she liked to do. If she was good at soccer or ice-skating or drawing pictures. Only her family can say how much they miss her. How empty their house must feel. How they probably keep the door to her room closed because of the reminders.

I imagine that. Coming home to a house with a room and a crib and a baby blanket and a stroller. It has to make the loss even worse. To see the signs of her everywhere, even though she's gone.

The woman next to me keeps sniffling and holding tight to her son, who has tangled himself around her leg. He's little and only comes up to the top of her hip, making him younger than Sequoia but old enough to be singing with those kids onstage. I take a couple of steps away. Like I should give this mom and her kid distance from someone like me. What would she do if she knew who I was and what I did?

What would this whole crowd do?

Mob mentality.

My dad had me write a paper about it last year. I didn't entirely understand the point at the time, but I do right now. I attempted to dissect Shirley Jackson's "The Lottery" and how an entire town went along with the ritual of stoning a woman to death for no other reason than the fact that everyone else was doing it. It was what they'd always done because it was what they'd always known.

What if that happens now?

What if someone from the hospital is here? Recognizes me? Calls me out? What if someone read the notification the CDC representative from the hospital said she was going to put in the newspaper and figured out who I am? What if I'm pushed to the ground? Kicked and trampled? Destroyed?

Maybe that's what I deserve.

Because this town seems like it was better off before I got here.

I grab my board and roll away from the crowd to hover on the outskirts, mapping out an escape route in case someone figures out who I am.

A stern voice booms behind me. "Hey! You!"

I turn. Freeze. A police officer and his flashlight are in my face. His name tag says ALVAREZ. I'm pretty sure I start shaking. My upper lip trembles. Why did I come here? Was I secretly hoping I'd be caught?

"Do you have a helmet?" he says. "Anyone under eighteen is required by law to wear a helmet while biking or skateboarding in Playa Bonita."

I shake my head. How do I tell him I took off in a fit of fury, leaving my annoying parents in my dust? I barely had time to grab my board, let alone a helmet. "It's at home. I left in a hurry. I guess I forgot."

"Technically, there's a ticket and a fine for that."

"How much?"

"Presumably enough to make you not forget your helmet again." He turns off his flashlight. "I'll let you off with a warning tonight. Considering you came down for a good cause."

"I appreciate that. Thanks."

I wobble on my board. Realize I should get off it altogether. I disembark and let it dangle from my fingertips as my other hand grips my melting candle, the wax dripping onto the doily.

He looks at the checkerboard Vans on my feet. Assesses. "You haven't been drinking or anything, have you?"

"Just Frappuccinos. Well, samples of Frappuccinos."

He smiles and pats his stomach. "They're pretty good, aren't they?"

"Yeah, they are."

My voice quivers.

The pain in me breaks.

Because sometimes, someone says something so simple, at just the right moment, and it makes all of you want to open up. I'm pretty sure that's exactly why I imagine myself sitting down on my board and spilling my guts. But I'm also done with this night.

I want to leave.

I tighten my grip on my board.

Blow out my candle.

"Will you be able to get home okay?" he asks.

"Yep."

He taps his head. "Next time, a helmet."

"Uh-huh."

THIRTEEN

I stand in front of my house and stare at the orange-yellow glow of the living room lamps lighting up the downstairs windows and the stained-glass cutout at the top of our front door. It's cozy. Warm. Safe.

Home.

Even after what happened before I bolted through the back gate and skated to the urgent care clinic.

Inside, my dad is probably sitting in his comfy chair, reading a mystery. *Dun dun dun*. And my mom is checking on Poppy and Sequoia or writing in her dream journal. My family. So familiar in their funky ways. It's funny how I can feel two things at the same time. That I can love them but not like them right now.

I brace myself and go inside.

"June!" My mom hangs up the phone in the middle of a conversation—probably with the missing persons department at the police station. She rushes to me. Draws me up in a hug.

But my dad is mad. I can see it in the creases on his forehead. "Where have you been?" he says. "We were worried sick. It's one thing to take off in a huff to clear your head. It's another thing to disappear for hours. You left without a flashlight or money or a helmet."

"Believe me, I know. The police weren't happy about it, either."

"The police!" my mom shouts. "What are you talking about?"

"I got stopped by a cop for not having a helmet."

"Oh, that's great," my dad mutters.

"Don't worry. He let me go with a warning."

"Well, good for you." My dad yanks the band loose from his man bun and refastens it. A nervous habit. "This is unacceptable, June. We're still getting settled here. It's not like before, where you knew everyone in town. You can't go traipsing all over Playa Bonita with no thought to the fact that your parents are at home worrying about where you are and who you're with."

"Ha! Right. Who would I be with? You just said it yourself: Everyone I know is six hours away from here. I don't even have a phone to keep in touch with them. I go to school in our kitchen instead of across the street. I have zero social life."

My dad talks right over that complaint. "It's Sunday night. You know Sunday night is family night."

"Poppy and Sequoia are sick in bed. What would we be doing for family night? Taking each other's temperatures?"

"Where did you go?" my mom asks.

I consider lying but settle on the truth. "I went to the vigil at the pier. The one for the baby who died."

"Oh, June! Why would you do that to yourself?"

I toe the frayed edge of the throw rug. The one my grandma once told me my mom learned to walk on. "I needed to be there."

"You did not," my dad says.

"It doesn't seem like the best idea," says my mom.

I remember the candles and the people and the songs and the prayers. I also remember the guilt and the sadness. "I'm glad I went. It helped me figure out some stuff."

"What stuff?" My dad spits out the words like they taste bad in his mouth. Also? I'm sure he wants me to use more sophisticated vocabulary than *stuff*.

"I decided something tonight, and I think it's important you know it, too."

"Go ahead," my mom says.

"I want to be vaccinated. Any shot I haven't had, I want to have it. Meningitis. Tetanus. Whooping cough. Whatever I need."

"Your mother and I chose not to have you kids vaccinated," my dad says. "That's the end of the story."

"But what if my choice for my body is different than yours?"

"I'd say you're sixteen and don't get to decide."

"That's bullshit and you know it."

"Language," says my mom.

"The consequences of vaccines are SIDS, seizures, autism, paralysis—" my dad goes on.

"The consequence of no vaccinations is death!" I shout. "And autism has been totally disproven. Are you even aware of a thing called science?"

"Science can be wrong." My dad paces the worn hardwood floor like he's giving me a kitchen school lecture. I'm waiting for him to roll out his chalkboard. "Research backfires. Look at the drug recalls happening all the time. Something that's supposed to help you not have a heart attack ends up giving you cancer. There was a drug in the sixties called thalidomide that was supposed to help pregnant women not have morning sickness, and guess what? It ended up causing birth defects. Babies were born with malformed limbs." He angles a hard stare at me. "Something might look good on paper or in the lab, and then ten, twenty years down the line, lo and behold, science was wrong. Nothing is guaranteed, and the only way your mother and I have to protect you is not to put any of it into your body in the first place."

"And there's no guarantee that not putting something into my body will protect me, either." I fold my fists at my sides. Bang them against my legs. "I got the measles because of your choices."

"And I still firmly believe that was the healthier option," my dad says.

"June." My mom reaches for me, but I flinch away. "The choices Dad and I have made for you and Poppy and Sequoia are because we want you to see things differently. We want you to think outside the box. There are too many sheep, doing whatever their neighbors and their friends do without thinking. The world and the choices in it aren't so black and white. We want you to grow up to be a free thinker."

"News flash: I won't get to grow up to do anything if I die from polio at sixteen."

My dad glares at me. "That's some extreme hyperbole."

"How can you say that when a six-week-old baby died from the measles? When I ended up in the hospital because of it?"

He shakes his head, and some strands of hair come loose from his hair tie. "You are not a six-week-old baby. You are a healthy, strong sixteen-year-old girl. And the fact that you're standing here right now is proof you didn't need the measles shot. You're better off having contracted the virus and created natural immunities. You'll come to see that eventually. This is a lesson from the world, and the world is your classroom. Listen to it."

"The world?" I throw my hands up in the air. "Please.

The kitchen is my classroom. That's the whole problem. It's boring, and nothing happens there besides scrambled eggs and dirty dishes."

"Oh, don't pull that. You spend plenty of time outside. Hiking. Surfing. You know your mother and I encourage it."

"But I want to meet people. And do real school things like joining clubs and going to football games and the prom. I can't do that by going to school in our kitchen with my sister and brother. Don't you get it?"

"Nobody is stopping you from making friends. Have at it." My dad riffles through a pile of papers on the table. "We just got a brochure yesterday." He tosses it to me. "Take an art class. Volunteer for a beach cleanup."

I crumple the brochure in my hand. "Teenagers don't go to beach cleanups to meet people. They make friends at school. If I get my vaccinations, I can go to Playa across the street."

"Juniper," my dad huffs, "even if you could attend the school across the street without vaccinations, we wouldn't let you go. That is not how we've chosen to educate you and your siblings. And since you're a minor who would need parental permission to enroll, that's how it's going to stay."

"So I'll never have a social life."

"We'll be starting field trips again soon. You'll meet other homeschool kids," my mom tries. "And honestly, June, every one of those things you mentioned about high school is entirely overrated. I went to a traditional high school, and all I got was four years of bullying and a nervous tic."

"Well, Mom, I'm not you. I'm me. And I don't really care about your tragic teenage years right now."

She sinks dramatically to the couch. Shakes her head at my dad. "I don't know what to say here."

"I do," my dad says, pointing at me. "You will be homeschooled and that's that. Vaccines are not an option in this family. You are receiving a perfectly fine education, not to mention the kind of practical guidance that will prepare you for the real world."

"Are you even listening to yourself? You want to prepare me for the real world. You tell me to think outside the box. To stand up for myself and my beliefs. But when I tell you I believe something different than you do, you can't handle it. You don't want me to be my own person with my own ideas. You want me to be just like you."

"June," my mom says in her sad, defeated way.

"I have a question. If I stepped on a rusty nail, say it was lodged so deeply into my foot that you had to take me to the ER, just like you had to do when I had the measles, and a doctor there said I needed a tetanus shot, what would you do? Would you say no thanks, we'll rub some of our sham essential oils on it and hope for the best?"

My mom laughs sarcastically. "I don't know where you think you're going to step on a rusty nail."

I hold up my hand. "Wait. That's what you got from what I said?"

My mom rubs her temples, trying to stave off a stress headache.

My dad sputters, "For one, we'd have to hear a darn compelling argument to be willing to inject you with anything."

I stand up straight. Square my shoulders. Look him in the eye. "You love your convictions more than you love me."

"That's not true," my mom says.

"Are you sure about that?" I look at her hard. "Because it doesn't feel like it. Maybe you need to think about it."

"I don't need to think about any such thing. All the choices we've made are because you are our top priority."

"Whatever. I'm going to bed."

"Good," my dad says. "Because this discussion is over. I'm tired of fighting with you about this. It ends right here, right now."

I pound my way up the stairs, not even caring if my heavy footsteps wake Poppy and Sequoia.

In my room, I take out a piece of paper and draw a line down the middle of it. On one side, I write down the alleged cons of vaccines, according to my parents: *autism, paralysis, allergic reaction, Big Pharma, government scam.*

I write the pros: *NOT DYING. NOT CAUSING OTHERS TO DIE.*

I underline that sentence. Add exclamation points, pressing the pen so hard it makes holes in the paper. I crumple the list in frustration. Toss it across the room.

My dad said we'll never discuss this again. I'll obviously have to figure out a way to do this on my own. Dr. Villapando told me to get a good attorney. He wasn't serious. But I am.

I'm going to sue my parents.

FOURTEEN

It's my first Monday back at the farmers market, and it's weird to be here. I already feel like I'm keeping a secret everywhere I go, but it especially feels like that here. In this place. Where I had contact with Baby Kat.

I made sure we brought the pop-up canopy today. I work on opening it as my mom organizes sprigs of herbs tied in twine and essential oils along our folding table.

Mary strolls by with a bin of apples in her arms, backtracking when she sees me. "Juniper Jade, where have you been, sunshine? This place hasn't felt the same without your smile."

"I was sick," I say. My mom ruffles my hair like I'm a two-year-old and the blowup fight in our living room didn't happen last night. "Poppy and Sequoia, too."

"Oh, my. It must've been bad for you to be out for so long. What did you have?"

I open my mouth to talk, but my mom cuts me off so hard with an arm across my chest that she practically knocks the wind out of me.

"It just seems to be one thing after another when you have three kids," my mom says.

"Ah, yes. I remember those days." Mary pulls her apple bin closer and takes a step away from us. "We all saw a CDC notification in the paper about a person who had the measles being at the farmers market. I hope it wasn't that. Ten confirmed cases in California is the last I heard. And of course we all know about that baby who died."

My eyes dart to my mom and back to Mary, who's studying me intently.

"It wasn't the measles," my mom states firmly. "We're all fine and back at school."

"In the kitchen," I say.

"Well, that's good."

"It certainly is," my mom says.

Mary smiles at my mom. "Welp. Here's to good sales today."

My mom gives her a thumbs-up. "Back atcha, Mary."

I turn my back to my mom and roll my eyes as I tie my apron around my waist. *Melinda Jade: Queen of Overkill.*

Once Mary is out of earshot, my mom hisses at me, "That woman is the biggest gossip in town. Don't you dare tell her a thing. Nobody needs to know you had the measles. Keep it to yourself."

I clutch bottles of essential oils in my hands, wanting to grip them tight enough to shatter them. The crowds are smaller today. Maybe because summer is over and nobody wanders in from the beach for snacks and fresh fruit. Our stand is never as busy as the others, but today, we hardly sell anything.

At one point, I notice Mary huddled up with another woman. My heart skitters because I recognize her. First from here and then from the urgent care clinic. The severe bun. The perfectly put-together outfit. The woman who reminds me of Mimi. Mary pulls in two young moms pushing babies in strollers. They lean into the elderly woman's hushed whispers. Their eyes follow her finger pointing at me. Land. Judge. They pull their strollers closer, trying to create distance. Then one of them snaps a photo of my mom and me with her phone.

Why is she taking a picture?

My gaze jerks away from them when the woman with the business suit and the flip-flops stops at our stand. "Do you have mint?"

"We do," I say, staring at her shoes. I want to ask her why she wears them. Does she actually get away with it at the office? Does she have an office? Or does she always work from a table at Starbucks? Instead of asking her any of those things, I untangle sprigs of mint from each other. "How many would you like?"

"One is plenty. I like it for my tea."

She pays me, and I shove the money into the front pocket of my apron. "Thanks for stopping by. It's been a little slow today."

"Yes, well, things always seem to slow down once summer has ended," she says.

"I guess." I stop myself from saying more. "Enjoy your mint. And tea."

She holds the bundle up in the air as if to say *cheers*. "I will."

When we're packing up a few hours later, that same elderly woman with the severe bun passes our stand.

She glares at my mom and me.

I square my shoulders. Stare back.

"I know who you are." She says it like a threat. And it sends a chill straight to my bones.

FIFTEEN

The next afternoon, long after I've spent the morning diligently listening to a Kitchen School lecture on chemical compounds, and the buses filled with students have pulled away from the high school across the street, I interrupt my dad from his copyediting to tell him I'm going to the library to do some research.

"Very well," he says.

One thing he will admit is that this house lacks the necessary resources for proper research. Case in point, my grandma's 1989 encyclopedia collection. On top of that, we have one computer for the whole family, including my dad's work, and one tablet. A tablet Sequoia is currently glommed onto, doing a math tutorial, which is the closest he'll ever get to playing a video game. So I really do need to go to the library, but it's not my fault if my dad assumes today's trip is for the English paper he assigned instead of figuring out how to sue him.

Our house is only a block from town, but there's the smell of storm in the air, so I pull up my hoodie and hurry down the sidewalk, trying to beat it. Playa Bonita is small, and the postage-stamp-size library in the middle of downtown reflects it. The orange carpets are old and well-worn, as if they haven't been replaced since the seventies, and there's a constant musty scent that emanates from the pages of the books lined up along the metal shelves. When I push through the front door, my ears are assaulted by energetic singing and the annoying clang of a tambourine from Preschool Story Time in the back corner, where toddlers bounce on their stubby legs, attempting to dance, and moms and nannies alternate between clapping along and snapping photos with their phones.

I usually head straight to the young adult fiction section and tuck myself into one of the overstuffed beanbag chairs. But today I need the computer lab, which is a glass-enclosed room housing twelve Apple computers and two printers. I have to check in with the attendant first. The last few times I was here, an elderly woman wearing a Christmas vest in the summer was working. But today, there's someone new—a lanky teenage guy with floppy curly hair wearing a Playa Bonita High School T-shirt. His backpack sits at his feet, the seams busting open from too much academia, as he thumbs through a copy of *The Crucible*.

I like *The Crucible*.

I like boys who read.

I like floppy hair.

My dad told me to go out and meet people in an art class. How about a person right here at the library?

"That's a good one," I say, pointing to his book. I hear the nervous quiver in my voice, but I hope he doesn't. "I read it, too." I roll my eyes at myself. "Obviously. I mean, I wouldn't say something was good if I hadn't read it."

"I believe you." He focuses his big brown eyes on mine and smiles. My knees go floppy like his hair. "It's kinda brutal, though, don't you think?"

"Oh, definitely. Mob mentality." I stop myself from pulling up a chair and telling him all about the paper I wrote for my dad. "Brutal stuff for sure."

"Scary stuff." He shudders. "People are scary."

Not being vaccinated is scary. I remember why I'm here. "I need a computer."

"Take your pick." He waves his hand at the bay of computers and accidentally smacks the wall. His clumsiness is comforting, and I try to decide how I'd describe him to someone: *lanky and slightly awkward but comfortable in his own skin.* "It'll cost you one library card, though."

"Why? Do people actually try to steal computers?"

He twists his mouth into an amused smile. "You know, I'm not really sure. It's kind of a weird rule, now that I think about it."

"Stealing a computer from the library definitely seems like too much work. Heavy. Awkward. That dangly cord." I twirl my finger in a curlicue, then fish my card out from the front pocket of my backpack and hand it over.

He studies it. "Juniper, huh?"

"That's me."

"Cool name."

"Not really."

"I get it." He points to himself. "I'm Nico. People seem to like my name okay, but I don't."

"I like it better than Juniper."

"That's something, I guess." He grins and his brown eyes light up. "I think my parents tried too hard to name me something cool, and there's no way I can live up to it."

"It's funny how names say more about the person who picked them than the person with the actual name."

"Huh." He nods and his hair flops. "I never thought of it like that."

I shrug. "Maybe I've thought about it too much."

"Doesn't seem possible to think too much."

"If you say so." I shove my hands into my pockets and look around the room. "So . . . computer."

"Right. Which one do you want?"

There's only one other person in the lab right now—a middle-aged woman with a website pulled up on Beanie Babies. She scans the stuffed animals, stopping every few seconds to scrawl a note onto the yellow legal pad next to her.

I point to the computer as far away from her as possible. "That one, I guess."

"Lucky number seven," Nico says as he places my library card into the corresponding pocket of a numbered plastic cardholder hanging from the wall.

"There's no such thing as a lucky number."

"Then how do you explain the lottery?"

"Math."

"What about people who win the lottery twice?"

"Still math. Did you know there was a lottery in Bulgaria where the same six winning numbers were drawn within four days of each other?"

"Really? That sounds rigged."

"Not rigged. Look up *The Improbability Principle* sometime. All that stuff you think is rare actually isn't. Coincidences happen all the time, but people chalk it up to luck."

"Huh." He scratches his head. "That's no fun."

"Reality rarely is."

"Truth."

"Sorry to bum you out."

He smiles. "You didn't."

"Okay. Good."

He pulls his book back up to his face as I take a seat at my assigned computer and open Google. After some trial-and-error searches for my rights to be vaccinated, I stumble across some information about custody battles, where one divorced parent wants to vaccinate a child and the other one doesn't, but I can't find anything for a teenager who has never been vaccinated for polio trying to do so.

I do learn that if I want the HPV vaccine or mental health treatment or STD testing, I can do that without parental consent. In California, I can have an abortion without telling my parents. It makes no sense to me how I can get medical treatment for those things but not a meningitis shot.

Maybe doctors have never had to deal with someone like me.

Maybe I have to be the first.

Maybe I have to lead the way.

I find some pages on the pros (and alleged cons) of vaccines. I want to study them more closely, so I print them out for ten cents a copy to read later. Now I'm free to spend the rest of my time here in one of those comfy beanbag chairs with a good book.

"Thanks for not stealing a computer," Nico says as he hands my library card back to me. "I don't run very fast."

"Neither do I."

I spend the next hour gorging on a story about a girl fighting off metaphorical monsters the summer before college, but I eventually get a crick in my neck, so I decide to check the book out from the librarian and finish it at home along with my vaccination reading. When I get outside, the ground is wet from what was probably a five-minute downpour, and I see Nico unlocking a bright green ten-speed from the bike rack next to the book return box.

"Hey, Juniper with the cool name," he says as I pass.

"Oh." I shift from one foot to the other. "Hi."

He walks up next to me. Instead of sitting on his bike, he stands to the side of it, with one foot on the pedal, while we wait for the traffic signal to say WALK. He looks over at me and smiles, and I can't help but smile back, because he has a good smile. And good teeth. Like someone who had braces.

"So your shift is over?"

"Yep. Done for the day."

"Do you like working at the library?"

He shrugs. "It's okay. It's a job. Plus, I get holidays off. Well, except Halloween."

"Maybe one day Halloween will be the national holiday it deserves to be," I say, and Nico nods enthusiastically.

"It's a pretty good one."

"Yeah, it's a pretty good one." I sigh. "On another note, I want to get a job. The library seems like a cool job. The books are the best part, but I guess you don't really have a lot to do with them."

"Yeah. They stuck me in the computer lab because I can troubleshoot and reload the printer ink. It's a whole thing. But I'm allowed to read as much as I want while I'm there."

"That's pretty cool."

"It'll be good in the summer. But so far, I've only been reading books for school."

"I'm guessing you go to Playa Bonita?" I gesture at his shirt.

"Yeah. Do you? I haven't seen you there."

"I go to school in my kitchen. Homeschool. Our mascot is basically a vacuum cleaner."

He laughs, and I like the sound of it. Rich and real. Straight from his belly. "I've never met someone who's homeschooled. It seems like a sweet deal. More freedom and stuff."

"I hate it."

"Like you hate your name?"

"My parents are obviously the worst."

"That sucks."

The light changes, and instead of pedaling away on his bike, he hops off the single pedal he's been standing on and steps into the crosswalk to walk next to me.

"Do you live this way?" I ask, wondering if he's a neighbor I haven't met yet.

"Nah. I have a film club meeting at school at six."

I glance at my watch. "I think you're going to be late. It's six oh seven."

"I'll be fashionably late," he says. "Are you this way?"

"I'm across the street from the school, actually."

"Do you like movies?"

"I love movies. Not that I've watched a ton of them."

"Wanna go to this film club meeting with me? We're screening *Stand by Me* as part of our Stephen King series."

"Is this the part where I tell you I've never seen it?"

"That's the whole point."

I laugh. "Right."

"So do you want to come be a film geek with me?"

I glance down the street at my house. My mom is fiddling with the planter boxes underneath the front window. Her back is to me.

"Let me just . . . I'm going to go ask my mom. Wait here. Okay?"

"Um, okay. But I can come with if you want. I'm not weird about meeting parents."

"No. It's better if I go by myself."

"Okay."

I rush up to the house, while Nico stands on the sidewalk, holding up his bike with one hand on the seat.

"Mom," I call out as I hustle toward her.

She turns around, dirt stains all over her gardening gloves. "Goodness, Juniper, where's the fire?"

"Sorry. I'm in a hurry, that's all. I was at the library and I met these other kids working on the same book as me for English." I can't tell her I want to go watch a movie. She'll have to know the name of it so she can look up the plot and parental rating, which will take forever. "They're having a study group at the school tonight, and I was wondering if I can go."

She swipes her wrist across her forehead, leaving a smudge of dirt behind. "That's quite a coincidence."

"I know, right? I didn't even have to go to a beach cleanup to meet people."

"Humph. You'll just be at the school? Right across the street?"

"Yep."

"For how long?"

"A couple hours."

She pulls down the top of her glove to look at her watch. "That should give you until a little bit after eight o'clock. Seems reasonable."

"Thanks, Mom." I want to hug her for not making a big deal out of it.

"Mm-hmm." She glances down the street toward Nico. "Is that boy the only one in the study group? Where's everyone else?"

"They're already there. Nico stayed with me so I'd know where to go."

"He could've at least come over to meet me."

"He wanted to. I told him it was okay if he didn't."

"It would've been more okay if he did. Remember that next time."

"I will," I say over my shoulder as I open the door. I drop my library book on the table in the living room and grab the book I'm reading for Kitchen School. And then I hurry back down the street to Nico before my mom tries to shove homemade oat-and-flaxseed bars in my hands so I can share them with the other kids to clean their digestive tracts.

Nico raises his eyebrows. "Well?"

"I can go."

"Yeah?"

I laugh. "Yeah."

"Cool," he says, grinning a grin that makes my insides flip.

So cool.

SIXTEEN

By the time we get to the classroom, the movie has
already started. The lights are off and I trip over my own
feet trying to find a place to sit in the dark. Nico sets his
backpack by the door and reaches his hand toward mine.
I let him guide me through the maze of wayward desks
and the legs of students sprawled out across the floor.

I've never held a boy's hand before. But this isn't
like holding hands for real, so I should just calm down.
Anyway. I like the feel of it. Nico's grip is firm but not
forceful. Confident. Nice. And when he seems to give
my fingers a light squeeze, I try not to dissolve into a
fizzy puddle. I barely notice when he grabs a pizza box
from a nearby desk.

He finds us a place to sit on the floor. Somewhere we
can rest our backs against the wall. We're in our own
space, away from everyone else. He sets the pizza down

between us, opens the lid, and shines the light from his phone screen.

"Sausage and pepperoni," he whispers. "Hope you're not a vegetarian."

I whisper back, "At home we usually make pizza with cauliflower crust and pile veggies on top."

"I can get something different."

He closes the lid and pushes off the wall to stand up, but I stop him by putting my arm across him like my mom does to me when she suddenly has to slam on the brakes in Bessie. "No, it's okay. I'm not at home."

"You sure?"

"One hundred percent."

"Well, then dig in," he whispers.

I can hear my dad's lecture about processed meats in the back of my mind. I flick him away like an annoying bug, grab a slice, and take a bite. The pizza is salty and spicy and greasy, and it's so good that I let out a literal moan that makes Nico laugh. I freeze, waiting for the people watching the movie to shush us.

Nico leans closer so only I can hear. "The best, right?"

"Oh my god." I take another bite. "Where has this been all my life?"

"Arnoldi's makes killer pizza. They swear it's because they ship their water in from New York for their crust."

After two slices each, Nico moves the box aside and we settle back against the wall. On-screen, a kid is being chased by a dog through a junkyard, and a titter of laughter wells up.

"This movie is one of my favorites," Nico whispers in my ear, and the breath from his words makes my neck tickle. I can feel it all the way down to my fingertips. And the base of my spine.

I try to watch the movie, but the truth is I'm too distracted by how close Nico's sitting to me to fully focus on anything but his breathing. Every time he draws in air, his shoulder pushes against mine just the tiniest bit. I wonder if he notices it, too. All I can think is that I miss holding his hand.

Reel it in, Juniper. It's a movie and some free pizza, not a promposal.

Still. His shoulder won't stop touching mine.

When the movie ends, nobody hurries to get up and turn on the lights. Especially not me. I'm glad Nico doesn't, either.

He lets out a happy sigh. "That's the sign of a good movie," he says in my ear, and my whole body goes fizzy again. "Sometimes you have to sit in the dark for a little bit after it's over, just taking it in."

"I get like that with books. Sometimes I'll finish the last page and literally hug it. Like I need a minute to collect myself or whatever. To inhale. Or exhale. I don't know." Nico tilts his head to the side, studying me. "What? Is that weird?"

"Not at all."

"Okay, good."

"So what's your favorite book-turned-movie?"

I scrunch my forehead. "You're asking me to go deep on something I don't know very well, because I don't watch a lot of movies. How about you tell me yours instead."

"Probably *The Shining*." He leans in. Nudges my elbow with his. "But don't tell Stephen King."

"I'll try to remember. I mean, we are like this." I cross my index and middle fingers together.

He locks his eyes with mine. Smiles. "Lucky you. He's a genius. I hope he teaches you everything he knows."

"You do know he makes books, not movies, right?"

He nods. "So have you lost all respect for me because I know his movies better than his words?"

"No."

"Cool."

"But why shouldn't I tell my BFF Steve *The Shining* is your favorite?"

"Well, I don't know him like you do, but he's been pretty vocal about not liking Kubrick's adaptation. Calls it misogynistic. Says it lacks emotional depth. It's a whole thing."

"Really?"

"Yep."

"Do you agree?"

"I can see what he's saying." Nico stops like he's

thinking. "It's just . . . *The Shining* is so aesthetically awesome, you know?"

"I don't know, because I haven't seen it. Are there any adaptations he does like?"

"Supposedly this one. *Stand by Me.*"

"Well, I'm glad I saw it, then."

"Me too."

The lights finally flicker on. Nico pushes his back against the wall and raises his arms high above his head to stretch. I can't help but notice the way the bottom of his T-shirt rises up to expose a sliver of skin from his stomach.

"So you enjoyed that?" he asks.

At first I think he means did I enjoy that sliver of stomach, but he means the movie. "It was good. Even the barfing scene."

"Sorry we got here a little late. Maybe we can watch the whole thing from the beginning sometime."

"Definitely." I want to ask when. Like give me the exact time and place and I'll ditch school in the kitchen to be there.

In one fluid motion, Nico jumps to standing, hovering above me. He puts his hand out to mine. I grab it and he pulls me up from the ground, giving my hand an extra squeeze I know I'm not imagining this time. But then he lets go.

And we're standing there facing each other, only a few inches between us, until a stocky guy with Real

Woodstock Jimi Hendrix hair and a smattering of chin pimples accidentally bumps Nico hard enough on the shoulder with his camouflage backpack that Nico goes toppling into me. My hands automatically grab his waist to steady myself, and I suddenly feel like we're slow dancing.

"Dude," Nico says to the guy, "watch the backpack."

"Sorry, man. Just wanted to say cool pick on the flick."

I turn to Nico. "Wait. You picked the movie?"

He shrugs. "Yeah."

"Why are you acting all shy and embarrassed? You did a good job," I say.

"Thanks."

"I've got the next one," the guy with the backpack says excitedly. "So get ready. You know I like my sci-fi." He rubs his hands together. "I'm thinking *Brazil*. Or *Blade Runner*. Or both."

"Figures." Nico shakes his head. "Juniper, this is Jared, by the way." Nico waves his hand between his friend and me. "Jared, Juniper."

Jared tilts his chin at me. "Hey."

"Most people in our club are here simply because they like movies," Nico says. "But Jared wants to go to film school same as I do, so we appreciate each other on another level."

"We do," Jared says. "Which is why I was trying to decide if I was gonna give Nico a hard time for bringing a newbie tonight. But you seem cool enough."

"Ah. But how do you know I'm cool?" I grin. "We've barely talked. I could be a total asshole."

He laughs. "Nah. Nico doesn't really hang out with assholes."

"Except you," Nico jokes.

"Dude. That hurts," Jared says, pressing his hand to his heart in mock pain.

I use the sleeve of my hoodie to hide a giggle.

"Did I mention he wants to be an actor, too?" Nico tells me. "In the movies that he writes *and* directs? Which I'm sure he'll accomplish, because he's really good."

"You know it. I'm gonna be a triple threat." Jared points at me as he walks away. "Juniper, thanks for coming. Maybe I'll see you next week."

"Yeah, maybe." I glance up at the clock. Realize it's ten minutes past eight. "I should go. I told my mom I'd be home around now."

"Oh." Nico grabs his backpack from the floor. "I'll walk you."

I was hoping he'd say that.

SEVENTEEN

We stroll out of the classroom with a few others from the film club, all of them chatting excitedly about the movie, debating symbolism and the duality of the characters as they straddled childhood and adulthood. Nico's enthusiasm is palpable, and I'm struck by how much respect the others seem to have for what he has to say.

I should probably chime in with my thoughts, but I'm too distracted by being in an actual high school hallway and the distinct stink of cafeteria grease and hormones. Body spray and deodorant. Books and sweat. Yet I still want to stop and read every single flyer taped to the red-and-yellow-striped walls of this building. I want to swipe my hand across the lockers. I want to peek into the classrooms and see the rows of desks lined up and read the assignments on the whiteboards.

I want to belong here.

My focus narrows in on a hand-painted banner

hanging above the double front doors, advertising Playa Bonita's Homecoming next week. I wonder if Nico is planning on going to the game, or if he's taking someone to the dance.

Bids: $20 for a single or $35 per couple.

Will he use money from his job at the library to buy a ticket? Or tickets?

The group disperses at the steps in front of the school. Some shove empty pizza boxes into the nearby recycle bin. Others pile into cars. A few take off on foot. But everyone leaves with the promise to see each other tomorrow or at the next meeting. I want friends like that. And the assurance of when and where we'll see each other again.

It's one more reason I want to go to regular school. I wish my parents would change their minds.

"Do you like school?" I ask Nico as he unlocks his bike.

"I guess. But, I mean, it's *school*. Does anybody really like school?"

"What about the parts that aren't school?"

"Like film club? Yeah."

We walk past the flagpole and onto the sidewalk, the windows of my house glowing bright across the street.

"We obviously don't have stuff like film club in home-school. I'd be the only one going."

"Is that why you don't like it?"

"That and a lot of other reasons." I sigh. "I think I'd like the nonschool parts of regular school. Clubs. Football games. The cafeteria." *Homecoming.*

"Juniper, nobody likes the cafeteria."

"They don't? I feel like I'm missing out on a crucial part of the American high school experience."

"You're really not."

"If you say so."

It's impossible to convince someone the things they take for granted are worth longing for. So Nico doesn't think the cafeteria is all that great. The food is probably gross. And the walls probably smell like oily tater tots, and there are probably cliques at every other table, like this movie I watched with Mimi called *Mean Girls.* But it's a room full of teenagers, and that alone makes me want to be smack-dab in the middle of it.

"Why don't you just go to Playa?" Nico asks.

"My parents would never agree to it. And since I'm a minor, I'd need to have their permission to enroll." I won't even mention the vaccinations.

"Don't take this the wrong way, but can I ask what their reasoning is? Is it a religious thing?"

"No. It's a hippie thing."

"Ah, sure."

"Yeah."

"Well, you know you can come to our film club anytime you want, right? You can be an honorary member."

"Sweet."

"We'll always have film club," he says dramatically, and it makes me laugh.

"Ugh, that makes me sound so pathetic."

"I meant it like, 'We'll always have Paris.' You know? From *Casablanca*."

I look at him, confused. "Is that a movie?"

He waves his hand. "Forget it. It's not even that funny." He gestures toward my house. "This is you, right?"

"Yeah." I look up and stop short on the sidewalk.

I gasp and pull my hand to my mouth. Holy hell. *My front door.* Who did that? And why? I almost sink, but Nico balances me.

There's a giant letter *A* painted in red paint on our front door. The point of it hits the exact middle of the top of the door, and the rest of it drips right over the original stained-glass inlay, across the threshold, and onto the doormat.

My eyes dart around our house and land on the lawn, where the word *anti-vaxxer* has been spray-painted in the same scarlet-red paint across the grass. *A* for anti-vaxxer. I get it now.

"Juniper?" Nico says.

My name sounds far away and garbled.

I shake my head. Tremble. Push the tips of my thumbs into the corners of my eyes to try to keep from crying. Our house. Our door. "Oh my god."

"Juniper, what's going on?"

"I need to go." I run to my front door.

"Juniper!" Nico drops his bike on the ground, and it lands with a clatter. He scurries behind me, but I manage to get inside and shut the door before he gets to me. I lock it, worried that if I don't, he'll turn the knob and come in after me. But he doesn't. He doesn't even jiggle the handle. He knocks instead. Because he's polite. He calls my name again.

My dad comes in from the kitchen, dunking a metal tea steeper into a mug of steaming water. "Who's at the door?"

"Nobody."

Nico knocks again.

"Doesn't sound like nobody." My dad pulls the door open. The scarlet *A* reveals itself to our living room in all its horrific glory, but my dad's too busy looking at Nico on the front porch to notice. "Can I help you?"

"Someone painted a giant *A* on your door," Nico says, pointing.

And that's right when my mom comes down the stairs.

"What on earth?" she shouts, rushing to the door. She touches her hand to the paint, and her fingertips come back tinged with red. "Russ! Our home has been vandalized! Who would do this? What does it mean?"

My dad narrows his eyes at Nico. "Was it you?"

Nico holds his hands up. "What? No way."

"Dad, why would he knock on the door to tell you about it if he did it?"

"Who are you?" my dad says to Nico, his voice rising in that serious way he has.

"Russ, this is Juniper's friend. They were studying together at the school."

I look sideways at Nico like *don't you dare tell them we were watching a movie.*

"I'm Nico Noble," he says, all calm and collected, and I remember him telling me he's not weird about meeting parents. "I go to Playa and work at the library."

My dad gives him a half-hearted handshake. "Nice to meet you." He turns to me. "So you two didn't see who did this?"

"I'm pretty sure we would've noticed someone defacing our front door," I say.

My mom paces, wringing her hands. "What do we do?" she asks my dad.

My dad motions Nico into the house, then walks outside and bangs the door shut to examine it from a different angle.

"Unbelievable," he shouts from the porch, and comes back inside, the door slamming closed behind him.

All the noise is enough to make Poppy and Sequoia come stumbling down the stairs together—Sequoia with his blue pajama bottoms pulled too far to the right, making them look twisted and uncomfortable. Their rashes have peeled, but their skin is still a little blotchy and pink. I stand in front of Nico, as if that'll be enough to shield him.

"Have you had the measles shot?" I ask him under my breath.

His eyes crinkle in confusion. "Um, yeah. Why?"

"Just . . . you should go outside. It's a cesspool of germs in here."

"Honestly, Juniper," my mom says, her arms flapping at her sides. "Nobody is contagious anymore."

My dad points his finger in the air. "I'm calling the police."

"Daddy, what's wrong?" Sequoia asks, his voice cracking with fear. He pulls his stuffed animal closer. "Is someone getting arrested?"

"God willing," my dad says.

"Mom?" Poppy says. "What's happening?"

"Come here." My mom sits on the couch and pats the cushions on each side of her so they'll sit down, too.

"I'll be right back." I motion toward the door so Nico will follow me outside.

"What's the deal?" he says when we get to the sidewalk. "Why would someone do this to your house?"

"Trust me, you don't even want to know."

"Just tell me. I'm not that easy to shock. What's going on?"

"My parents are anti-vaxxers. With a great big capital *A*." I gesture toward our vandalized front door. "It's why I don't go to your school."

He shakes his head, confused. "Wait. You've never had a shot for anything? Ever?"

"Nope. That's why I got the measles. And then my siblings got them."

He gasps. "No way."

"I thought you weren't easy to shock."

"No. It's just . . . pretty much everyone in town has been talking about the measles since that baby died. Everyone's trying to figure out how she got it. They're worried there's going to be an outbreak, because a few others have already gotten sick."

"Yeah. She got the measles from me."

He shoves one hand into his pocket and the other through his hair. Takes a step back. "Jesus."

"It's a lot to take in, I know."

"It's just . . . ," he tries, flummoxed. "Yeah. It's a lot."

I nod.

He pulls out his phone.

Glances at the time.

He wants an out.

I give it to him. "I should get back inside."

"Yeah. I should probably"—his eyes run across the word scrawled in scarlet paint in our grass—"go."

"Totally. I get it."

He takes another step back. Pulls his helmet free from the handlebar. Fastens it under his chin. A huge sticker of a film reel takes up the whole left side of it, and I miss the idea of him already. "Maybe I'll see you around."

"Yeah. Maybe."

He flicks on his bike light. I hug myself around the middle to keep myself from crumbling as I watch him pedal away.

EIGHTEEN

My stomach revolts a few hours after I've fallen asleep. I wake up sweaty and rush for the bathroom. I worry for a second that I have another deadly virus I should've been vaccinated for, but throwing up pizza is an instant reminder that it's only because my body isn't used to eating things like greasy pepperoni and sausage.

I'm sure the stress of the scarlet *A* on our front door didn't help, either.

After Nico left, a police officer was a towering presence in our living room, taking statements and scaring Sequoia by being there. My brother kept eyeing the handcuffs dangling from his belt. And the gun in his holster.

"Where does this go from here?" my dad asked as Officer Cooper closed up his little notepad and shoved it into the front pocket of his shirt.

"We'll put our feelers out," Officer Cooper said. "If I

were to guess, I'd chalk this up to the local youths. You live across the street from the high school. It's a small town. Word gets around."

"And you want to go to school with these people!" my dad said to me. Like the sole act of sitting in a math class across the street would make me complicit in vandalism.

When I'm done being sick, I flush the toilet and brush my teeth with the DIY toothpaste my mom mixes herself in order to avoid toxic triclosan and fluoride. It's flavored with cloves and leaves my mouth tasting like pumpkin pie, which makes me want to barf all over again. Why can't she use peppermint like everyone else?

I go downstairs for a glass of water to wash out the taste and notice a scratching sound coming from the front door. Unbelievable. I know my parents would want me to call the police or come get them first, but if it's some local teenager from the school across the street, as Officer Cooper suggested, I want to catch them in the act. I quickly pull the door open. My mom screams and drops the scrub brush she's holding. It lands with a splat in the bucket of soapy water by her feet. I flick on the porch light. It doesn't light up the whole house like a spotlight, but it illuminates things enough for me to be able to see my mom's face.

"It's just me, June." Her voice catches.

I scurry outside, shutting the door behind me. "What are you doing?"

She retrieves the brush from the soapy water and scrubs at the red paint splattered across our front door. "I need to get this cleaned up before morning. Before the neighbors see."

"They probably already saw."

"I hope not."

"Maybe our neighbors are the ones who did it."

"That's unconscionable." She sniffs.

"Are you crying?"

"I'm having a moment."

"What kind of a moment?"

"The kind of moment where I feel like I'm in middle school all over again and people are making fun of me in the hallways."

"That happened to you?"

"Yes, Juniper. Every day."

"That's really awful, Mom."

"It is. Or it was." She clenches her eyes shut, like she can convince herself not to cry if she just concentrates hard enough. "But even when things were at their worst back then, nobody came around vandalizing my house."

"Is there another scrub brush somewhere?"

"Under the kitchen sink."

"Do you want some help?"

"That would be nice. Two of us will finish it faster. Your dad's going to get up early with the lawn mower to see if it'll help with the yard. It's too dark right now."

I go to the kitchen, grab the scrub brush, and down a

glass of water. Then I return to my mom and plunk the brush into the soapy bucket.

"How about I take the right side and you take the left?" she says.

"Okay."

"Teamwork." She dunks her brush in the bucket. Rinses it. "What are you doing up, anyway?"

"I was sick."

She looks at me, concerned. "What kind of sick?" The fact that I hear an edge of panic in her tone is interesting. Like maybe she really does stay awake at night worrying that Poppy, Sequoia, and I could've ended up like Baby Kat because of the choices she's made.

"Puking sick."

She reaches for my forehead to check my temperature but remembers her hands are wet and soapy.

"I'm not *sick* sick. I think I ate a little too much."

"What did you have for dinner, anyway? You weren't here."

"Pizza."

"Pizza!" She spits the word out in horror. "What kind of pizza?"

"Real pizza. From this place in town called Arnoldi's." I want to twist the knife even more. "With pepperoni and sausage."

She throws her hands up in exasperation, and water goes splattering against the wood wall behind her. "Well, there you go."

"It was really good."

"It made you sick."

I think of Nico and the way his shoulder felt against mine. And the way he whispered in my ear. And the way his hair flopped all over the place. And how he made my insides fizzy. I think of how good it was, even if it was for only one night. Even if I'm never going to see him again.

"It was worth it."

NINETEEN

A few days later, my mom and dad take Bessie in for new brake pads. Instead of doing homework, I scramble to the phone attached to the wall in the kitchen and start dialing.

"Burns, Menendez, and Watson," a bright voice chirps from the other end of the line. "How may I direct your call?"

"Is there anyone there who would talk to me about suing my parents?"

"How old are you?"

"Sixteen."

The woman laughs so loud through the receiver it practically shatters my eardrum. "What's wrong? Your mom took your iPhone away because you missed curfew?"

My face heats with anger. "No. I have a serious issue to discuss. About vaccinations."

"Sorry. We don't represent minors."

I collect myself and try again. "May I please talk to someone who might be able to send me in the right direc—"

She hangs up on me.

"Well, that's real professional," I mutter as I stand there with the dial tone blaring in my ear.

I slam the phone back on the hook and turn to the next page of the Yellow Pages. This copy is so old that half the legal practices don't even exist anymore. After a few wrong numbers, the next person is nicer. She says she can take down my name and contact information and have someone call me back.

"I need to talk to someone now," I say. "I can't risk anyone calling my house." I sound like I'm in the witness protection program.

"Well, you can try again tomorrow morning." I can hear her tapping her fingers against her computer keyboard, like talking to me is secondary to forwarding an email.

"Maybe," I say, and hang up.

So much for that one. I can't exactly get up in the middle of Kitchen School to call my attorney.

I continue to thumb through the Yellow Pages.

Poppy waltzes into the kitchen. "Whatcha doin'?" she says.

I slam the phone book shut. "Nothing."

"Sure." She eyes the Yellow Pages.

"Don't worry about it."

"I won't." She opens the fridge and pulls out a pitcher of fresh orange juice. Fills a glass. Takes a sip. Leans against the counter. Studies me. Sips again. "Need help with your nothing?"

"No."

She takes another sip. Makes the same smug *ahh* sound my dad makes when he drinks his boring black coffee. I tap my fingers against the wall.

"Why not?" she says.

"Are you staying here all day or what?"

"Depends. Are you?"

"Not with you."

She lets out a dramatic sigh and finishes off her orange juice. "Fine." She rinses out her glass and leaves it in the sink. "I'll leave you alone to call your boyfriend."

"I don't have a boyfriend."

"Then who was that *boy* who came over here the other night? The tall one who looks like he doesn't comb his hair."

"His name is Nico, and I'm sure he combs his hair. It's just . . . floppy." I get discombobulated remembering Nico and his floppy hair. I'm not sure my mouth can make words. I try anyway. "There's a difference between a friend who's a boy and a boyfriend, by the way."

"Whatever you say."

"And anyway, he's neither. He doesn't want to see me again."

"Oh. Why?"

"Why do you think?"

She shrugs. "I don't know."

"There was way too much drama here the other night. It scared him off. Our family is a freak show."

"Speak for yourself."

I roll my eyes. "Can you please just go now?"

She finally leaves. I shut the phone book. It's outdated and useless. I need to figure out something else.

TWENTY

There's nothing suckier than having to go back to the library after what happened with Nico, but my dead-end Yellow Pages calls have made it clear I need to get online if I'm going to find an attorney. I just have to be stealthy. So after the weekend, on Tuesday afternoon, one week after meeting Nico, I tiptoe around corners and peer into the computer lab to make sure he isn't there.

I don't see him.

The problem is, I don't see anyone.

The lab is completely empty.

But the hours are posted by the door, so I know it isn't closed.

I pace back and forth. Do I go in there? Or will I get in trouble for not checking in with someone? Will I lose my lab privileges if I don't hand over my library card to promise everyone I won't steal a computer?

I peer around the corner again. Still empty. Is he working or not? Because if he is, I can't go in there. No way.

I decide the front desk is my only option.

"Hi, I'd like to use a computer, please."

"Oh, is nobody in there?" The librarian's eyes dart around the library, past the bookshelves and the DVD rental section. "The attendant must've just stepped out for a moment. Would you like me to page someone?"

"No!" I shout. I don't mean to be so loud. "I'll just wait."

I don't wait in the lab. I wait behind a bookshelf around the corner. I can see the lab if I move two books aside. Not creepy at all.

I scan the books along the shelves, pretending to be enthralled by the World War II collection in front of me. I run my fingers along the spines, reading the titles. I casually pull books from the shelves. I try to read the jacket copy, but my eyes glaze over.

Finally, the person working the computer lab returns, and it's not Nico. *Thank you.* I rush over, vowing to get my work done quickly in case Nico has the next shift or something.

I give him my library card and ask for computer number seven, just for nostalgia's sake.

The guy working doesn't look at my card and comment on my name or wait for me to tell him everything I know about the lottery in Bulgaria. He just slips my card into the corresponding slot and tells me to "get to it."

I sit down. My fingers quickly glide across the keyboard, pulling up a directory of local attorneys, all still in business, unlike the ones in our phone book at home. I send the list to the printer and log out. I wait until I hear the printer stop churning out papers before I get up and walk over to collect and pay for my copies.

The guy hands my card back to me, and I stroll out of the library like the whole trip was painless.

Maybe I can trick myself into believing it.

I decide to reward myself by checking out the free samples at Starbucks. It's only a couple of blocks away, and I enjoy the walk through town. The weather has cooled and it feels like fall. Crisp and clean.

The café line is short, but there aren't any free samples today. Thankfully, I have money left from the five-dollar bill I brought for printing pages at the library. I order a plain old drip coffee. Since they're in the middle of brewing a new vat of it, I have to wait. If I were a normal person, I could scroll through my phone to pass the time like everyone else waiting for their drinks. But I'm not. I'm me. So I stand by the counter and watch the barista make foamy milk at the espresso machine instead.

"Juniper?" a voice calls.

It isn't because my coffee is ready.

It's coming from behind me, and I recognize it instantly.

My heart skitters. Please just let me disappear. I don't care if I have to become microdust that blends in with the cement floor. Just please don't make me have to look Nico in the eye right now.

"Juniper," he says again.

I turn around slowly, hoping I'm wrong and it isn't really him.

But it is. With his floppy hair and his big brown eyes looking up at me from the long table filled with students, including Jared, doing their homework. He has a book propped open and an orange highlighter in his hand. Literally my favorite highlighter color. I realize this is a dorky thing to call favorites on.

"Hi," I mumble.

"Hi," Nico says, smiling like he didn't peel off on his bike, leaving me in his wake, the other night.

"Hey, Juniper," Jared busts in, all loud and enthusiastic. "Sit with us." He shoves his camouflage backpack aside to make room for me.

"I can't right now. But thanks."

Nico stands and edges cautiously closer to me. When I take a step away, he shoves his hands into his jeans pockets and pushes back on his heels. "Hey," he tries again.

"Hi." I look around the café, like maybe I'm meeting someone here. Like maybe I have friends, too. Like maybe I can sit at a long table with a bunch of people and know all their names just like he does.

But I don't know anyone here besides Nico and Jared. And I don't even really know them.

Thankfully, the barista calls my name for my coffee order. I swipe it up, gripping the warm cup in my hands.

"Just sit with us while you drink your coffee," Jared says. "Since you're not contagious or whatever."

My face drops.

I look at Nico, my chin wobbling. My voice comes out like a whisper. "You told him?"

"I mean . . ."

"I can't. Oh my god."

I make a beeline for the door.

"What the hell?" Nico says to Jared. Then, "Juniper, wait."

I don't.

I walk faster instead.

Because I can hear his footfalls behind me.

I push the front door open and hurry away, past the bike racks and the bus stop bench. One, two, three, five paces ahead of him.

The mail carrier tells me to have a good day as I walk by.

"Juniper!" Nico calls again when I have to stop at the corner. Stupid red light.

I turn on my heel. Glare. "You told Jared about me?" I lower my voice. "About the measles?" I don't say it quietly enough, because two people standing next to me on the sidewalk turn to check me out. Are they taking mental notes? On my height? My face? My hair? Will they take a photo like those women at the farmers market? "Why did you tell him?"

"I don't know. Maybe because I was freaking out a little and he's my best friend. He told me I was overreacting." He steps forward. "He won't tell anyone. Jared's not like that."

"He practically announced it to all of Starbucks just now."

"I'll talk to him."

"Please don't. Don't say anything else to anyone. You've done enough already." I jab my finger at the crosswalk button half a dozen times, willing the light to turn faster. "Don't you have to do your homework?"

"I do. I'm just . . ." Nico lets out a long sigh. "Can I please talk to you? For a minute?"

I pull my drink to my chest. It's warm against my heart. Comforting me somehow. Holding me together. "Why?"

"Look, I'm sorry I left like that the other night."

"It's fine."

"No, it's not. I think I hurt your feelings."

I shrug. "Whatever."

He runs his hand through his floppy hair and it sticks out everywhere. I want to run my fingers through it to tamp it down.

"I'm sorry," he says. "I didn't know what to do, so I left. But it was kind of a dick move."

"It's fine. Really."

"It's not fine. I'm trying to apologize here."

I look past him. I focus on the bookstore display window behind him. At the cars driving down the street in the distance. "Okay. Thanks for the apology." I take a sip of my coffee, trying to feign indifference. It's gross. It's hot and bitter and I want to spit it out. How does my dad drink this?

"Juniper, come on." He stubs the toe of his red Converse against a crack in the sidewalk. "Can we please hang out again?"

"I don't think that's a good idea."

"Why not?"

"I have a lot going on."

"Like what?"

"Everything." I'm so embarrassed that it's hard to even look at him. "Our house being vandalized. Other things. I'm not a great person to be around."

"But I want to be around you."

I crinkle my eyes at him, genuinely confused. "Why?"

"Because you're cool. And smart. And funny."

"I'm really not cool. I eat pizza with cauliflower crust. My dad treats sinus infections by burning a hollowed-out candle in my ear canal. I wash my hair with shampoo my mom makes from egg yolks and lemons." I wince. "Do you have any idea how bad that smells?"

"But you don't smell bad. You smell like . . ." He thinks for a second. "Coconut? Like sunblock."

"Right. My homemade deodorant. Even better."

He runs his hand through his hair again, and it flops all over. He needs to stop doing that. It's reeling me in. "I don't care about any of those things."

"I do. I'm embarrassed, okay? My family isn't normal."

He laughs. "How do you even define normal? It's not any one thing. It's a perspective. There's no such thing as normal." He knocks his shoulder against mine. "And you know cauliflower crust isn't even that weird, right? We do that at my house, too. And you can order pizza that way at California Pizza Kitchen."

"You can?"

"Yeah."

"Oh." I clutch my coffee cup.

"If you want to swap embarrassing stories, I have a million of them. Want me to tell you all about the time my shorts fell down when I was running the mile in PE?"

The light turns but I don't move. "Go on."

Nico takes a step closer. "I'd had the flu. Lost a bunch of weight. They didn't fit anymore. It was a whole thing."

"Really?"

"Actually, no. But I'll pretend it's true if it makes you feel better." He grins and I laugh.

"Stop. That's not funny."

"Then why are you laughing?"

"Because you're ridiculous."

"Okay. But if you want real embarrassing, I can come up with tons of stories for you. How about if every time I see you, I tell you one?" His eyes are bright and hopeful.

"Why would you do that?"

"Maybe because I think all the things you think are weird about you actually make you interesting. And I like that you liked *Stand by Me* almost as much as I did. And I like that you know random stuff about the lottery in Budapest."

"Bulgaria."

"Tomato, tomahto."

"Tomato, tomahto? How old are you?"

"Sixteen."

"Are you sure?"

"Look." He shoves his hands into his pockets. "I messed up. I bailed the other night and I shouldn't have. But I hope you'll give me another chance. Because I want to hang out with you again." He looks at me hopefully. "Can we?"

I kick my foot at the ground. Thinking. "What would we do?"

"We can watch movies and eat pizza and play the lottery."

"Technically, you have to be eighteen to play the lottery."

"So I'll have my brother buy our tickets. But we'll have to wait until winter break, because he goes to Northwestern."

I study his face. His big brown eyes and the curve of his mouth. "I guess we can go to the beach or something."

"I don't generally do outdoor activities. You can probably tell from my pasty pallor." He gestures to himself with a wave of his hand. "I've got bee allergies. And peanut allergies. An EpiPen. Benadryl. Is that a deal breaker?"

"No."

"Okay, good. Because I love bees, but I can't hang out with them."

"Well, yeah, bees are pretty awesome." I study him. "So you never go outside?"

"Well, I'm here now, aren't I? I'm basically risking my life for you." He grins. "I can go outside. It's not that I *never* go outside. I just have to be good about being prepared. Like wearing long sleeves and stuff."

"Got it."

"So." He nudges my elbow. "Do you want to come back and drink your coffee with us?"

I don't answer. Instead I take a sip of my coffee. Shudder. "This is so gross."

"You don't like it?"

"It's bitter."

"Well, come back and add cream and sugar." He smiles at me. Tilts his head toward Starbucks. "Come on."

"Okay."

He pulls out his phone as we walk. "You know where to find me, but can I add you to my contacts? Snapchat? Insta? Something else?"

"No phone." I point at my skull. "My dad says they cause brain cancer. Do you want to hang out with me or what?"

"I so do, Juniper."

TWENTY-ONE

Another week passes and I'm sitting in an uncomfortable chair in the waiting room of an attorney's office in the middle of town. I finally found someone willing to make time for me on his lunch hour. As far as my parents know, I'm at the art supply store.

The window over my shoulder looks out to the park across the street. It's the same park where my mom packed a picnic dinner and made my whole family go watch a band sing cover songs from the eighties for the town's Summer Sundays concert series this past July. The band wore long-haired wigs and black lipstick and pastel polo shirts with popped-up collars in a nod to every fashion trend from the decade. A guy and a girl took turns singing into a microphone while my mom and dad sat on top of the patchwork quilt they'd spread out to eat dinner and bounce along to the music. My mom fell all over herself when they played a Duran Duran song, and my dad got super into anything remotely punk because I think it made him feel cool.

Poppy sat under a shady tree and read a book.

Sequoia managed to make friends with a group of kids his age, and they chased each other around the park playing some Star Wars game I'm sure he didn't completely understand because he's never seen the movies. Maybe he'll eventually get a chance to visit Mimi and Bumpa alone like I finally did—without our parents—and get a Star Wars introduction from Bumpa, who owns the entire collection on DVD.

At the summer concert, I scanned the crowd for sympathetic eyes from other sullen teens whose parents had dragged them there. I couldn't find any.

Still, the thought of that night makes me a little wistful. Because it was before the measles. When my family could blend into a crowd like everyone else's.

"Ms. Jade?" The receptionist stands up from her desk, interrupting me from my pity party. "Mr. Graff will see you now. I'll take you back."

I stand up and smooth out my clothes. I tried to look professional today, with a white button-down shirt tucked into a navy-blue pencil skirt, but when I went to put on my nice shoes, I'd outgrown them. My most decent option was a pair of strappy sandals more suitable for Coachella than meeting an attorney, but maybe I'm pulling it off, like the woman at the farmers market with her business suit and flip-flops.

We pass a coffee station as we head down the narrow hallway with carpet so thick I nearly trip over it. The receptionist stops in her tracks and I almost bump into her.

"Oh! Coffee?" she asks, like she's suddenly remembering it exists.

The coffee machine is set up on a small white folding table covered in sugar granules and ringed stains. A box of wood stirrers has toppled over, and they're now scattered like a game of pick-up-sticks. The carnage makes it seem like everyone here is too busy doing important things to clean up after themselves.

Maybe that's a good thing. Maybe someone here will work hard for me.

As much as I want to drink coffee just to make a statement about the fact that my dad won't let me do it at home, I turn it down. That coffee I had with Nico the other day didn't taste very good, even with the milk and sugar I added. Plus, I don't need the caffeine. I'm jittery enough as it is.

The receptionist reaches her hand out to knock on the door at the end of the hallway, and a bellowing voice directs us to "come on in."

The door swings open with a *swoosh* across the thick carpet. "Mr. Graff, I have Juniper Jade for you."

"Thank you, Evelyn," Mr. Graff says.

I walk into his office, and the receptionist pulls the door shut behind me.

Mr. Graff pushes his half-eaten sandwich aside and stands up from his desk as marble rye bread crumbs fall off the front of his shirt and onto his desk. He's tall and slender, with a receding hairline of fine blond hair. I'd guess he's somewhere around my dad's age. He sticks his hand out to mine, and the necktie he'd swung over his shoulder falls back into place along the buttons of his shirt. After we shake, I restrain myself from wiping the residue of his damp palm on my skirt.

"Sit, sit," he says to me. I take a seat in one of the two chairs opposite him and fold my hands in my lap. "What brings you in today?"

"I want to sue my parents."

He shakes his head and chuckles lightly, but stops when I don't join in. "Oh, you really mean it." He pulls a to-go cup of soda closer and sucks the drink up through a paper straw until it's drained and there's nothing but the echoing sound of air and ice. "Why?"

I twist my fingers together. "I want to be vaccinated, and my parents are anti-vaxxers."

He taps his chin. "Interesting."

"Really?"

"Interesting, but not possible."

I sit up straighter. "Why not?"

"Remind me of your age."

"Sixteen. Seventeen in April."

"Well, sixteen, seventeen in April, I say you should wait until you're eighteen."

"But I can't wait. I'm legitimately worried about my health."

"How so?"

I tell him all about the measles and the hospital and my brother and sister. About Katherine St. Pierre and the rest of the Playa Bonita community.

"You knew the baby who died?" he says.

How do I explain that I didn't know her at all, really? That I met her once? But I carry her around with me like I always knew her. I know her as a part of me now. And it's a part of me that will always hurt. "She got the measles from me."

He looks confused. "Was she a family member?"

"No. She's someone I met at the farmers market before I knew I had the measles. I didn't do it on purpose."

"No, of course not," he says, shaking his head. "But it's very sad, isn't it?"

"Sad is an understatement." I look at him sharply. "So you can see why I don't want to wait until I turn eighteen to get my shots. If I can help it, I don't want what happened to that baby to happen to someone else."

"I understand."

"I want to make a difference."

"That's virtuous." He grunts. "Teenagers seem to be a little too virtuous these days."

I press my back into the chair. "It sounds like you don't like teenagers very much."

"I love them. I have two at home. But they don't always know what they want, even when they think they do."

"I know what I want."

"But do you really? You're talking about wreaking havoc on your family. Creating dissension between you and your parents. For what? To prove a point?"

"I'm trying to save my life."

"Hmm." He looks at me seriously. "Is there more to this? Is it not safe for you at home? Are your parents hurting you, Juniper? Anything you tell me is confidential."

"What? No!"

"Okay. Good. That's good."

"I love my parents. I just think they're wrong about vaccinations."

"There's always emancipation."

"What's that?"

He leans back in his chair. "Emancipation would give you legal independence from your parents."

"Meaning?"

"Your mom and dad would no longer be responsible for you in any way, thus allowing you to make your own medical choices. As such, you'd have to prove you're capable of taking care of yourself. Are you?"

"I can cook and clean and do my own laundry." I wonder if this is what a job interview feels like. I sit up straighter. "Actually, I can do a lot of things."

"Do you work? You'd have to prove you could support yourself financially. And you'd have to find your own place to live, separate from your parents. Those things are necessary for emancipation."

"I don't have a job. I want one. But I don't. And even if I did, I wouldn't want to move out. I like living with my family. Poppy and Sequoia need me."

"So like I said, wait till you're eighteen." He eyes his sandwich like he wants me to leave so he can finish his lunch now. Like there's really nothing more to say.

I clear my throat, and he manages to look at me instead of his sandwich. "I got really sick from the measles, Mr. Graff. I don't want something like that to happen to me again."

He sighs. "Juniper, I appreciate what you're doing, but this is California law. Other states may handle it differently, but here, your only option is emancipation."

"So I'm basically defined by my zip code."

"Pretty much." He leans forward, and his tie creases against his desk. "There's no federal precedent for this."

"Lots of things don't have a federal precedent. And then someone fights hard enough to make them happen."

"Unfortunately, those someones aren't usually sixteen-year-old girls." His words make my blood boil. I'm so sick of being dismissed. He leans back in his chair. Cradles his hands behind his head. "Look, you came to me for a professional opinion, and I'm giving you one. I know it sounds impossible right now, but you should just wait until you turn eighteen."

"I don't believe in impossible." I smile. "I can't."

"Well, then, I wish you the best."

I leave his office and jump on the city bus, knowing it will take me to the courthouse. Maybe I can find an attorney there who will help me. One coming out of a courtroom or milling around the front steps on a break. I can walk up to them and tell them my story.

TWENTY-TWO

My trip to the courthouse was a total bust. It seems attorneys at a courthouse don't want to be approached by strangers asking for legal advice. I should've known better, but I was so eager to find help that I didn't adequately think through my plan.

Thankfully, I can concentrate on something else today, because it's a couple weeks before Halloween, and everyone is completely recovered, so my parents have decided to take the whole family to the local pumpkin patch. Like everything in this town, the Playa Bonita Halloween Patch is over the top, with a hayride, fresh-pressed apple cider, tons of pumpkins, and a petting zoo.

"So cruel," my mom says, shaking her head at the goats and alpacas bleating behind the temporary mesh fence.

Maybe it is cruel. But I still feel bad for Sequoia when he tugs on the hem of my mom's sweatshirt, begging her to take him to pet the animals. I try to distract him with the one-hundred-pound pumpkin on display instead. I even help him climb on top so my dad can take a photo. And then my dad directs my mom, Poppy, and me to stand next to Sequoia. My mom takes a whiff of the crisp October air and hugs a smaller pumpkin like she's posing for a cheesy fall catalog for gift baskets instead of a picture for my dad.

After taking a few photos, my dad says, "You know what'd be even more awesome? All of us in the picture." He turns around, holds out his camera. Asks, "Can you, please?" when a woman passing by looks up from her phone. She glances back at her phone again, recoils from us, and shakes her head no. Her reluctance sends a chill through me. The same chill I felt when Mary and the elderly woman and the young moms at the farmers market huddled together to whisper about my mom and me. Still, my mom, my sister, my brother, and I stand by awkwardly, holding up the line of people also wanting to climb on top of the giant pumpkin to take a photo while my dad keeps trying to find a photographer.

"Let's just forget it," I say to my mom.

"It's fine," she says even though her forehead creases with worry.

But a dad with a kid finally says yes. We all pose with fake smiles while my dad talks him through operating the complicated camera he insists on using because it takes much better photos than any camera phone.

143

And then the woman who told us no before walks up and pulls the kid away. When the man I assume is her husband turns to face her, the lens of my dad's camera brushes her elbow and she flinches.

"What are you doing?" she says through her clenched teeth like a ventriloquist, but I can still understand her. "That's them. The ones from the picture online."

Her husband looks confused. "What picture? Online where?"

"I just checked to make sure." She holds up her phone, and I see a sharp photo of my mom and me standing behind our table of herbs and essential oils at the farmers market. "I knew I recognized them from the Facebook group."

A woman passing by squints at the photo, looks at us, pulls her daughter closer to her side, and hurries away. I notice others nearby with their heads pushed toward each other. Whispering. I catch the word *measles*. I spot the side-eye.

Does everyone know who we are?

This woman doesn't want her husband to touch my dad's camera because she thinks it's covered in germs.

She thinks we're covered in germs.

Untouchable. Contagious.

"Mom," I say, "we should go."

"We should," she says. "Russ, get your camera back."

"No!" Sequoia shouts. "I'm not going." He slides off the giant pumpkin and darts into the nearby patch.

"We just got here," Poppy says, crossing her arms. "I haven't even picked out my pumpkin yet." My sister doesn't love Halloween, but she does love carving pumpkins. It's art. She's been working on designs in her sketchbook all week, including on the car ride over here.

"We need to go," I say. "Look around."

People passing by are staring and whispering, their words spreading like a disease.

Is the person who painted the scarlet *A* on our door here? Is it that woman wearing the fancy rain boots, even though all we got was some drizzle two hours ago? Is it that man with the cup of apple cider? Or that couple with the double baby stroller?

We slowly back away from the giant pumpkin and step toward the patch to retrieve Sequoia so we can go.

"Hey!" a mom in workout gear shouts as she pushes her kids behind her. "We know who you are. You killed that innocent baby. You're murderers."

I rack my brain trying to figure out how so many people know who we are.

Who told? Who is spreading our story? My mom and dad and Poppy wouldn't tell. Who would?

My dad looks flabbergasted. My mom looks like she might pass out from shock.

"Mom?" Poppy says, her voice shaking.

Sequoia hears the shouting and ditches the pumpkin patch to run to my side for protection. Because a crowd has gathered and they're closing in.

Mob mentality.

People push forward. Wanting to see. Like we're at the scene of an accident.

But my family is the accident.

I take a step back, fear pulsing. My instinct is to protect Poppy and Sequoia. I pivot my body to shield them. It's my mom's instinct to protect all three of us, so she angles her body in front of me.

"We don't want you here!" The mom in workout gear has gotten close enough that I can see her spittle hit the air when she shouts. "This town didn't sign up to be victims of your negligence." One of her friends tries to pull her back, calm her down, but she shakes her off. She points her finger at my parents, her face red with rage. "You have blood on your hands. You know that, don't you?"

Sequoia looks at my mom's hands, confused.

My dad's mouth is a slash. He balls his fists at his sides. I'm genuinely afraid he might punch someone. *A woman. A mom.*

"Don't you dare," he says, standing tall, chest puffed, arms out, in front of all four of us. "Don't you dare take another step closer to my family."

My mom spreads her own arms, hands shaking.

"Oh, sure, protect your kids but no one else's!" shouts a voice in the back.

"Hey now," someone else shouts. "Let's be reasonable."

146

"Oh, are you an anti-vaxxer, too?" comes the response.

Some people have pulled out their phones. They're filming everything. Others type, frantically texting the chaos to those who aren't witnessing it in person because they have errands or soccer games.

"Russ," my mom murmurs, "let's get out of here."

Sequoia stomps his foot. "I want a pumpkin."

"I'll make sure you get a pumpkin later," I tell him. "I promise."

Tears are forming in his eyes. I look to my mom for help, but she has tears in her eyes, too. Are they from guilt? Humiliation? Is it middle school all over again?

My dad stands taller. "Back up," he says to the crowd. When he lunges forward, they push away from him, not because he's scary and forceful, but because they're afraid he might get them sick. He puts an arm around Poppy and leads us, single file, to Bessie.

"Thank you," the mom in workout gear says, clapping her hands dramatically. "Thank you for leaving. Tell you what, why don't you leave this town altogether? You're not wanted here."

"Oh my god," Poppy mutters in full-on exasperation. "Go to yoga and calm down."

Her words fill me with a weird mix of pride and horror.

On the way home, Sequoia sits in the back seat, twisting his hands together. It's like I can see his brain cycling through what happened. Eventually he says, "Who did we kill?"

"What?" my dad says, his knuckles turning white as he grips the steering wheel.

"It's not like that," Poppy says.

"What's it like, then?" Sequoia says, looking at me.

"Not now," my dad says, struggling to stay calm as he looks at us through the rearview mirror.

"Was it with a gun?" Sequoia asks.

"We don't have a gun," my mom says.

"But how do you murder someone without a gun?"

Poppy and I lock eyes. We both know there are so many other ways to kill a person. Neither of us will be the one to tell our brother.

"Not now," my dad repeats.

"But that lady said we murdered someone."

My dad twists in his seat to face us when we stop at a traffic light. "We don't have a gun. We would never have a gun. Nobody was murdered. End of discussion."

The signal changes and we lurch forward.

Sequoia lets out an exasperated sigh and crosses his arms in front of his chest. I want to help him under-stand, but how do you explain to a second grader what happened to Baby Kat?

I lean against the window. My eyes dart to Poppy's sketchbook, still open on the cushion between us, her jack-o'-lantern designs on display. A cat. A pirate. A witch. None of them will be carved today.

And Katherine St. Pierre will never carve a pumpkin. She'll never wear a costume or go trick-or-treating or watch a scary movie. She'll never grow up and go to college. Or have children of her own.

And that's our fault.

Whether it happened with a gun or not.

TWENTY-THREE

On Halloween afternoon, I still don't have the pumpkin I promised Sequoia. I've made attempts to return to the pumpkin patch, but I always chicken out as soon as the entrance is in sight, remembering the way everyone closed in on us. Shouting and snapping photos. I don't want to go back alone. Even though I haven't seen Nico since running into him at Starbucks at the beginning of October, I definitely haven't stopped thinking about him. So I decide to head to the library, because I remember him saying he works on Halloween. Maybe he'll go to the pumpkin patch with me when his shift is over. When I walk in on him in the computer lab, he's too engrossed in the book he's reading to see me. I sneak up behind him, lean over, and whisper, "Boo" into his ear.

He jumps in his seat. Fumbles his book to the floor.

I can't help but laugh. "You okay?"

"You just pulled off a classic jump scare."

"What's that?"

"A movie thing. Jared loves them."

"Still not following."

He waves his hand in the air. "It's when the visual suddenly changes on-screen, something pops up out of nowhere and scares you so bad it makes you jump."

"Hmm. I guess I should've been able to figure that out."

"Don't worry about it." He looks up at me. Smiles. "Hello, by the way."

"Hello."

"You remembered where to find me."

"I did."

I move closer. Let my hand linger along the edge of the back of his chair as I stand behind him. His hair looks even floppier from this angle. My fingers ache to run through it. To feel the silky strands fall between my knuckles.

"Do you want to go to the pumpkin patch with me when you're done?" I say.

"The pumpkin patch?"

"Yeah."

"I don't think that's a great idea."

"Why?"

"Juniper," Nico says, running his thumb across the edge of his laptop sitting on the desk in front of him. "You should probably see something. I just don't like having to be the one to show it to you."

"Now you're scaring me."

"Well, it is Halloween." He grudgingly flips the laptop open and clicks his way to Facebook.

And there it is.

A video frozen. The triangle play button in the center of my mom's face.

Poppy, Sequoia, and the one-hundred-pound pumpkin.

My dad off to the side.

And me, shell-shocked.

Then and now.

I press play.

The room is filled with the horrid words of the woman in workout gear all over again. *Negligence. Blood on your hands.*

Murderers.

Nico winces. "It's really bad. I'm so sorry."

My legs can't hold me. I sink into the chair next to Nico. "Where did you find this?"

He looks at the computer. He can't look at me. "Everywhere. But it started on the Concerned Citizens of Playa Bonita page on Facebook."

I lean in closer, notice the page has 4.2K followers. That's a lot. Almost one-third of this town.

"Is that all there is?"

"Not exactly."

"Show me."

He scrolls through the page, and there are several photos of my mom and me at our booth at the farmers market. All of them from different angles. Some close, some zoomed in. A caption loud and clear. *These people gave Katherine St. Pierre the measles. Keep your precious babies away from them.* I had no idea that many pictures were being snapped. I only remember the one the mom with the stroller took after Mary gathered a group of them to huddle together and whisper. To point and judge.

There's also a photo of our house with the scarlet *A* on the door before my mom scrubbed it off. *Stay away*, the caption says.

Another photo of my mom and Sequoia in the front yard. *Evil*, says that caption.

One more of my mom and dad climbing out of Bessie in the parking lot at the auto mechanic. *This is them, right?*

My whole body shakes. "So that's how everyone knows who we are. They're basically stalking us. And they've been talking about us on this page for weeks."

This is what my mom meant when she told the CDC representative that she didn't believe we'd actually be kept anonymous. *It's only a matter of time before they know who we are*, she'd said.

"I think they're under the impression they're doing something good by warning everyone about your family," Nico says. "But it's not okay. It's totally invasive."

My knee knocks his knee. Our shoulders touch. I stay there because I need the solid and steady feel of him next to me to keep me from shaking. The video has over three hundred comments. Nico clicks onto the next empty box and starts typing:

You can't put the blame on someone who didn't even know she was sick. And shaming them won't lead to genuine dialogue. These people aren't murderers. All they wanted to do was go to the pumpkin patch. I'm ashamed of my hometown right now. This is a bad look, Playa Bon—

I stop him from typing by placing my hand on top of his.

"Thank you," I say. "But you don't have to get involved. It's not okay to drag you into this."

"Don't care." He finishes typing, presses enter, and the comment posts. Someone responds immediately:

Screw you pussy.

"Dumb shit forgot the comma," Nico says.

I shut the laptop cover. "I don't want to see any more."

His gaze on me softens. "They're wrong, Juniper. You know that, right?"

"No. I kind of agree with them. A baby died because of me."

He shakes his head. "You need to stop saying that."

"It's the truth."

"Okay, technically, yes. She got the measles from you. But it wasn't like you set out to do it." A muscle in his jaw twitches. "And don't be mad at me for saying this, but if anyone's really responsible, it's your parents."

"You're not entirely wrong. It's their fault *and* mine."

He raises his eyebrows. "So have you told them that?"

"I've told them a lot of things." I shrug. "Like that I want to be vaccinated and go to regular school. And when they disagree, I tell them they're elitist and ridiculous."

"I'm pretty sure I'd be grounded for life if I said something like that to either of my parents."

I sit up straight and talk in a deep voice, imitating my dad. "Yes, well, being outspoken is part of the Jade Family way." I laugh sarcastically. "We shouldn't be afraid to say what we think simply because we're kids. We're not censored. We're encouraged to argue our point of view." I sigh. "That's the theory, at least. But my parents are hypocrites, because they refuse to hear me."

"So what are you gonna do?"

"I'm going to fight them on it."

"How?"

"I don't know. So far everyone has told me it's impossible."

"Is it?"

"I guess we'll see."

I stand up because I can't sit still any longer. My eyes dart to the exit.

Nico scoots his chair back. "Wait. Maybe I can leave

early. The computer lab doesn't exactly get swamped on Halloween. Do you want to get out of here?"

"I really do. Can you take me someplace far away?" I stare dreamily at the ceiling. "Can we go to the moon?"

He bumps my shoulder with his. "How about a movie? A bunch of the film club members are meeting up at Playa Cinema because they're screening all the *Halloween* films today."

"As much as I'd love to disappear inside a movie theater, I promised my brother I'd get him a pumpkin. And I know Poppy would like one, too." I motion to the computer screen. "But you're right. The pumpkin patch isn't a good idea."

"Um, have you seen our display? The library has more pumpkins than we can handle. I can get you some."

"Are you sure?"

"Positive."

TWENTY-FOUR

About thirty minutes later, Nico shows up at our house in the library's golf cart, the back row full of pumpkins.

I pat the steering wheel. "Aren't they going to miss this sweet ride back at the library?"

"Nah. It's for a good cause." Nico grins. "Wanna help me unload 'em?"

We haul the pumpkins to the backyard. Poppy is beside herself, literally shivering with excitement. She inspects each one, trying to find the most perfectly round and least marred of the bunch.

"Thankyouthankyouthankyou," she says, like one long word, when she finds it.

My mom sets up carving tools and a bowl for pumpkin guts on the picnic table. Poppy gets out her sketchbook to revisit her designs. Sequoia grabs a pumpkin and hugs it like it's one of his stuffed animals.

"This was very sweet of you," my mom says to Nico.

"As you can see, you've made two kiddos very happy." She tries to smooth down Sequoia's flyaway hair. "I really appreciate it."

"No problem, it was easy. The library has plenty of pumpkins to spare from their Halloween decorations."

"Well, we are grateful," my mom says.

I turn to Nico. "Thanks for helping. But you don't have to stay. I know you want to go to the movies."

"Juniper, I've seen the *Halloween* movies more times than I can count. I'll survive."

"You're saying you want to carve pumpkins?"

"I'm saying I'd love to carve pumpkins."

The tip of Poppy's tongue sticks out of the side of her mouth as she fine-tunes the details of her cat design on her pumpkin before carving. Sequoia is less intense. He's happy to trace a traditional jack-o'-lantern face for me to cut out, and then he accessorizes it with stickers and glitter and slashes of Sharpie marker to look like a row of stitches.

"It'll be a monster pumpkin," he says.

"Ooh," my mom says. "Frightening."

Nico knocks his knee against mine under the table. "Which one are you gonna carve?" he asks as I thumb through Poppy's sketchbook.

"I don't know. Poppy's designs are good. There are too many choices." He leans over my shoulder to check out my sister's art and a flop of his hair tickles my cheek. I breathe him in and decide I want to bottle the smell of him and spray it on my pillowcase. "What're you carving?"

"Pennywise. From *It*." He holds his pumpkin up for inspection. "Trying to, at least."

"Didn't even have to think about it, huh?"

"Nope."

"Did you read the book *and* see the movie?"

"I saw Chapter One of the reboot five times." He shudders like just the thought of it scares him. "What about you?"

I shrug. "I don't really like scary stuff. Real life is scary enough."

My mom untangles slimy, wet pumpkin strings from her fingers and tosses them into a bowl. "A natural moisturizer," she chimes. "Antioxidants. Zinc. I'm going to mix a face mask. Who wants to join me?"

I cringe. Lean into Nico and whisper, "See what I mean?"

"I'll join," Poppy says.

"Me too," says Sequoia.

"Welcome to my weird," I mutter.

"I like your weird." He knocks his knee against mine again.

"Good. Because it doesn't end here."

My dad collects the pumpkin guts for the compost bin after my mom has fished out all the seeds for roasting and set aside her face mask portion. By the time the sun sets, there's a bowl of roasted pumpkin seeds on the coffee table and five fantastic pumpkins lined up and lit on our front porch.

Sequoia bounces off the walls, ready for trick-or-treating. We've always been allowed to go out and get candy, but we have to drop it off at a collection bin at the fire station that they donate to veterans. Anything that isn't candy is okay to keep, so Sequoia stakes out houses for stamps and stickers and pennies and bubbles. I'm sure this would lead to a massive meltdown in most households, but when you don't know another way, I'm not sure you think about it.

My brother is eager to hit the sidewalks as soon as it's dark out, while Poppy falls back dramatically on the couch, her hands clutching a book.

"I'm too old for trick-or-treating," she says.

"You can stay home and pass out toothbrushes with us," my mom tells her.

I feel a prickle in my scalp.

I have to pull my parents aside and tell them about the video I saw at the library. About all the comments. And the anger. It's not safe for us to welcome trick-or-treaters to our home. In fact, we should blow out the candles of our jack-o'-lanterns and bring them inside. They'll look just as cute on the back porch. Right?

I ask my mom and dad to follow me to the backyard, where Nico pulls up the video and photos on his phone.

My mom's eyes well up. "Russ," she says to my dad, grabbing his arm. "This is awful."

My dad pushes the phone away. "I've seen enough."

"We can't have trick-or-treaters," I say.

My dad nods. "You're right."

"Maybe Sequoia shouldn't go out, either," my mom says.

My brother will be crushed. I can see the meltdown now. "He'll be in a costume," I point out. "Nobody will recognize him."

"That's true," my dad says.

"I'll break the news to Poppy about the tooth-brushes," my mom says.

My dad takes her hand, and Nico and I follow my parents back into the house.

They're worried, but they put on their game faces for Sequoia because he's excited to hit the sidewalks with his treat bag.

I turn to Nico. "Do you want to come with Sequoia and me?"

"Sure." He grabs his backpack and unzips it.

"What're you doing? Do you carry an emergency costume in there or something?"

"Nah. Just a sweatshirt." He pulls a hoodie over his head. I laugh when he turns around and I can read the back of it: BIRTH. MOVIES. DEATH.

"Such a film geek," I say.

"I try."

My dad helps Sequoia dress up as a detective from a mystery novel. *Dun dun dun.* The hat and plastic glasses with a mustache attached make him hard to recognize. It's also for this reason that, in addition to my usual jeans and sweatshirt, I wear one of my grandma's Mardi Gras masks when we head out the door. It's gold, purple, and green, with feathers and ribbons hanging down the right side of my head like a ponytail. The mask is big enough to cover my face from my forehead to my upper lip, making me unrecognizable.

"Be safe," my mom says.

"We're trusting you'll keep an eye on your brother," my dad says.

"I will."

I shake my head at the treat bowl my mom had set up by the front door.

"Can you believe they were going to pass out biodegradable bamboo toothbrushes?" I mutter to Nico.

He laughs. "Yep. You're *that* house." He presses his hand to my lower back. Leans in. "It's a good thing, you know. Saving the planet. Preventing cavities."

"I know it's a good thing. It's just . . . why do they have to make such a *statement* all the time? Just because they knew kids would be getting boatloads of candy tonight, they wanted to be the house that reminded them how bad that is. Can't they just take a night off for once?"

"They are taking a night off, aren't they?"

"Right. By force."

Nico shrugs. "I don't know. I think it's kind of cool in a way. They're passionate about what they believe in.

How's that any different than me liking movies and you wanting to get vaccinated?"

I let the words sink in, pondering. I know he's right. My parents do a lot of good things. Biodegradable bamboo toothbrushes are a *good* thing. But judging kids for eating candy on Halloween is over the top.

Sequoia yanks at my hand impatiently. "Come on," he groans.

We head out the front door and my mom turns out the lights. Our house goes dark. Off-limits. Do not enter. I leave it behind me and walk into the cool evening. It feels good to be outside, caught up in the excited energy echoing underneath the moon and stars. The air smells like fall. Like roasting marshmallows and wet leaves and chimney smoke.

Sequoia pulls me along yet insists he's big enough to go to the doors of houses on his own. Fine. Getting mixed up in a clump of kids will make him stand out even less.

Nico and I hang back on the sidewalk, trying to stay out of the way of wobbly toddlers and their overzealous parents taking videos on their phones.

"What'd you get?" Nico asks Sequoia after he returns breathless from the first house.

"A peanut butter pumpkin thing."

"Ooh, the good stuff." Nico takes a step back. "But keep it away from me. I'm allergic."

Sequoia shoves the candy into the reusable shopping bag my mom gave him. "You're allergic to candy?"

"Peanuts."

"I'm allergic to baths," Sequoia says.

I laugh. "I think that might be true."

And before I know it, my brother has raced up to the next house, disappearing into the throng of Teenage Mutant Ninja Turtles and Wonder Women.

"Halloween, man." Nico laughs and shakes his head. "I almost want to be a little kid again."

"What's the best costume you ever had?"

He twists his face, thinking. "Zombie."

"A movie zombie?"

"Is there another kind of zombie?"

Sequoia runs past us to the next house, and we move forward a few more steps.

"Right. Silly question." I bump his hip with mine. "What's your favorite scary movie?"

"Oh, man, there are so many good ones. Even the ones that are so bad they're good."

"Like?"

"*Return of the Living Dead*, for instance." Nico's voice takes on that excited tone it gets whenever he talks about movies. "The title tricks you into thinking it's related to Romero's *Night of the Living Dead*, of course."

"Oh, of course." I look at him and grin. "I mean, I totally assumed it."

"You have no idea what I'm talking about, do you?"

"Here's what you sounded like to me." I make air quotes. "'*Blah blah. Blah blah blah blah.*'"

"Harsh." I'd worry I had actually hurt his feelings if it wasn't obvious that he was trying not to laugh.

I put my hands up in defense, playing along. "My sincerest apologies. I didn't mean to offend."

He sticks his arms out and clomps toward me, letting out a bellow. "Bah ha ha! Zombies don't get offended."

"You are such a dork."

He continues his uneven forward stomp. Grabs for my waist. Presses his fingertips into my hips, electrifying every one of my nerve endings. We're standing in the middle of a crowded sidewalk, but so what? I fall into him. I slide my mask on top of my head, bury my face in the nape of his neck, and inhale. He is campfire smoke and citrus shampoo. And safety. His skin is soft and warm against my nose. His arms tighten around me, hugging me closer.

"I'm really glad you came to the library," he says softly in my ear. "Before and today."

"Me too."

Kids rustle past us, their plastic pumpkins full of candy bumping our legs. My heart skitters in my chest. All I want is for Nico to kiss me. I wait for it.

But then he pulls back. Squints. "Doesn't your brother know he's supposed to skip the houses with the lights off?"

I look over my shoulder to find Sequoia pounding furiously against a darkened front door two houses down.

"Ugh. Obviously not." I break away from Nico and rush to collect my brother as I pull my mask back on. "Sequoia! Come here!"

He gives me a quick glance and pounds again. I grab his hand and pull him away.

"Stop! I'm trick-or-treating! None of these houses have stickers. It's all candy."

"You don't knock on the doors where the lights are off. They don't have treats."

"Oh. Sorry."

"Don't apologize. You didn't know. But now you do."

As we make our way back to the sidewalk, the automatic garage door of the darkened house groans open and a forest-green SUV pulls into the driveway.

"They're home," Sequoia shouts, and goes rushing to the car. "Trick or treat!"

Taken aback, the woman presses into the driver's seat.

"Trick or treat," Sequoia says again as I scramble up behind him.

The woman sits there silently, almost confused, like she didn't realize it was Halloween until just now.

"Oh, honey. I don't have any candy," she says as she cautiously exits the car.

And then I can't suck in air.

Because I recognize her immediately.

Baby Kat's mom.

This town is too small.

She doesn't look bright and vibrant like she did at Mary's stand at the farmers market, when she showed off her newborn with the little white bow in her hair. When her baby was tucked tight and safe in a ladybug sling, away from people like me. It was her first time out. I remember her saying that. She'd been nervous. Worried. Maybe deep down she knew.

I take a step back, thankful for my Mardi Gras mask.

"That's okay. I'll take pennies or stickers," my brother says.

"Sequoia!" I'm horrified. "He doesn't know all the rules," I tell her.

I turn my brother around by the shoulders.

"No. Wait." Her voice is thin behind me. I turn back. Stand still in front of her.

I say, "Okay," even though I really want to leave. Because maybe she recognizes me after all. My voice. My mannerisms. Maybe she wants to grab her husband so he can punch me in the face and wring my neck to get even. So he can leave me in a bloody heap that someone will confuse for gruesome Halloween decor.

But she rummages through her purse instead. Her hands shake. She drops it. Scrambles to pick it up again. She digs around, and I hear keys and spare coins jingling, until she unearths an orange lollipop. She hands it over to Sequoia.

"This is all I have," she says.

"What do you say?" I ask him.

"Thanks."

"Thank you," I tell her. "I promise to talk to him about skipping the houses with the lights off."

She sighs. "I don't like that we're that house." She looks at the ground. Shakes her head. "It's been a rough few weeks. I didn't have it in me."

"I understand," I say.

She looks at me sharply. "Do you, though?"

My face falls, but it's hidden behind my Mardi Gras mask. I feel like I know everything about her, but she knows nothing about me. To her, I'm anonymous. Just a person in a mask. "I mean . . ."

She waves her hand. "I'm sorry." How ironic it is to stand here, listening to Baby Kat's mom apologize to me when I wish I could apologize to her. "That was so rude of me. I had no right to say that to you."

"It's okay."

"It isn't."

But it is. She has every right to go off on me. If she knew who I was, she'd probably have a lot more to say. I study her. The dark circles under her eyes. The way the light has left her face. She's broken.

I need to go. I steer Sequoia away. I grab the lollipop from my brother, shove it in my pocket, and race to the sidewalk, with him trailing behind me.

"Why the hustle?" Nico says.

"That was Katherine St. Pierre's mom," I tell him,

taking big strides toward the next house, trying to get away as quickly as I can.

"Oh, man." He walks faster to keep up with me. "Are you okay?"

"Not really." Sequoia runs up to another house. I can't even care where he goes right now, because it won't be any worse than where he just went.

Nico reaches for me and I shake him off. "Juniper."

I put up my hand. "Don't."

Nico looks at me, and his eyes are sad and shiny. "I want to be able to say the right thing, but I don't know what it is."

"There's nothing to say. I have to live with this. But those parents have to live with something far worse because of something my family did."

"Do you want to go home?"

"No. I want Sequoia to have fun."

And I do. I'm committed to it. We tromp toward the next house, even though every step feels like a chore. I want to give my brother what I don't have. A fun night. No worries. Because even with my Mardi Gras mask, I can't be invisible. Not even to myself.

I know who I am and what I did.

We go house to house for the next hour, and my brother's candy bag gets heavier and heavier. The weight of it eventually makes him slump to one side. His candy will probably fill the whole donation bin at the fire station.

When he hands his bag to me because he can't carry it anymore, I say, "I think we're done." I turn to Nico. "I really do want to go home now."

We manage to make it the few blocks back to our house, where Sequoia runs inside to sift through his treats, trying to find the few non-candy items he can keep.

"Thanks for coming with us," I tell Nico.

"I still had fun," he says as we stand on the sidewalk in front of my house to say good-bye. "I hope you did, too."

"It was great until . . ."

"Yeah." He kicks at the edge of the grass between the sidewalk and the street. "Wanna try again tomorrow night? There's a football game. Playa's in the playoffs."

"Really?" I do want to go. I want to spend more time with Nico. But I'm also scared of going out in public. Of being recognized.

"I've got study group after school. Kickoff's at five, but I can stop by here a little before. Cool?"

I nod. "Yeah." Because I'm willing to take the risk for Nico.

But right now, I need a good cry. The tears are already slipping before I've shut the door to my room. I throw myself across the bed, and the mini Milky Way bars I swiped from Sequoia's trick-or-treat bag fall from my sweatshirt pockets and scatter across my quilt, along with the orange lollipop from Baby Kat's mom.

I let out a sob and it shakes me, racking my chest.

I don't want my parents to hear me and come to my room, so I shove my fist against my mouth, trying to muffle myself. I burrow underneath my covers, knees to my stomach like a ball. The candy is lost to my sheets somewhere.

I can hear my dad making monster noises through the floor, and Poppy and Sequoia screeching and giggling. That makes me cry more.

Apparently, I'm not stealthy enough, because my mom taps on the door a minute later.

"Juniper, can I come in?" she asks.

"Whatever."

She opens my door. "I'm choosing to translate 'whatever' to mean yes." She shuffles over to my bed, and I pull the quilt up to let her in.

"What's going on?"

"Everything."

"Did something happen with Nico?"

"No. He's fine."

She shifts positions, and a Milky Way bar rustles underneath her. She pulls it free and holds it up to me, raising her eyebrows, but she doesn't say anything as she sets it on the nightstand. "He does seem like a kind boy."

"He is." I sniff and shove the edge of my quilt to the corners of my eyes to soak up the tears.

"So what's got you so upset?"

"Sequoia rang the doorbell at the St. Pierres' house tonight."

My mom freezes. "Oh no."

I clutch a handful of quilt in my hands.

"You and Dad keep saying nobody's to blame, but I don't think that's true. Our family isn't innocent in all of this," I sputter. "The St. Pierres lost everything, because I wasn't vaccinated. And from where I'm standing, that was a terrible choice."

"Oh, Junebug." She looks at me resolutely. "I know you think you know everything, but you don't. Your dad and I did not come to our decision lightly. We read articles and did our research. And there was real-world experience. The little boy who lived down the street from us when I was pregnant with you, for one. He started showing signs of autism right after his MMR shot."

"Mom, the link between the MMR vaccine and autism has been debunked."

"Nevertheless . . ."

"No. There's no nevertheless. It's not true. There's no link. Besides that, do you even realize how offensive your argument is? You make it sound like it's worse to have an autistic kid than a dead kid. That's so messed up."

"Every decision I make, I make for you," she murmurs.

I want to talk to her calmly. Rationally. But I can't help sobbing into the quilt. "I don't understand how you can see me upset like this and still tell me I can't get the vaccinations I want." She reaches for my hand, but I pull away. "So much of what you and Dad do, what you've taught us, is about making the world a better place for *everyone*. Vaccinations do that, too." I look her right in the eye. "I don't want this to happen again, Mom. Not to me. Not to anybody."

She angles her face to the ceiling and closes her eyes. Like it hurts too much to have them open.

Like it hurts too much to see the truth.

TWENTY-FIVE

The football stadium smells like wet grass and popcorn. I hold tight to Nico's hand as we push through the excited crowd, trying to find a seat. The bright fluorescent floodlights buzz above us, and my eardrums vibrate with the echo of cheers and the chatter of students in the stands. It's so packed, so busy, that part of me wants to curl up and retreat. But Nico's hand is soft and warm, pushing me forward.

"My friends and I usually sit somewhere around here," he says, pointing out two empty seats at the end of a cement bench in the middle of the student section.

I'd expected we'd sit off to the side somewhere. Inconspicuous and away from people who might watch online videos from the local pumpkin patch on an endless loop. Because they still haunt me. The yells. The taunts. The spittle. The threats.

Murderers.

"What if someone recognizes me?" I say.

"Nah. Most of the people I know aren't paying attention to stuff like that."

He's so sure, so confident, that I can't help but trust him. I square my shoulders. Commit. "Lead the way."

We walk up alternating steps of red and yellow, painted in school colors, to take our seats. Various people say hi to Nico along the way. The constant greetings make me feel like all eyes are on us, but when I really look at everyone, we're merely a blip and they've gone back to focusing on the band marching through the middle of the field, pounding drums and blaring horns, while color guard girls wearing red and yellow sweaters and silver skirts that catch the light twirl flags and batons. I sit down, pull the red knit hat Poppy made me last Christmas lower over my ears, and tuck my hair into the back of my sweatshirt.

A guy in front of us turns around. Says, "What up?" to Nico.

Nico greets him with a lift of his chin and a "hey."

A girl from a few rows behind us calls out Nico's name. He turns around and waves.

"Come sit up here," she shouts.

"We're good," he calls back, then turns to me and rubs his hands together in anticipation of the big game.

"Are you the mayor or something? You know everybody."

"Nah. Just been in this small town since kindergarten."

He bumps my shoulder and places his hand on my knee. When his fingertips sink into the skin between the rips in my jeans, it makes my heart skitter. "All good?" he asks.

I nod and watch the field. If I look him in the eye, I'll give away everything. Like how much I like him.

I focus on the sights and sounds instead. I break into a smile, my cheeks somehow warming despite the cold air.

I can't believe I'm really here.

I'm finally in this.

I know enough about football from what Bumpa taught me watching games on TV at his house on Thanksgiving and Christmas, but I've never been to a game in person, where I can actually feel the vibrations of the ground under my feet. Hear the metallic pom-pom tassels swish through the air. See the vibrant green of the grass.

The hickory scent of chimney smoke wafts through the stadium, and I wonder if it's coming from my house, where this fall's football games have only been an echo through my kitchen as my family ate dinner together. Garbled. Distant. Not mine.

There's a screech of feedback through the stadium speakers, and people put their hands to their ears to protect them from the shrill sound. A booming voice announces the team. "And now, it's my pleasure to present to you, your Playa Bonita Condors in their first playoff appearance since 2016!"

People in the stadium chant, "Caw, caw!" and I can't help but laugh.

"I still can't get over the fact that your mascot is a practically extinct California vulture."

Nico laughs. "Gotta represent."

A cannon fires and I startle in my seat as the team comes crashing through a hand-painted banner held up by cheerleaders. I hear the rip of the paper. Fans in the bleachers stand up, chanting and clapping. Nico stands too, pumping his fist in the air. I look up at him, debating whether to join.

"School spirit!" he says, urging me to join him. "Come on! You wanted the full experience, right?"

I give in, getting on my feet and cheering with him, unable to deny the rush of adrenaline it gives me.

The first quarter passes in a whir. First down. Third down. A field goal. A touchdown. Through it all, the cheerleaders flip in the air and the band plays "Seven Nation Army" by the White Stripes. The drumbeat pounds a trancelike rhythm that reverberates in my belly and my fingertips. The student section locks their arms across each other's shoulders and bounces side to side in unison. One row goes to the right while the other goes to the left. I wonder what we look like to the fans of the opposing team sitting in the shabby wooden bleachers across the field from us. Intimidating? Doubtful.

Nico locks his hand over my shoulder and pulls me with him as our row bounces and sways to the music.

The drum section takes over, and my skin prickles with goose bumps as the crowd chants along with the beat, "Oh, whoa, oh, oh, oh, oh."

I take my free hand and swipe at my face and swear I feel tears. Of happiness. Because I've always wanted this. To be a part of something. To belong.

At halftime, Playa is up by a touchdown and the team runs, all muddied and sweaty, to the locker room as everyone in the bleachers stands up at the same time, making a collective rumbling sound.

"Want a Coke or something?" Nico says, looking toward the snack stand in the distance.

I brush off the back of my jeans. "Sure."

Soda. Another thing that's not okay for Team Jade to consume, but I go with him anyway. I won't tell him my dad calls soda "sugar water."

Nico holds my hand as we weave through the crowd, bumping and jostling against the throng of bodies all heading to get food at the same time. Someone stops Nico to say hi every five seconds. When he turns to talk to a guy with dreadlocks, a tall girl in a short skirt clips my shoulder.

"Oops," I say. A knee-jerk reaction.

"Try sorry," she hisses.

"Sorry."

She laughs. "I'm just messing with you." She glances at my hand entwined with Nico's. "You're here with this guy," she says, motioning to Nico. "You can't suck too bad."

"Oh."

"Have fun," she says, and walks away.

"Who is that?" I ask Nico before she completely disappears.

"Who's who?" He looks all around.

"Do you know that girl?"

"There are a lot of girls here. You have to be more specific."

"That tall girl with the plaid skirt who was just talking to me."

He shrugs. "I didn't see her. But I'm sure we've hung out at some point."

"Is hanging out code for something?" I want to shove the words back into my mouth. "Forget it." I flutter my free hand between us. "I don't know why I said that."

Nico crinkles his eyes to study me, like he's taking in every inch of my face to understand me better. And then he smiles, leaning his head closer to mine so that our foreheads almost touch. "You do realize I'm here with you, right?"

"Yeah. I know."

"Okay, good." He presses his forehead to mine. "Because I'm hoping this isn't just a one-time thing. And I also hope it's more than hanging out."

Every nerve ending in my body fizzes. "Yeah. Same."

"Cool. Let's go get some food."

We pinball our way through the thick crowd as we make our way to the snack stand. As we stand shoulder to shoulder in line, I jump when someone bumps into me again. Jared from film club.

"Juniper! You're here!" he says, with genuine excitement to see me. "Did Nico tell you about our next meeting? We missed you at my sci-fi double feature."

Nico buries his face in my hair like he's telling me a secret. "Longest night ever." I feel his smile against my ear. His lips. His breath. My insides fizz again. He's close, but I want him closer.

"Sorry to have missed it," I say.

"You should come to the next meeting," Jared says, twisting to fist-bump a guy walking past him with Air-Pods shoved into his ears. "We're screening classics from the eighties."

"You'll love it," Nico says, pulling back from me. I reach for his hand to keep him near. "We're gonna watch high school movies." He playfully nudges his elbow into my rib. "Lots of cafeterias. Your favorite."

I elbow him back. "Are you making fun of me?"

Nico grins. "Not even. Come. I want you to."

"Okay. I'll ask my parents."

"Sweet," Jared says.

We move forward an inch at a time, and when we finally get to the front of the line, I can't bring myself to actually order a Coke. I remember the pizza and the way it made my stomach sick. Maybe some of my parents' rules aren't the worst. I order hot apple cider instead and pull a dollar bill out from the back pocket of my jeans. But Nico pushes my hand away.

"I got it. Don't worry."

"Oh." I put my money back into my pocket. "Thank you."

We make our way back to our seats and sit down in our cement row of bleachers right as the band finishes up their halftime show. I sip my cider and watch band members take their places in the section of bleachers reserved especially for them. The team runs back onto the field and before I know it, the game starts up and that energy returns along with the cheers and the swaying and the pom-poms and the crackly commentary over the loudspeaker.

With two minutes left in the fourth quarter, the game is tied. But Playa has the ball. Everyone in the bleachers is on their feet. I try not to bite my nails, but I'm not sure where else to focus my nervous energy. My stomach flips, and I wonder how I can care so much so quickly. But I really want Playa to win. Maybe it's because I just discovered this magic and I'm not ready to walk away from it yet. If they lose tonight, they're out of the playoffs and the season is over. I want another game. Another night like this.

With Nico.

With everyone.

At under a minute left to play, the stadium hauls in a collective breath when Playa takes a chance on a critical fourth down. I dig my fingernails into the palm of my hand. *Please get it. Please*, I chant in my head. Without thinking, I grab Nico's hand and bury my face against his shoulder.

"I can't watch."

"We have to watch." He nudges my cheek with his shoulder so I'll look. "Our team needs us. This is a classic movie moment right here. You can't miss it."

I open my eyes just as Playa players push forward, all together, and we manage to get the inches needed for a first down. The stadium erupts in cheers. But on the next play, Playa almost loses the ball. Everyone groans. And finally, with four seconds to go, Playa has gotten within field goal range. The kicker runs out to the field, surrounded by a wave of cheers and shaking pom-poms.

We all watch nervously as the ball is snapped.

The kick is good.

Playa wins.

I jump up and down. All the students scream in celebratory glee. Nico hugs me and I want to sink into him and stay there forever. And then, in the heat of the moment, in the excitement, he does it. He kisses me. A quick swipe of his lips on mine. Everything inside me flutters. I smile against his mouth.

When we pull away, I look up at him. He's staring back at me. His big brown eyes are happy. Dancing. I know mine are, too. Because I'm pretty sure this is the best night of my entire life.

TWENTY-SIX

After the game, my cheeks are cold from the wind as Nico and I roll to a stop in front of a craftsman bungalow a few blocks from the school. I only know the house is called a craftsman bungalow because it's the same as the house we live in. They're popular in Playa Bonita. Nico's on his bike. I'm on my skateboard. Both of us with helmets intact. We unsnap them in unison.

"Dorks times two," I say.

He uncoils his bike lock, loops it through his back tire, wraps it around a skinny tree trunk, and clicks it closed. "If *dork* were a sound, it'd be a ten-speed bike lock clicking shut around a tree in front of a high school party."

"Well, you don't want anything to get stolen."

"Yep. Gotta keep things safe," he says, patting his bike seat.

I can't help but laugh.

The party is bigger than I'd expected. Crowded with people like something out of one of the CW shows I watched at Mimi and Bumpa's house over the summer. When I see the swell of bodies packed inside through the big front window, I feel claustrophobic already. And then there is laughter. Screeches. The heavy thump of music seeping into the street.

I pull my skateboard closer to my hip like a shield.

Nico eases my skateboard free and shoves it underneath the braided metal of his bike-lock tether. It'll do nothing to protect my board, but it looks like it's secure in theory. "The party's gonna be fine. I'm right here with you. It's basically the football game with beer and music."

"And drunk people I don't know."

"The beauty of drunk people is precisely the fact that they're drunk. They have no idea what's going on."

I nod my head, trying to exude confidence. "Okay. Let's go."

The front door is unlocked, and Nico walks right in like he lives here. We're instantly assaulted by a too-sweet strawberry-scented vape cloud. I cough. The guy who blew it bobs his head at me and inhales again. Thankfully, he blows the smelly cloud over his shoulder into someone else's face this time. We land in the living room, where the coffee table is filled end to end with empty red plastic cups and a half-drained bottle of clear liquid that I'm pretty sure isn't water. There are two couples making out on the couch. Two guys on one end and a girl and guy on the other end. Everyone's hands wander to places that make me feel like a perv for watching, so I turn away.

I focus on the video game playing on the TV instead. It's one of those first-person shooter games where you only see the back of someone pushing through an empty warehouse with a gun. It's the kind of game Sequoia will probably want to play someday and my mom will have to curl up into the fetal position in the corner of her bedroom, crying and asking where she went wrong. I can't even tell who's playing, since there are too many people here and the couch is taken.

"Another room?" Nico says.

"Good idea."

We push through the throng of people. A drunk guy goes off-kilter, banging into my shoulder. I grab for Nico's hand and our fingers lock. He squeezes. And I'm suddenly back in that classroom with the movie playing and the pizza steaming and Nico all excited about Stephen King. Here and now, he turns around and smiles at me. I smile back.

In the kitchen, there's a line for the keg, and people in it that shouldn't be because they're already too drunk. But who am I to say?

We lean against the counter, where empty chip bags are scattered across the black-and-brown-speckled granite. I can only imagine how disgusted my dad would be. "Heart disease in a bag," he'd say.

I admit there's a part of me that wants to clean up this mess. To sort it out between bins for recycling or composting. I hold Nico's hand tighter to stop myself.

Next to us, a girl dumps a bag of peanut M&M's into an empty bowl. Nico flinches. *Peanuts*. She leaves.

"Do you drink?" Nico asks.

I shrug. "I haven't. But I can. I guess?"

"No pressure, okay?"

I nod. "None felt."

We get in line for beer. Everyone pushes forward until my knee bangs into the side of the metal keg with a clang. I quickly regain my balance so Nico can let go of my hand to grab cups for us. I have no idea how to work the faucet thing, but Nico handles it like he does it all the time.

"Maybe just halfway?" he says to me, and I nod.

He fills my cup first, hands it to me, then knocks his own full cup against mine. Some beer burps up over the rim and gets my thumb wet.

"Cheers," he says.

"Cheers."

He takes a sip.

I take a sip.

The beer is bitter and bubbly and foamy. It's gross like black coffee in a different way. I want to spit it out, but I swallow it down instead. I'm pretty sure I wince, because Nico slants his head to the side. Softens his gaze on me.

"You cool?" he asks.

"If you mean am I cool with the beer, yes. If you're asking if I'm cool in general, not even close."

He smiles. Points at himself. "Dork with the bike lock, remember?"

"How could I forget?" I tap my elbow to his. "But your winning film knowledge makes me swoon, so . . ."

"Does it now?" He leans against the counter, his brown eyes locked on mine. "What else makes you swoon?"

"I don't know." Everything. "What makes *you* swoon?"

He grins. "Oh, Juniper, where do I start?"

"Wherever you want."

"Well . . ." He leans forward just as some guy pushes into me, spinning me out of the way so he can get to the keg. My hip bone digs into the edge of the counter. "Dude," Nico says to him as he grabs my elbow to steady me.

"My bad," the guy says, stumbling away and bumping into everyone else in his way like a bowling ball knocking down pins.

Nico presses his hand to my hip where it hit the counter. "You okay?" he asks. His fingers skim the space between the top of my jeans and the bottom of my sweatshirt. I can feel the heat of his fingers through the cotton. I want to feel his fingers against my skin instead.

"I'm okay."

"Yeah?"

"I mean, I'll be lucky to leave here without bruises." I squint at the crowd. "This place is more packed than the football game. Do you know all these people?"

He looks around. "Pretty much. I've probably hung out with everyone here at one time or another."

"So whose house is this?"

"Mason and Mercy Miller's."

"That's a lot of M's."

He takes a long chug of beer. "Mmm."

"So they're married?" I say, emphasizing the M.

"Clever." He knocks his cup against mine in cheers. "They're twins."

"Do you know them more than sort of?"

"Mason and I were on the same Tee Ball team in first grade. Mercy and I did cotillion together in sixth."

"So it's been a while."

"You could say that, yeah." He takes another sip. "But this town is so small that everyone still knows each other, you know?"

"I don't. So far I know you. And Jared, I guess."

"Well, that's about as good as it gets, so . . ."

A roar goes up over Nico's shoulder as a Ping-Pong

ball lands in a cup of beer. Everyone around the table chants, "Drink! Drink!" and the guy drains his cup without coming up for air.

Someone else at the table holds a ball up to Nico. "Noble! You in?"

He shakes his head no.

I turn toward him. "I love how your last name is Noble. Like a noble fir Christmas tree. You're so festive. I want to drape you in tinsel."

"Do you now?"

My face flushes red. Oh jeez. What am I saying? "I mean . . ."

He smiles. "Forget the tinsel. My name's all about being tall and sturdy and shit." He pounds his chest.

I look him up and down. "But you're not that tall."

"Ah, but I'm sturdy." He raises an eyebrow at me.

"Wow."

"I aim to wow."

"You're pretty good at it, honestly."

"Yeah?" He takes a sip of beer. Smiles over the edge of his cup.

I take a sip, too. Smile back. "Yeah."

"Good to know."

A sloshy, wobbly girl leans against the counter next to us. She points at me as approximately twenty metal bracelets as thin as pencil points slide up her wrist toward her elbow.

"I know you," she slurs. "You're that girl my mom

showed me. The one from the video at the pumpkin patch."

I shake my head in a mixture of trying to clear it and also faking a *nope, not me.*

"You are. Oh my god. Your family is totally evil." She pulls on the collar of an enormous guy, all muscle and brawn and clearly a football player, standing behind her. "Teddy, this is her! The girl from that family that got the measles."

"Whoa," Teddy says. "Did you have 'em, too?"

The girl slaps him on the shoulder. "Dude. That's literally what I said."

"Actually, it isn't," Nico mutters.

"Sorry." Teddy holds up his cup to the girl. "I'm kinda . . ." He makes a face that I assume is supposed to indicate that he's out of it.

"You're such an idiot sometimes," she says.

They fall into each other, laughing sloppily.

Nico angles in sideways, creating a shield between all of us.

"Seriously, though." The girl looks at me and shudders. "Are you still contagious?"

"Dude, she wouldn't be here," Teddy says. "Unless she wants to kill us all."

"Not us. We've all had the measles shot. She just wants to kill babies."

I drop my cup on the counter with a thump. Take a step back.

"That's enough," Nico says. "Leave her alone, Avery."

I know I should say something. I want to say something. The right thing. The same way Nico wanted to say the right thing on Halloween. But I don't know what that right thing is.

"You should go home," Teddy says to me. "For real."

Avery throws her head back and laughs. "You're so brutal, Teddy."

Teddy snorts obnoxiously. Pumps his fist in the air. "Go home! Go home!" he chants the same way the group at the table behind us chanted, "Drink! Drink!"

I don't even think before I do it. I just push on his chest with my hands. And Teddy goes tumbling to the floor in a tangled mess of limbs and muscles. Laughter erupts all around him. He rights himself, lifts up on his elbows, and looks at me with rage in his eyes.

"What's your problem?" he says.

"You deserved it," says Nico.

"You little . . ." He scrambles back to his feet, lunges for Nico. "You're dead, dude."

We both duck and Teddy stumbles into the breakfast nook, his head hitting the light dangling above it. He falls into one of the built-in benches almost like it's on purpose. Like he's going to sit up and eat scrambled eggs now. But he doesn't. That last hit sobered him up, and he grunts his way to standing and hulks out in front of us.

"Teddy," Nico says, putting his hands up. "Let's not do this."

Teddy's nostrils flare. "Oh, we're doing it." He balls his hands into fists. Releases. Balls them again.

A bunch of girls scream, which alerts five huge, scary guys to rush in from the other room. *Great. The football team.* They look left and right and up and down, clearly trying to find someone more intimidating than Nico from the film club.

"Stop," I say, blocking Nico.

Teddy stands in front of us, breathing hard through clenched teeth.

"Look, I don't know who you are," one of the other football guys says to me. "But you better get out of the way while these two work this out."

Teddy sways from side to side. Grunts like a bull in the ring.

The kitchen is chaos. Filled with people. Screams. Empty cups flying. And why is the music so loud? The guns from the video game are still shooting. All the noise hurts my head and my brain. I hold my hands to my ears.

"Stop!" I yell. It comes out long and screechy, filled with O's. "We're leaving."

I grab Nico by the elbow and pull him through the sliding glass door to the backyard.

Teddy pushes toward us, but a couple of guys pull him back.

"Let him go," one of them says. "It's not worth it. Playoffs, Teddy Bear. Remember?"

Laughter swells up behind us.

"How do we get out of here?" I say, fumbling with the latch on the side gate that will lead us to the front yard. My hands are shaking and I can't grip it. I look over my shoulder to see if anyone's coming. Nico stands there silently.

I finally unhook the latch and pull us into the front yard as the gate slams shut behind us. I stride toward his bike. Loosen my skateboard from underneath the metal tether. I yank my helmet over my head.

"I should've taken care of that better," Nico says.

"No. I don't need saving. I don't need you swooping in like some superhero every time I mess up."

"That's not what I mean."

I turn to him. "You couldn't have taken care of that even if you wanted to. It was six against one, Nico. Did you see those guys? They were drunk and irrational and they would've killed you."

"But you didn't even let me try."

I turn to face him, my helmet slipping. "Try? Are you kidding me right now?"

He shrugs.

"Look, I'm not into all that fighting stuff. If that's your thing, if you're the kind of person who goes to parties to get into a fight, we shouldn't hang out anymore. As much as my parents annoy me, they taught me to be a pacifist. I don't like what I just did back there. I'm down with the peace and love thing."

"I'm not that guy. I've never even been in a fight before." He shakes his head. "But maybe I could've talked to them."

"Yeah? And what would've happened when they didn't want to listen?"

"I guess they'd kick my ass."

"Exactly."

He angrily wraps his lock around the handlebars of his bike. Then he shoves his helmet onto his head and fastens it. He turns to face me, frustration still biting at the corners of his eyes.

I can't help it. I burst out laughing.

"What?" he says.

"If you could see yourself right now, you'd know why I dragged you out of there. You do not look like someone who should attempt to take on six football players."

He leans against his bike. It teeters. "You're really saying I couldn't take them?" He flexes his biceps.

"Not even close." I lean closer to him. My mouth is practically touching his. "But that's why I like you."

"Yeah?"

I nod. "Yep."

He wraps his hands around my waist, his fingertips pressing into the space between the bottom of my sweatshirt and the top of my jeans again. He grabs at the edge of my shirt underneath. Lifts it up just enough to let his fingers skim my skin. "So you like me."

"I do. When you're being you."

"Good. I like you, too."

He leans in closer.

Closer still.

My eyes flutter shut.

Because I'm pretty sure Nico's going to kiss me again.

But now that I have time to think about it, a million things go through my mind at once. Do I tilt my head? Do I hold my breath? How do I start? How do I stop?

He presses against me.

I sigh happily.

And then, as it's about to happen, the tops of our helmets bang against each other, preventing our lips from meeting.

We both bounce back in shock.

"Oh, come on," Nico says, yanking off his helmet and throwing it to the ground.

He bends his knees so he can get up and underneath my helmet, and then his lips touch mine. Soft and sweet, like the Nico I know. Not like the Nico who wanted to punch Teddy five minutes ago in the kitchen. And even though I've never kissed anyone until tonight, my mouth somehow knows what to do. Maybe it's because Nico's guiding me in his own gentle way. A nudge. A swoop. I stop thinking and melt into him. Our hip bones pressing together. His hands still pushing into the small of my back, urging me closer.

TWENTY-SEVEN

I pull back from Nico because I suddenly remember Teddy and the rest of the football team. I told them we were leaving.

"We should go before anyone realizes we're still here," I say.

Nico kisses me again—one more quick peck—and climbs onto his bike.

"Yeah. Let's go," he says.

I admit getting on my skateboard instead of standing in the yard and kissing Nico all night long is the hardest thing I've ever had to do. I sigh in frustration.

"We could go to my house," he says.

I smile so wide it threatens to break my face. "Okay. I just have to tell my parents first."

"No problem."

We stop at my house to make sure it's okay if I go to

Nico's for a couple of hours. Since it's only nine o'clock, I'm hoping my parents will still be okay with the eleven p.m. curfew I had before we moved here. It takes a little convincing, and Nico promising he'll drive me home, but they say yes.

Nico's house is at the end of a cul-de-sac. It's two stories high, with a perfectly manicured front yard and a basketball hoop hanging above the garage door at the end of a long driveway.

"My brother's." He nods up at the hoop. "It sits sad and lonely while he's at college."

"That's kind of depressing."

"Yeah." He gestures to the side of the house. "This way." We go through the gate, which Nico leaves open as he parks his bike against the wall.

I prop my board up next to it. "Safe and sound."

"Now excuse me while I go earn the big bucks." He dashes back through the open gate and to the curb to wheel in a trash can, then does the same with the big blue recycling bin. "Okay. Now we can go inside."

A few feet up, along the same wall where Nico propped up his bike, there's a door that leads us into the kitchen. I follow Nico inside and he goes straight to the farmhouse-style sink to wash his hands.

"Nico, honey? Is that you?" a woman's voice calls from a nearby room.

"My mom," he tells me.

"I figured."

"Yeah," he calls back to her. He fills a glass of water from the sink and drains it in one take.

His mom rounds the corner into the kitchen. "Oh, good. I'm glad you're home. I kept hearing sirens, and I get nervous when you're out there on your bike."

He pats himself down. "I'm here. In one piece. All good."

Mrs. Noble reaches her hand out, pushes his floppy hair back from his forehead. "Did something happen? You look disheveled." She tugs at the front of his sweatshirt. "Your pocket is ripped."

"I fell off my bike. But I'm fine." He turns to me. "Mom, this is Juniper."

She turns to me, looking so much like Nico. The same dark eyes and hair. Hers falls in loose waves over her shoulders. "It's lovely to meet you, Juniper."

"You too."

Nico's mom turns to him. "Who won the game?"

"We did."

"Hooray! Go, Condors!" She pretends she's waving a pom-pom in the air.

Nico cringes, looking embarrassed. "Mom, you're gonna weird out Juniper."

"I was a cheerleader," she whispers to me, and waves her pretend pom-pom. She turns to Nico. "You should just be glad I'm not doing the kicks and the tumbles."

I can't help but smile. My mom would probably tell me some story about how the cheerleaders were mean to her in high school, but Nico's mom seems nice. And genuine.

Nico refills his water cup. Asks me if I want one too by raising his eyebrows at me, then the faucet. I nod.

"So we're just gonna hang and watch a movie or something," Nico tells his mom. There's the slightest undercurrent to his tone that says it's okay for her to leave now.

"Oh. Right. Okay. I've got some work to go over anyway."

"It was nice to meet you," I say, taking a seat on one of the stools at the kitchen island.

"Likewise."

"Sirens." Nico shakes his head as she leaves. "She is such a worrier." He pulls off his hoodie, and it takes half the T-shirt underneath with it. I sit there watching, trying to figure out how someone who says he sucks at sports manages to look that good without a shirt on. After his T-shirt falls back over his stomach, he empties his jeans pockets onto the island. Student ID. Some crumpled-up dollar bills. An EpiPen. Cell phone. He turns his attention toward the fridge. "You want some food? We have leftover lasagna."

"Nah, I'm good. I ate dinner early. Before the game."

"My mom makes the best lasagna. You'll be missing out," he taunts as he walks back to me, peeling the tin-foil off the top of a half-empty casserole dish. He sets it down between us. Then he opens a nearby drawer, grabs two forks, and hands me one. "In case you change your mind."

"Have you ever had to use that?" I ask, pointing my fork at the EpiPen.

"Nope. And hopefully never will." He takes a bite of lasagna. Chews.

"Do you know how to use it?"

He grabs the capped EpiPen and holds it a few inches from his outer thigh. "Pop the top off and jam it in." He quickly swings his arm toward his thigh like he's pitching a softball. "No hesitation."

"That seems scary."

He takes another bite of lasagna. Talks around it. "Not as scary as suffocating because your throat is closing up."

"True."

I dig my fork into the lasagna and take a bite. "Oh, wow."

"Good, right?" He takes another bite and so do I.

My eyes dart to the sleek stainless-steel appliances and the soapstone countertops of Nico's kitchen. So different from my house, where we still have my grandma's avocado-green refrigerator and the linoleum floors to match. Nico's house screams new and modern, while ours screams time warp.

"You want more?" Nico gestures to the casserole dish. I shake my head, and he refastens the tinfoil and shoves the pan back into the fridge. "Movie?"

"Definitely."

I follow him into another room with a flat-screen so big it practically takes up the entire wall. There are speakers affixed to the ceiling in the corners of the room and a big, cushy leather couch with built-in cup holders and seats that recline.

"It's like your own private movie theater," I say.

"That's the goal."

"Lucky you."

"So we can stream something, or you can choose a movie from the old-school collection. But be warned, a lot of them are my mom's." He opens a massive cupboard filled with DVDs and VHS tapes. "Pick whatever you want."

I walk over to the cupboard. Run my fingers across the spines. "It's almost better than a library shelf." I look at him over my shoulder. *"Almost."*

"I won't fault you for liking books better than films."

I pull some movies out and read the synopses on the backs like I would do with books at the library. I ponder one called *10 Things I Hate About You.*

"This one?" I say.

"I'm not surprised you picked that one. It's a modern-day *Taming of the Shrew*. And a classic teen film."

"No way. I'm so in."

I settle onto the couch while he sets up the movie. And by the time the opening credits start, he's sitting next to me, my hand in his, which is exactly what I've been waiting for since we snapped our helmets shut outside the party. I zero in on every detail of the opening credits, especially when one guy points out all the different school cliques to the new guy as they walk through campus.

"Is this what it's like in the cafeteria?" I ask.

"Your fascination with the cafeteria is adorable."

A few seconds later, Nico laughs at a joke I don't get, but I don't care because the sound of his laughter makes my heart trip.

I try to keep my focus, but all too soon, my eyes wander from the screen to look at Nico. At the way his hair and eyelashes fall. At the faint sprinkling of freckles across his nose. At the way his jaw twitches when he thinks something's funny on-screen.

He turns to me. Smiles. "Hi," he says.

"Hi."

He leans closer. And then there's no movie.

There's only us.

TWENTY-EIGHT

My eleven o'clock curfew comes before the movie ends, and Nico's mom is fine with him driving me home. I feel a little ache in my chest about tonight almost being over. I'm sad that I'm going home now. But I'm also excited for all my next times with Nico.

He unlocks the car and we both get in, me with my skateboard between my legs.

"Seat warmer?" he asks, his finger hovering over a button on the dashboard.

"Seriously? Seat warmers. Sunroof." I twirl my finger at the dashboard. "That fancy digital screen with the map on it and the radio stations. This car is the complete opposite of Bessie."

"Bessie?"

"Our crappy family van. And yes, my dad actually named our car."

"Well, my mom's car is *too* fancy. Why do you think she makes me ride my bike instead of driving? I only get to use it on special occasions. Like tonight. Otherwise, it basically lives in our garage or at the courthouse."

"Courthouse?" I remember my useless trip there, where every attorney looked at me like I was pathetic when I asked them if they could help me. "What does your mom do?"

"Attorney."

"Really?" I perk up. "What kind of attorney?"

"Boring real estate stuff."

"Oh."

He looks at me, confused. "Why?"

"I need an attorney."

Nico laughs. "For what? Did you rob a liquor store and not tell me?" He backs out of the driveway and presses the remote attached to the sun visor to shut the garage door.

"I've actually been trying to find an attorney to help me figure out how I can get my vaccinations. Since I'm a minor."

"Oh, right. Of course you'd need an attorney for that."

I shrug. "Yeah, well, it'd be nice if I could actually find one willing to help me."

"My mom might know someone. I can ask."

"Thanks. I'd appreciate that." I'm not very optimistic,

but it's worth a try. "I can't pay anyone. Not much, at least. I do have some birthday money saved up, but I thought I might need to use it to pay for actual shots."

He shakes his head. "We'll figure it out."

He looks at me and smiles.

My stomach leaps. My nerve endings shatter. And I smile back.

"Okay, cool," I say, turning on the seat warmer to indulge myself. "That's really cool."

"It is." He flicks his blinker, looks over his shoulder, and switches lanes.

I burrow deeper into the bucket seat. It's heating up, and I don't hate it on the first night of November. I don't hate anything about this night except for what happened with Teddy and Avery at the party.

We pull up to the curb in front of my house, and Nico puts the car in park. Across the street, you'd never know a huge football game had gone down a few hours ago. Everything is dark and closed up for the weekend.

"Wanna hang out again soon?" he asks.

"Yeah."

"Cool."

"But can we take your mom's car? I think this is the most comfortable ride I've ever had. Way better than a skateboard."

"I'll ask."

"I bet she'll say yes."

Nico leans across the center console. "Can we stop talking about my mom now?"

"Oh, did you want to talk about your dad instead?"

"Funny." He pokes me. "But for the record, my parents are divorced and my dad lives in Washington. The state, not DC. I visit him in the summer."

"Ah. Okay." I pretend to jot down notes in a notebook like the one Officer Cooper held in our living room the night of the scarlet *A*.

Nico pushes my fake notepad away with his hand. "Can I kiss you good night now?"

I put my hand to my forehead and fall against the seat dramatically. "If you must."

And he does.

And I decide kissing Nico only gets better and better.

TWENTY-NINE

Monday morning. Kitchen School. Maps out. My dad has his boring black coffee. Poppy has her colored pencils. Sequoia has his almond milk. I have my dreams. It was a good weekend. With the football game. And the rush of winning. And Nico. But now Nico is back at school across the street and I'm stuck here with my family, talking about geography and places in the world.

"If you could step outside and go anywhere you wanted, right this very second, where would it be?" Poppy asks as her purple pencil hovers over a map of the world.

Sequoia's thinking hard as my mom comes in from the garden and plunks her cardboard box of herbs on the counter.

"Not the farmers market," I mutter.

"Oh! Oh! I know! The Middle Ages!" Sequoia shouts.

"Duh. Real places," Poppy says. "That we can go to now."

"I think the Middle Ages sounds interesting," my mom says, sorting out bundles.

"This is the problem with Kitchen School," I say. "I'm supposed to be talking all serious about going to Singapore or something, and instead I'm here with a second grader who wants to go on some fantasy time-travel trip."

"June," my dad admonishes. "Tone."

"Okay, fine." I fold my hands on the table like a serious student and look at my brother. "Why do you want to go to the Middle Ages?"

"Dragons." He crosses his arms, all proud of himself.

Poppy slams her purple pencil down. "There weren't actual dragons in the Middle Ages."

"How do you know? You weren't there!" Sequoia shouts.

Poppy picks up her pencil again and points it at him. "I know because I'm alive in the world. And I pay attention when Dad tells us history stuff. Dragons are something people made up to scare each other so everyone would stay in line."

"Not to mention they gave chest-pounding dude bros an excuse to go off on big adventures all in the name of slaying," I add. I bet Teddy and those friends of his from the party would've fallen all over themselves to slay dragons.

"That's not true," Sequoia insists.

Poppy tosses an exasperated look at him. "What

really happened is dinosaur bones were showing up all over the place and nobody knew what they were. So bam! They made up dragons."

My dad smiles triumphantly. "That's one theory," he says. "Does anyone remember others?"

"Something about the Bible," I mumble. "Dragons were Satan."

"Gold star," my dad says.

I twirl my finger next to my head. "Whoop-de-do."

"Oh, June, honestly," my mom says, shaking out some herbs. "Don't be such a teenager."

"News flash! I *am* a teenager. I'm sixteen years old. I can't exactly not be sixteen years old. Therefore, I can't not be a teenager."

My whole family starts laughing.

"What?" I say.

"You're so literal," Poppy says.

"Literally," my dad says, and everyone cracks up again.

I push my chair back from the table. "Fine. I'm going to recess."

Sequoia rolls his eyes. "We don't have recess."

"No kidding," Poppy says, looking up from her map to watch me sit down again. "Now she's being the opposite of literal. Ironic. Or sarcastic? Which one is it, Mom?"

My mom studies me. "She's being Juniper. That's what she's being. Acting like she's a caged bird and we've clipped her wings."

"If we were in the Middle Ages, you could go out and slay dragons," Sequoia tells me. "To have an adventure. And be a hero."

"You know," my mom says, "we had Vikings in our family on Grandma's side. Do you think our ancestors were dragon slayers?"

Sequoia rubs his hands together. "Ooh." His gaze wanders dreamily to the ceiling, like he's imagining all of it.

"I think it's in our blood," my mom continues. "To get out there and conquer the world." She looks at me. "I understand you more than you think I do, Juniper Jade."

"We both do, Junebug," my dad says, and winks at me. I wiggle uncomfortably in my chair. "After all, your mom and I did pack up an old Toyota and drive ourselves to Woodstock with only twenty dollars each. Yet somehow we made it through by innovation and perseverance."

"Please no. Not the Woodstock stories," Poppy moans.

"Wannabe Woodstock," I correct.

"The rains were great that day," Poppy begins like she's narrating an epic poem.

"And the mudslides even greater," I finish.

"Oh, you two," my mom says. "You know you wish you could've been there."

"Um, no," I say.

"Oh, come on," my dad says. "It's basically like that Coachella thing you want to go to now."

My mom stops with the herbs and sidles up to my dad, who is still sitting in his teacher chair. He puts his arm around her waist and pulls her closer. He doesn't think about it. He just does it automatically. Because they have this unspoken way about them. It's their history, I guess. The years together. The Wannabe Woodstock stories and living unconventionally and driving a beat-up Toyota into the sunset. Then getting married and having kids and teaching them about dragons in the kitchen.

I feel tears prick the corners of my eyes.

I complain a lot about my life, but at the heart of it, there is this. There is here. My family. All together. Laughing in the kitchen.

Even in all their quirky weirdness, I love them.

But what will happen to this calm after I get an attorney, assuming I can find one to take my case? Do we go to court? Could my parents get in trouble for being negligent? Will someone take Poppy, Sequoia, and me away from here and everything we know?

From my mom and her box of herbs to my dad adding a last-minute note to his geography lesson. From my sister coloring in all the parts of the big, wide world on her map to my brother dreaming of dragons.

Can I really risk losing this?

Can I really risk losing them?

THIRTY

Later, my mom and I unload Bessie at the farmers market, setting boxes down and unfolding our table in our assigned spot. As we're arranging the essential oils into rows, a woman with bobbed hair and a clipboard comes marching up to our booth.

"Stop there," she says to my mom. "I need a moment."

"I'm sorry, do I know you?" my mom says.

"I'm Kayla Kaye from the city council." She says it fast, so it runs together like one word. Kaylakaye.

My mom wipes her hands on her apron. "How can I help you?"

"We've received a petition." Kaylakaye holds up her clipboard. "It was started by the Concerned Citizens of Playa Bonita."

Oh no. "Like the Facebook page," I say.

Kaylakaye continues, "The petition has been signed

by five hundred people, the required number of signatures needed to ban your booth from the farmers market."

"You can't be serious," my mom says, laughing. "Let me see that." She holds her hand out. "You must have me confused with someone else."

Kaylakaye pivots slightly, pulling the clipboard out of my mom's reach. "You are Mrs. Melinda Jade, are you not?"

My mom nods.

"The Playa Bonita community has serious concerns about your product, Mrs. Jade. They're afraid it could be contaminated."

My mom stares, wide-eyed. "With what?"

"Well, it's our understanding that your family recently contracted the measles."

"How do you know that?" my mom asks.

"So it's true?" Kaylakaye says.

I toss her a hard glare. "I assume you saw us on Facebook?"

She rolls her eyes. "Everyone saw you on Facebook."

"Well, we're not contagious anymore," I say.

She grips her clipboard and clears her throat. "There are other concerns."

"Like what?" my mom says.

I feel the weight of people and realize there's a crowd gathering. It's like the pumpkin patch all over again. They've been waiting for this. They knew. They all signed the petition. And someone here surely started it all in the first place. But who?

Kaylakaye says, "Other possibilities of contamination. Other . . ." She clears her throat. "Other viruses, perhaps. We understand your family is against vaccinations."

I want to shout, *Not me!* I'm torn. I agree with Kaylakaye and all those people who signed that petition, but I also want to defend my mom. "Anybody here could have a virus. Even you. You could be exposing all of us to a cold or something right now."

She fumbles. "Yes, well, I understand that. But we're not talking about colds. We're talking about deadly viruses. Ones that were thought to have been eradicated in the United States."

My mom looks at Kaylakaye. Pleads with her eyes. "Surely you can be more reasonable."

"We have a right to stay," I say.

"I'm sympathetic, I really am," Kaylakaye says. "But Playa Bonita has spoken, and as their representative, I'm afraid I'm here to tell you that you'll need to go."

"Today?" my mom says.

"Right now."

"We can't even finish our booth this afternoon?" I ask.

"I'm afraid not."

"Very well," my mom says, then looks at me. "June, let's pack it in."

My hands are balled into fists. I'm frustrated for my mom, but I'm more frustrated for me. Kaylakaye isn't saying anything I haven't already tried to say. How many people have to shun us before my parents get it?

"You can't be surprised by this," I say, but my mom doesn't respond. She just shoves things into boxes without organizing them.

Kaylakaye tries to shoo the crowd away.

The crowd doesn't budge.

They watch us as we pack, taking photos for Facebook and passing more judgment. I stare down every single one of them. I promise myself I'll yell if they come one step closer. It'll be a huge scene for all of Playa Bonita to see. Let them put it online. I don't care.

My mom keeps her gaze low, not making eye contact, as we cart our boxes away. It's a relief when we finally climb into Bessie and peel out of the parking lot.

"There are a dozen more farmers markets we can go to," my mom rants, like she had to wait until we were out of earshot to speak up. "Surely some of them have openings. Even if we have to drive a bit, it'll be fine."

I can see it now. Sweating in Bessie with no AC as we drive to markets an hour away from here only because nobody will know us.

"Maybe we should just take a break," I say.

"Never," says my mom.

THIRTY-ONE

On Tuesday a week later, when the school lets out across the street, Nico knocks on my door to ask me if I can come over later for dinner.

"My mom invited a friend who she thinks can help you." He lowers his voice so only I can hear. "She's cool. An attorney and a marathon runner."

"At the same time?"

He laughs. "Probably, knowing her."

I like that the woman who might be my attorney runs marathons. It means that she has endurance. That she knows how to keep pushing.

It takes a little bit of persuading to get my parents to let me go because it's a school night, but once I explain that my essay for tomorrow is already written, and I can finish the rest of my homework before Nico comes back to pick me up at six, they agree.

A few hours later, Nico and I walk through the front

door of his house and into the savory smells of basil and garlic. We find Mrs. Noble and her friend standing at the kitchen island, glasses of wine and a bowl of salad in front of them, and pots bubbling on the stove behind them as they chat animatedly. When her friend turns, I recognize her immediately.

The woman from the farmers market. Business suit. Flip-flops. Though tonight her feet are bare, her flip-flops probably left by the front door.

"Oh, good, you're here!" Mrs. Noble greets us enthusiastically. "Juniper, I want you to meet my friend Laurel Ward. She is smart and fabulous, and Nico and I told her all about you."

Ms. Ward reaches her hand out to shake mine as Nico's mom crosses to the stove to pull the pot of pasta from the burner and drain it in the sink. "It's wonderful to meet you, Juniper. Call me Laurel, please."

I shake her hand. "I've actually seen you before. I sell herbs at the farmers market . . . or I used to." I see Kaylakaye and her clipboard. "You bought mint from me. For your tea."

"Oh, yes! You must have a way with remembering faces. Very impressive." I don't tell her it's the business suit and the flip-flops, not her face, that I remember.

"I heard you run marathons."

"I do when my toes aren't broken."

I glance at her feet, finally close enough to notice the way her three middle toes are gathered together with clear medical tape. "So that's what the flip-flops are all about."

She laughs. "You saw that, huh? I try to wear them with confidence, hoping people won't notice because I look like I'm okay with it."

"I noticed. But only because I thought it was pretty cool."

"I'm glad you think so, but don't worry, I'm just about done with them. The doctor says I'm ready to go back to regular shoes during the workday." She wiggles her toes. "Just giving them some room to breathe tonight."

"Laurel will be totes profesh," Nico says, reaching into the salad to pop a carrot slice into his mouth. His mom slaps his hand away, then turns to toss the pasta with the sauce still simmering on the stovetop.

"Well, phew. Because you know how I insist on totes profesh. I mean, look at me." I strike a runway model pose in my jeans with the ripped knees and my faded hoodie.

Laurel smiles. "We'll get along just fine."

"Shall we?" Mrs. Noble says, and we all follow her to the dining room.

Nico's mom grabs the pasta. I carry the garlic bread and Nico follows me to the table with the salad and tongs.

We talk about film club and this weekend's football semifinal. It's an away game, which is probably for the better. I don't exactly want to see Teddy and Avery again.

It isn't until the table is cleared and Nico and his mom are cleaning up in the kitchen, rinsing plates and utensils before loading them into the dishwasher, that Laurel asks me to tell her more about why I might need a lawyer.

"I saw a doctor who told me to hire a good attorney if I wanted to be vaccinated. He was only half-serious," I explain.

"That's nothing to joke about." She leans forward on her elbows. "We should go see that doctor together."

"Do you think we can convince him to give me my shots if you're there?"

"It's worth a try. It's more likely I'll gather the information I'd need for filing a petition on your behalf."

"Petition?" I remember Kaylakaye had a petition at the farmers market. I knot my fingers together. "Would it need to have five hundred signatures?"

She waves her hand. "No. It would only be between you and your parents. We'd submit a request to the court to give you permission to make your own medical decisions."

"I like how that sounds."

"How about you take me through what happened from when you contracted the measles until now."

I nod, lean back in my chair, and tell her everything while Nico bangs around in the kitchen.

Laurel listens sympathetically. She hears me and my story.

"It must be frustrating to be judged for your parents' decisions. For choices you've had no control over, especially when they affect innocent people like a baby."

"I want control." I grip the edge of the table. "I should be able to decide what happens to my body. It's mine."

"Exactly. That's our argument. Bodily autonomy."

"Yes." The weight in my chest lifts because Laurel really gets it.

"We're talking about real change here, Juniper."

"I saw another attorney in town. He told me that what I want to do is impossible. He suggested emancipation, which I can't afford. I don't have a job, so I can't get my own apartment. And I don't want to move out of my house anyway."

She harrumphs, and I can almost hear her muttering, *Silly man* under her breath. Instead she says, "It sounds like he doesn't have any confidence in himself. That's the difference here. I do."

"He made it seem impossible."

She pats both hands on the table. "Let's make the impossible possible together, shall we?"

"All these people signed a petition to kick us out of the farmers market. It's going to break my parents when they find out I'm signing one, too."

"We'll start with your doctor. Maybe it won't even have to go that far. I'd like to try to make it as quick and painless as possible."

"I don't have an actual doctor. I've only seen Dr. Villapando at the urgent care clinic. We moved here in May, and it's taking my mom a while to find someone who's willing to see unvaccinated patients." I scratch at my scalp in irritation.

"Can you go with me to see Dr. Villapando tomorrow?"

"Absolutely. As soon as possible." But then I remember. "How much is this going to cost, though? I don't think I can afford you."

"Nico didn't tell you? I'm working pro bono here. This case is important. I want to take it on. So what do you say? See you at the clinic at three tomorrow?"

"I'll be there."

Nico shows up in the doorway between the kitchen and the dining room, patting his hands dry on a dish towel. "Sounds like you have a plan."

"A start anyway."

"One step at a time," Laurel says.

"Cool," Nico says.

His mom walks in with the bottle of wine Laurel and she had been sharing in the kitchen, and Laurel holds her glass out for a refill.

"Well, I'm sure you two have a movie or something to watch," Mrs. Noble says.

Laurel turns to me. "Juniper, I'm honored you came to me."

"I'm honored you listened."

I want to hug her. Because she's the first person who has made me believe I have a fighting chance. She has made me trust there are other people out there who believe a sixteen-year-old girl has the right to make decisions about her own body.

THIRTY-TWO

"Come out back," Nico says. "I want to show you something."

"Smooth."

He bumps his shoulder against mine. "Right?"

He slides open the screen door and we step onto a stark tile patio. No flowers. No greenery. Yet still gorgeous. There's a barbecue in the corner, a fire pit in the middle, and twinkle lights strung across the wooden slats of a pergola. I gasp when I look at the wall above the picnic table.

"You have a flat-screen. On your patio. Are you kidding me?"

"You're too easily impressed. But forget the TV. What I want to show you is over there."

My eyes follow where he's pointing. Past the patio, farther into the yard, is a big oak tree. Tucked high up into its sturdy branches is a rugged little tree house. A rope ladder hangs along the trunk, and Nico leads the way up the rungs to the entrance. We both have to wiggle our way through an opening barely bigger than a doggie door, and I land in an awkward tangle on top of the hardwood floor, like I've just been birthed.

"Smooth," Nico says as he scrambles to his feet, holds out his hand, and helps me up.

I brush off my knees and elbows. "I like to make an entrance." I sniff. "It smells like boy in here."

"Well, yeah."

I squint my eyes through the dark and see a small window behind Nico. On the floor there's a magnifying glass. Books and notebooks. An empty box of Pop-Tarts. There's a beanbag chair and a flashlight. A backgammon game. A chessboard. A deck of cards. There's a pair of broken earbuds. A pile of Pokémon trading cards. And a set of walkie-talkies and binoculars.

"You're like Encyclopedia Brown up in here. Do you solve mysteries, too?" I restrain myself from adding, *Dun dun dun.* "Or are you just a total creeper spying on all your neighbors?" I motion to the window, which has a perfect view of the house next door.

"Total creeper." Nico flicks on the flashlight and sets it upright like a lantern, bathing the inside of the tree house in a soft, warm glow.

"Nice."

He sinks down into the beanbag chair and the insides smoosh around as he burrows in.

"Sit with me. We can both fit." He's angled off to the side a little, but there's not a ton of extra space.

"You sure about that?"

He grins. "We'll make it work."

I attempt to settle in next to him. The only way to fit is if I lean my back against the tree house wall and drape my leg across Nico's. He rubs my calf, then spiders his fingertips up and around to pick at the ragged threads left over from the hole in the knee of my jeans.

"So," I say.

"So." He smiles.

"Do you bring all the girls up here?"

"Definitely. There's nothing hotter than a guy with a tree house."

"I'll say."

"Juniper." He looks at me seriously. "You're the only girl I've brought up here. For real."

I smile. "I'm honored. For real."

"I mean, look at this place. It's like my most embarrassing secrets exposed." He kicks at the Pokémon cards. "But I'm never embarrassed with you. You make me feel like I can always be myself."

"For the record, your tree house is cool. I need to lobby for one in my backyard so I can spend the whole day in it to escape my family."

"I only come up here at night."

"Because of the bees?"

"Yeah." He picks at my jean threads again. "Too dangerous in the daylight."

"You're like a vampire." I eye the game boards. "So do you play chess against yourself while you're here?"

"Nah, those are left over from when Matteo and I would face off."

"Your brother."

"Yeah." He raises his eyebrows. "Do you play chess?"

"Is my dad my dad? Of course I do."

"Wanna play now?"

I smile huge. I smile like Nico. "I totally do."

He leans over, gives me a quick peck on my cheek, and stands up. His leaving throws the beanbag off-kilter, and I have to realign myself to be able to stand up, too. Nico grabs a blanket from the corner and shakes it out before spreading it across the floor. I sit down, crossing my legs like a pretzel twist, and help him set up the board.

"Last piece," Nico says, holding up his queen. He kisses her. "Let's do this," he tells her.

I shake my head. "Wow."

"Hey. This is my tree house, which gives me free rein to dork out."

"Well done."

He rubs his hands together. "Get ready to get your ass kicked, Juniper Jade."

"You wish."

Nico opens the game by moving his queen's pawn.

"My dad has a timer." I mimic Nico's first move. "Thirty seconds per turn."

"That's some very serious Bobby Fischer–style game play."

"Isn't it, though?"

Nico maneuvers one of his pawns. "Is he exhausting? Your dad?"

"Sometimes. But not always."

Nico nods. "Yeah. I get it."

"Is yours?" I move again.

"I'm not sure. I don't see him much. Don't know him that well." He shifts his gaze from the board to me. "I was only three when my parents split up and my dad moved away. I feel like I have to get to know him again every summer."

"That must be weird."

"It's not ideal." He shrugs. "What makes your dad exhausting?"

"His inability to see his privilege." I sigh. "And I don't just mean about vaccinations. It's everything. Even the littlest things."

Nico leans forward to study the board. "Like what?"

I think for a minute. "Organic food, for instance."

"Not a bad thing."

"No. But my dad doesn't acknowledge that it takes money to eat and live organically. I'm sure there are plenty of people who'd love to make it a priority, but they literally can't afford to. My dad insists there are small things anyone can do, but buying the shampoo and the makeup and the mattresses and the food is more expensive. Even buying organic chicken for your whole family costs twice as much as nonorganic. It adds up."

"You've really thought about this."

"I have. And I've pointed it out, but . . ."

"Yeah."

"Yeah."

Nico moves another pawn. "So organic chicken and chess. Your house sounds like a real party."

"Oh yeah. My parents really know how to do it up. Remember the Halloween toothbrushes?"

"How could I forget?"

"And there are also concerts in the park in the summer."

"The park isn't so bad." He leans back on his hands. "I've always wanted to be one of those old guys who plays dominoes on the tabletops there, laughing and messing around with my other retired friends all day. How great would that be?"

"Living the dream."

"You know it. Me and my EpiPen and my box of dominoes. And a best friend who gets to our table before me." He laughs. "Some guy who wears a porkpie hat and loves Fellini films."

"You might've been born in the wrong generation."

"Possibly."

I study Nico and the faint smile on his lips as his hair flops over his eyes. "I'm glad you were born when you were." I want to push his hair back into place. I want to touch him. "So you can be sixteen right now." And adorable. I can't stop looking at him. I can't stop thinking about him. Even when he's right here in front of me.

"I'm glad, too."

"Are you sick of playing chess yet?" I ask.

He looks at me and smiles. "Maybe. Why? Did you have something else in mind?"

"Yes."

"Like what? Using my binoculars to spy on my neighbors?"

"Depends. Would you rather spy on your neighbors or kiss me?"

"No contest." Nico lifts up on his hands and leans across the chessboard. Hovers. Waiting. I push up on my own hands and meet him halfway. The stars sparkle through the window behind him. Some of the chess pieces roll away when I bump the board with my knee. "I'm probably never going to find my rooks again," he says as his mouth hovers above mine.

"I'll help you find them. Your bishops, too."

"Doesn't even matter. You're the best thing in my tree house anyway."

"Please kiss me."

And he finally does. I sigh happily and feel his lips shift into a smile.

THIRTY-THREE

I tell my mom and dad I'm going to skate by the beach but meet Laurel in front of the urgent care clinic to talk to Dr. Villapando instead. After being called back and having my vitals checked in the hallway, I wait in one of the now familiar exam rooms of the clinic. The paper cover of the exam table crinkles underneath my jeans and nervous sweat collects beneath my ponytail. I thrum my fingers against my knees and try to distract myself by studying an IS IT A COLD OR THE FLU? poster on the wall across from me. It's been years since I've had it, but influenza is miserable. I decide to include a flu shot in my list of requests. That doesn't seem exorbitant. I've even seen places giving them out for free. Businesses and schools and pharmacies in town.

My attorney is the perfect picture of calm. The opposite of me. Or my mom, who anxiously twisted the strap of her purse in her hands when she was here. I decide to let Laurel's calm make me calm. To give me hope we can really do this.

Finally, Dr. Villapando swings the door open. He instantly scowls when he sees me but collects himself quickly.

"Well, hello, Juniper," he says.

I give a little wave at the side of my hip. "Hi, Dr. Villapando."

He studies me, looking for rashes and other uncontrolled contagious things that could require alerting the CDC. "What brings you in today?"

"You told me to get an attorney, so I did." I motion to Laurel. "This is my attorney. We're here to get my shots."

He shakes his head, smiling. "You certainly are determined."

"Yes, I am."

Laurel holds out her arm to shake Dr. Villapando's hand. "I'm Laurel Ward." I appreciate how easy it is to take her seriously. I'm sure the business suit without flip-flops helps. But does her foot hurt? Meanwhile, I rode up on my skateboard, wearing jeans like any other day.

Dr. Villapando looks at me. "Is Laurel your legal guardian?"

"She's not."

"I don't want to vaccinate you without a legal guardian. If your parents aren't here, saying this is okay, I'm at risk of a malpractice suit. And I can't jeopardize the clinic or myself."

"I'm not going to give up."

He sits down in his chair with the wheels on it and slides closer to me. "I'm an advocate of vaccines. I've made that clear to you, and I appreciate your dedication to this cause." He turns his focus to Laurel, then back to me. "There are some vaccines, like HPV, to which you can consent, but I honestly wouldn't feel comfortable administering anything, even that, without your parents' permission. While I hate to lend any credence to their fears about vaccines, you're a patient who has never been vaccinated. And if you did have any sort of reaction to a vaccine, even something as mild and common as swelling at the injection site, your parents could make a case of negligence against me. I can't risk that."

"Do you know someone who will do it?" I ask.

"You can certainly go office to office, doctor to doctor, and state your case. You might find someone willing. They'll want to bring in their office's malpractice attorney, I'm sure." He thinks for a moment. "What I will say is that if you had your own legal paperwork in hand, I might consider it."

I look at Laurel. "Like the petition?" I ask her and she nods. I look back at Dr. Villapando and say, "I can do that."

"Come see me when you get it."

"We're working on it," Laurel tells him. "This was good information today. Thank you."

Dr. Villapando stands and shakes my hand, then Laurel's. "You two have a good day."

I lean back and bang my head against the wall behind me as soon as the door shuts. "Another day and still no shots."

Laurel shakes her head. "Don't get discouraged. We're on the right path. A petition is the way to go."

"So my parents will definitely have to know."

"I don't see any way around it. We're not going to be able to find a doctor willing to take on the risk of vaccinating you without an okay from them, even if your age is legal for consent with some vaccines. I can sympathize with that. So we'll take a more official route. A legal one. If we take the mature-minor angle, that'll give you medical emancipation, allowing you to make your own medical choices, while still living with your parents." She looks around the room, at the cabinets and the posters and the jars of cotton balls, then back at me. "We'll get this done, Juniper. I'm sure of it."

"It sounds like it's going to be a lot of work."

"It's the kind of work I like to do."

THIRTY-FOUR

I kneel down to plunge my gardening shovel into the soft dirt at the base of a shady tree to unearth another wild mushroom. It's the day before Thanksgiving, and my mom probably wants me helping back at the house, but I had to get out of there. I can't be with my family without feeling guilty. Laurel has been working on putting our case together for the last two weeks, and I don't want my parents to know anything about the petition until it happens. So I shrugged into my warmest flannel, grabbed my field guide, and set off to get mushrooms for tomorrow's meal. A customer at the farmers market once mentioned that this spot on the cliffs overlooking the ocean was a jackpot for chanterelle mushrooms—one of my favorites for cooking—in November. Their peppery taste will give a kick to our Thanksgiving stuffing.

Someone suddenly taps my shoulder from behind me. I startle, drop my shovel, and tumble to the side to see Nico standing there with his backpack sliding off his shoulders.

He scrambles away with his hands up as I stand. "Oh, man, I'm sorry. I shouldn't have done that when you were lost in a nature trance," he says.

"Or ever." I stand up and point my shovel at him. "Rule of thumb: don't sneak up on people."

"You're right. I wasn't thinking." He runs his hand through his hair, making it flop all over. "I wanted to surprise you. Your mom told me I could find you here."

"Well, I *am* glad to see you." Even though I've seen Nico almost every day since I went to his house to meet Laurel, not seeing him yesterday made it feel like I hadn't seen him in weeks.

He glances at my bucket. "How many mushrooms can one family even eat?"

"You'd be surprised."

I kneel again, and Nico squats next to me. He sifts through my bucket.

"So how do you even know how to do this?" he asks. "Aren't most mushrooms poisonous? How do you know which ones are which?"

"I literally took a class." I gently lift the last chanterelle into my hand and place it in the bucket. "Only about twenty percent of mushrooms are actually toxic." I tap the lip of the bucket with my shovel. "Those are real chanterelles, but there are false ones out here, too. You can tell the difference by the gills and coloring."

"Will I die if I eat a fake one?"

"The fake ones aren't poisonous, exactly. But they don't taste good. And eating them will make you sick to your stomach."

He shudders. "No thanks." He picks up a mushroom, studies it, and drops it back into the bucket. "I think I'd be afraid to risk it. I only trust the produce section at the grocery store."

I glare at him. "You can trust me. I know what I'm doing. I'm a legit member of a mycological society."

Nico squints at me. Smiles. "I don't know what that secret club is, but your confidence is superhot."

I don't like that it sounds like he's making fun of me. "I'm serious. I know the difference."

He puts his hands up in defense. "Okay. I believe you."

"Then eat one."

"What?"

"If you believe me, eat one."

"Right now?"

"Yeah."

He leans in, glances inside the bucket. "They're dirty." He holds one up to me. Twirls it around. "It has actual dirt on it. See?"

I shrug. "So brush it off with your shirt. Or we can go down and rinse it off in the ocean."

"You're serious."

"If you are."

"Fine." He twists the mushroom in his hand. Studies it. Sniffs. He gently rubs it against the hem of his shirt to brush off the dirt. He looks at me. Opens his mouth.

I yank his hand back. "Stop."

"What?" He drops the mushroom. "Why?"

"It won't make you sick, but it tastes gross if it isn't cooked. I just wanted to see if you would really do it."

"That's kind of mean."

"I know. Sorry." I sift through my mushrooms. "I was just annoyed that you didn't trust me." We stand and brush off the knees of our jeans. I pick up my bucket and push my shovel into my back pocket. "Ready?"

"Yep." Nico takes the bucket from me. Looks inside again. "Very impressive haul, by the way. What're you gonna make with these?"

"Stuffing."

"Less impressive."

We head down the dirt path toward the parking lot. There are scrubby bushes on both sides of us. Shady trees. The winking waves of the ocean to the right. The pale blue lifeguard tower below. A small boat in the distance.

"So my family is obviously eating mushrooms for Thanksgiving. What're you doing?"

"We're going to my aunt's house. Always do. She has four kids, all younger, so I'll babysit and man the kids' table with a napkin tucked into my shirt like a bib."

"Sounds like a lot of work."

"Nah, it's fine. Someone in the family needs to introduce them to the good video games and the best movies. I'm thinking *Planes, Trains and Automobiles* this year. A Thanksgiving classic. I prefer *The Ice Storm*. But my cousins are still too young for that."

Nico's phone dings with a text. He pulls it out. Reads. Groans. "Ugh, leave me alone," he says to his phone, shaking it.

"Who's that?"

"This group chat thing. My friends keep trying to convince me to go to winter formal."

"Oh." My chest stings a little. "With who?"

"With you, obviously." He looks at me seriously. "But I don't do dances. Plus, they scheduled it for the weekend before winter break, which is the worst timing when you have finals the next week." He types out a text with his free hand and shoves his phone back into his pocket. "Can you believe it's called the Snow Ball? Who comes up with this shit?"

"Aw, I think that's kind of cute."

He winces. "It doesn't even snow here. It's stupid. Dances are stupid."

"I wouldn't know. I've never been to one." I want to go, but I don't want to sound desperate.

"Trust me, you're not missing out."

"So even if I wanted to go, you wouldn't take me?"

"Even then." I try not to frown, but I can feel the

corners of my mouth drop when he looks at me. "What? I have to draw the line somewhere."

"Draw the line? You make it sound like I force you to do stuff."

"No. School dances are the only hard pass for me. I don't like dressing up. I'm fine taking you to do things you've never done as long as they don't require wearing a suit."

"Being fine isn't the same as enjoying it."

He turns to me, his fingers searching for my hand. "I enjoy showing you new things."

I push his hand away. "Now you sound like my babysitter or my teacher or something. Sorry it's so annoying to have to do all those dumb things with me."

"That's not what I meant." He runs his hand through his hair. Kicks at the dirt. "This isn't coming out right."

"No, it's not." I cross my arms. "This whole conversation is making me feel pathetic. Let's just go."

I reach for the bucket.

Nico suddenly swats at the air with it. I assume it's a game. Like he's trying to be cute and wrestle me for it. But I don't feel like playing.

He swats again. Ducks.

I maneuver my way underneath his arm and grab the bucket before he spills all the mushrooms.

And then he looks at me with his eyes bugged out.

"What?" I say, hoisting the bucket above my head like a trophy. "You're mad I won?"

He shakes the hand that was just holding the mushrooms. "I think I got stung."

I drop the bucket. "By a bee?"

"Yes. Oh, fuck." His voice has a tone of disbelief. "I shouldn't have risked coming out here."

"Are you messing with me?"

He snaps his mouth open and shut. Coughs. I grab his hand, looking for the stinger. His fingers are already swelling. He coughs again. He's not kidding.

I shake his hand. "Where's your EpiPen?" I shout.

He shoves his swollen hand into his pocket, fishes out the EpiPen, and drops to his knees. Coughs. His hand is too swollen to uncap the pen. I kneel down next to him to grab it. I yank the cap off with my teeth. Spit it into the dirt.

"What do I do?" My voice doesn't sound like my own. It's a high-pitched screech. Desperate. Trembling. "Nico! Help me!" I shake him. "What do I do?"

His mouth is swelling. His lips. His eyes. It's hard for him to talk. I wrestle with the EpiPen and try to remember what he showed me that night in his kitchen. The way he swung it like a softball pitch into his leg. I hold my arm up high, ready to swing. I hear Nico's voice from that night. *No hesitation*, he said. I plunge the EpiPen straight through his jeans and into his thigh. There's a clicking sound. I keep my wrist steady, holding the needle in place for at least ten seconds, then pull it out and drop it to the ground.

I lean over him. Grab his cheeks between my hands. "Are you okay?"

"Call 911," he gasps.

I scramble for his phone. Dial.

"This is 911. What's your emergency?" an operator asks. She sounds too calm.

"My friend got stung by a bee," I pant. "He's allergic." Nico locks his panicked eyes on mine. My own eyes are tearing up, I know it, but I focus on him. Make sure he sees me looking right at him. "It's going to be okay," I tell him.

"Is he experiencing anaphylaxis?"

"Yes. Yeah." I prop Nico up against me. He leans into my lap like a baby. I want to comfort him, but I don't know how. And I don't want to hold him too tight if he's having trouble breathing. I unzip his sweatshirt, hoping that will help. "I need him to be okay. He has an EpiPen."

"And he used it?"

"Yes."

"How long ago?"

"Right before I called you." Nico coughs again, and my heart thunders. I can't control my shaking. "We're out on a trail." My eyes dart left and right. "There might be more bees. Please send someone soon." I explain exactly where we are and look over my shoulder for the ambulance. Anything. Anyone.

"They're on the way. Would you like me to stay on the line with you until they arrive?"

"Yes." My hands tremble so hard I drop the phone. I scramble to pick it up again. "Are you still there? I don't know what I'm doing. Should I try to get him to the parking lot?"

"You're doing great," she says on the other end of the line. Her voice is like a warm blanket. Comforting. Calm. "I'm going to help you help your friend, okay?"

"Okay."

She asks me questions about Nico's physical state and how old he is. After what feels like forever, I hear sirens nearing. I hang up when the paramedics run toward us with their equipment. They tell me to step away as they check Nico's vitals and ask him more questions. He seems to be breathing better, but they still strap an oxygen mask over his face. I can't decide if he looks more or less swollen. Less, I think. Maybe I want to convince myself.

More people come. Police officers. Firefighters.

It all seems like so much.

"Is he going to be okay?" My voice sounds panicked. I am snot and tears. I wipe both away on the sleeve of my shirt.

"You did everything right," a firefighter tells me gently. "But we need to take your friend to the hospital to get checked out, okay?"

"Yes. Okay."

"Call my mom," Nico says to me as they prep him for the ambulance. "But tell her I'm okay. I don't want to scare her."

I run down the path behind them. I'm so technologically inept that I don't even know how to find Nico's mom's number, and I have to ask one of the police officers standing away from the ambulance how to do it, because I can't exactly ask Nico right now. The officer helps me find Mrs. Noble in his contacts list, and I walk closer to the cliffs so I can hear her. I do my best to sound as calm as the 911 operator when Mrs. Noble picks up. But I'm not calm. My voice wobbles. And my heart thumps through my chest and into my throat. I tell her we'll meet her at the hospital. But before I can run back to the ambulance and climb inside, it pulls out of the parking lot with the siren blaring.

A police officer asks me if I'll be okay to get home. I nod.

And then I'm left standing alone in the middle of the parking lot with Nico's phone and my skateboard and a bucket of mushrooms I couldn't care less about anymore. Because Nico drove away and we were arguing before he got stung. It doesn't matter if we don't go to the dance. He just has to be okay. For me. For his mom. For his cousins at the kids' table. I want to go straight to the hospital, but I have to go home first because it's too far away and I need a ride. I'll have to leave Nico's bike locked to the rack, because I don't know his combo.

I skate home as fast as I can. I bust through the front door, sweating and out of breath, and race to the kitchen, where my mom is slicing carrots and celery at the counter.

"I need you to take me to the hospital!" I shout.

She drops her knife to the sink with a clatter and rushes to me, grabbing my face in her hands the same way I did with Nico.

"Why? What's going on? What's wrong with you?" She rakes her eyes over my body, looking for injury.

"It's not me. It's Nico. He got stung by a bee and he's allergic. The ambulance took him to the hospital." My voice trembles. Tears prick. "Please, will you take me to him? Right away."

"Yes, of course."

She calls out to my dad to tell him where we're going and why as she snatches up the keys to Bessie from the table by the front door.

He rushes down the stairs, his hair falling loose from its elastic ponytail holder. "Hang in there, Junebug." He pulls me into a hug and kisses the top of my head before we go. "I've got everything taken care of here," he tells my mom.

We scramble into Bessie, and I wrestle with my tangled seat belt as we back out of the driveway. As soon as we get on the freeway, I want to scream. There are too many cars, too many people traveling out of town for Thanksgiving, and it slows us to a crawl.

I wring my hands in the passenger seat until we exit.

And when we finally do, I swear we hit every red light on the surface streets all the way to the hospital.

Meanwhile, my mom keeps asking me question after question about what happened. She can't believe I was there and had to inject Nico with the EpiPen myself.

"That shot saved his life."

"He's very lucky," she says.

"Yes, he's lucky there's a lifesaving shot that exists in the world. Who'd have ever thought it?"

She nods.

I can't believe she can't see the irony here. The connection I'm trying to make. Things exist in the world to save people. Antibiotics and defibrillators. Oxygen tanks and chemotherapy. Mammograms and blood tests.

EpiPens and vaccines.

It's not that hard to see. It's not that hard to understand.

"Mom, a shot saved Nico's life." I want to make her look at me. To see me. But her eyes are on the road. "A shot saved his life, just like an MMR shot or a Tdap shot or a meningitis shot saves people's lives every day."

"That's not the same, Juniper."

"But it is the same." I pound my fist against my knee. "How can you not see that?"

"You're comparing apples and oranges."

"Okay. So what if I had a bee allergy? Would you get me an EpiPen?"

She turns into the parking lot of the hospital. "We're not having this conversation right now. I'm parking and you need to see Nico."

She pulls into a spot and I jump out of Bessie before she even manages to set the emergency brake.

THIRTY-FIVE

The last time I was in a hospital, I was sick. Too sick to pay attention to the stark white walls and antiseptic smell. The odor crawls up my nostrils, making my stomach turn and my fingertips tingle as my mom catches up to me.

Inside here, people are being born and dying.

One day Baby Kat was born here and a few weeks later her parents brought her back, sick with the measles, and they didn't get to bring her home again.

Please let Nico be able to go home.

We head to the information kiosk in the lobby, where a man with a shock of white hair and tiny round glasses tells us Nico's on the third floor. He hands us bright yellow visitor stickers and directs us to the elevator doors.

Mrs. Noble is talking to someone at the nurses' station when the doors open on Nico's floor. I rush to her.

"Is he okay?" I ask breathlessly.

"He is. He's going to be fine, thanks to you."

"What a relief," my mom says, exhaling. "I'm Juniper's mom, Melinda," she says, reaching out to shake Mrs. Noble's hand.

"It's nice to meet you, Melinda. I'm Adriana."

My whole body decompresses with relief. "I was so worried."

"You poor thing," Nico's mom says, pulling me into a hug. She holds on tight, anchoring herself. "I'm so glad you were there," she murmurs into my ear. "My greatest fear, aside from this actually happening, was that he'd be alone if it did." She pulls away. Looks me in the eye. "Thank you."

"It was scary," I blurt. There's no reason to be anything other than honest. "But I'm glad I was there, too."

Nico's mom turns to mine. "You have an amazing daughter."

My mom smiles. "I think so, too. But it's always nice to hear it from someone else."

"I've been so impressed by her. She really goes after what she wants."

My backbone goes straight. If I'd been drinking water, I surely would've choked on it. Did Mrs. Noble say too much? Did she flat-out drop a hint? In my mind, she might as well have told my mom to expect a court notice in the mail any day now. But I guess it's only obvious to me, because my mom seems to take the statement at face value, saying thank you and moving on.

"Can I see Nico?" I ask, peeling the backing off the sticker and fastening it to the front pocket of my flannel. I probably should've changed clothes, but in the flurry of everything, I didn't think to toss my dirt-stained shirt into the hamper.

"Yes. I know he wants to see you," Mrs. Noble says, leaning closer. "Between you and me, I think he's afraid what happened might've scared you off."

"No way."

"Good." She loops our arms together at the elbows and pats my hand. "How about I show you to his room and then maybe your mom and I can grab a cup of tea downstairs." She turns to my mom. "What do you say, Melinda?"

"Yes. I'd like that."

"Great."

Great? What will they talk about now?

Mrs. Noble leads me down the hallway to Nico's room, while my mom waits by the elevator.

"Please don't tell her about Laurel," I say. "I can't deal with that today."

"I would never say anything. You have my word."

"Okay. I trust you."

She knocks, then pushes open the door to Nico's room. I run to his side. The swelling has gone down and he seems to be breathing fine without oxygen. But he still looks like he's been through hell. The color in his face is still faded, almost gray, and his eyes don't look as bright and excited as I'm used to seeing. They're filled with something else. A mixture of fear and relief.

"I'll give you some time together," Mrs. Noble says. "You're good, right, honey?" she says to Nico.

He gives her a thumbs-up. "Stellar."

"Love you." She blows him a kiss as the door clicks shut behind her.

I set his phone on the table by the bed. Grab his hand. "You look so much better."

"Sure. Aside from the hospital bed and the sick-person gown."

"Nah. Puke green is a good color on you."

"Thanks."

I look around the room. "How long are you stuck here?"

"They wanna keep me overnight for observation. Monitor stuff. It's a whole thing."

"One night isn't so bad."

He reaches for me and I sit down next to him.

"Are you freaking out?" he asks. I can hear the worry in his voice. I can see it on his face.

"Not even."

"You were freaking out on the cliffs when it happened."

"Well, yeah. Who wouldn't? I was afraid you were going to . . ." I can't finish the rest.

"Die."

"Nico. I was worried. I already have Katherine St.

Pierre on my conscience. I couldn't let anything happen to you." I brush the hair back from his forehead, and the warmth of his skin heats my fingertips. "But you're fine. Look at you." I realize I sound like my mom telling me I was fine after the measles. Dismissive. Because I wasn't fine, and neither is Nico. These kinds of things can change a person forever. "I mean, you're okay now. And hopefully it'll never happen again."

"There's no guarantee. Unless I walk around in a hazmat suit."

"That'd be kind of hot. Like a man in uniform." I nudge him with my elbow. "I probably wouldn't be able to keep my hands off you."

"Your hands wouldn't be able to get onto me."

"I'd make it work." I lean over him, and my hair slides down like a curtain around us. I press my forehead to his. "I care about you. So much." I kiss his mouth. "Please wear a hazmat suit."

"Should I wear it to the Snow Ball?"

I pull back. Crinkle my brow. "I thought dances were a hard pass."

"I changed my mind. I think I should go. I want to. With you."

"Are you sure? You'll have to dress up. In a real suit."

"Positive. I think I can handle wearing a tie for one night."

"I can't wait to see you in a tie."

I lie down next to him. Kiss him again. His mouth.

His cheeks. His forehead. I pull his hand to my lips and kiss it right where the bee stung him.

"You're good at making things better," he says.

"I try." I rest my head on his chest and look around the room. "So where's the remote, then? We need to watch TV all day."

"Ah. So the truth comes out. You're using me for my tiny hospital room television." He laughs and I love feeling the rumble of it underneath my ear.

"Never."

He kisses the top of my head. "It's okay. I don't mind."

"Okay, then. Maybe a little." I kick my feet excitedly as he hands me the remote. "Ooh, maybe we can watch that ice movie you were talking about."

"That ice movie? Call it by its name, please. You know I have high standards." He laughs into my hair. "Say it with me: *The Ice Storm*."

I poke him. "You're my favorite film snob."

THIRTY-SIX

Mimi and Bumpa arrived last night while I was at the hospital with Nico, so by the time Mrs. Noble dropped me off at home, they were already heading to bed, exhausted from their drive down from Sacramento.

I'm happy to see them now, bringing their good vibes to our house.

On Thanksgiving mornings, we usually pile into the car together to serve food at a local soup kitchen, but my mom is hesitant today, worrying nobody will want us serving food to anyone anywhere. I don't disagree. But my dad insists.

"I've said it before and I'll say it again," he says through gritted teeth. "I refuse to be a prisoner in my own town."

His conviction doesn't exactly make me feel better.

"But it's Thanksgiving," my mom says. "It's an especially bad day to make a scene."

My dad stands firm. "That's everyone else's problem, not mine."

"What's going on?" Mimi asks as she fastens her watch around her wrist. "Why is this even a big deal? We do this every year no matter where we are."

"Don't worry about it, Mom," my dad says.

"I have a right to know if you're about to feed me to the wolves," she says, clipping on her earrings.

"There are no wolves," my dad says. "Just a bunch of people who can't keep their noses out of everybody else's business."

Bumpa laughs. "Sounds like all your friends," he says to Mimi.

She gives him a playful swat. "Oh, you."

Mimi and Bumpa don't know the half of it. They've always been only mildly supportive of my dad's beliefs and the way he's chosen to live. As far as they know, my sister, brother, and I got sick with the measles a few months ago and got well. They don't know about the scarlet *A* or the angry mobs or the online videos. I wonder what they'd say if they knew. Maybe I should tell Mimi the whole story. I just don't think Thanksgiving Day is the right time to do it.

It's ultimately decided that my mom will stay home with Poppy and Sequoia and I'll go to the community center with my dad, Mimi, and Bumpa.

Things are already a rush of activity when we arrive. There are cooking stations and checklists and tables being set. I barely get my latex serving gloves on when one of the women running the meal prep sends me out back to help carry in supplies that have arrived with drivers. My stomach clenches when I see that one of the drivers is Mary, donating vegetables from her farm. Will more food come from farmers market booths? And if so, will everyone be cool with my family being here?

"Juniper!" Mary takes a cautious step away from me. "Hello."

"I'm here to help you unload." I'm matter of fact. No niceties. Mary doesn't want them and I don't want to give them.

"No need," she says. "I've got it."

"There's a lot to carry in and we're in a time crunch. Just let me help."

She rakes her eyes across my latex gloves. "You're not contagious with anything?"

"I'm good."

"You thought you were good before you realized you had the measles, too. Who's to say you're not harboring some new illness today? Maybe having you serve food isn't the best idea. Perhaps we should talk to someone." She looks toward the back door to the kitchen for help. "I'm sure we can put you somewhere that you aren't handling food."

"No," I say firmly. "I'm fine. It's an important event and I want to help."

"I guess carrying my boxes in can't hurt." She wrestles with the door handle. Looks over her shoulder at me. "This stubborn old van."

The door finally creaks open.

Mary's van doesn't have any seats aside from the two in front, so it's practically packed to the ceiling with cardboard boxes full of regular potatoes and sweet potatoes and romaine lettuce and tomatoes. It's a generous donation, and I tell her so.

"Just grab whatever?" I ask, and she nods warily.

We go back and forth from the van to the kitchen, where Mimi and others are waiting to peel and dice what we bring in. It takes us a few trips since there's only two of us. When I try to grab the last box, it's stuck in the back. I jiggle it, trying to slide it out. I give it a hard pull to loosen it. Whatever was keeping it in place comes tumbling out of the door and lands by my foot. I bend over. Pick it up. Turn it over in my hand. It's a can of red spray paint. Scarlet. Like the *A* on our front door.

I want to believe Mary used it for something else. A DIY project or the homemade banner of her farmers market booth. But that would make me a fool.

And I'm not a fool.

Mary yanks the can from my hand and throws it into the back of the van, where it bounces loudly against the metal floor. "Too much stuff in there." She pats her hands around her apron, flustered.

"It was you," I say.

She looks down at the ground. Some strands of gray hair fall loose from her ponytail. "What was me?"

"You know." I can never tell my mom. She thought Mary was her friend. It would crush my mom to know Mary vandalized our house. Like a high school bully all over again. "Why?"

Mary shifts from one foot to the other, looking desperately at the others arriving at the community center. More cars delivering food. Nuns carrying in pies. A family dropping off bottles of water.

"You met the baby at my booth."

Realization dawns. "You feel responsible."

Mary nods. "She was exposed to the measles on my watch. I told her mom to nurse her in my chair under my canopy shade."

"But you couldn't have stopped that baby from getting sick. You didn't know I had the measles any more than I did."

"And I'll have to live with that forever."

"*You* will? How do you think I feel?"

"I hope you feel terrible." She narrows her eyes until it feels like they're cutting right into me, leaving a scar. "I did this town a service by painting that *A* on your front door. I did it to tell everyone who you were so that maybe I could stop what happened to that baby from happening to someone else." She lifts her chin in defiance. "I did what I had to do. On your door and on Facebook. So don't you forget it."

"I can't forget!" I lower my voice when my shout stops people in their tracks. "I think about Katherine St. Pierre every day. I don't agree with my parents' anti-vax stance."

"You don't?"

"I want to be vaccinated, Mary."

"Oh."

I look at her hard. "But guess what? Sixteen-year-old girls don't get a whole lot of say about things in this world."

She shakes her head. "Juniper." Her voice is softer.

I put my hand up. "Don't."

She nods. "Understood."

"It's Thanksgiving." I pick up the one remaining box. "And it looks like this is the last of it."

She shuts the door behind me. Locks it.

"I'm sorry," Mary says. "I hope you get what you want."

I don't turn around. An apology can't wash away the fact that she vandalized my house and made my family feel unsafe. I'll always know what she did.

And so will she.

Lunch goes by in a rush, as a long line of people pass through the community center for a hot meal and a slice of pie. Mimi and I are on mashed potato duty, putting two round scoops on each plate. My dad washes dishes in the back. And Bumpa greets people at the door because he's friendly like that.

There are families and veterans. Single moms and teenagers. A girl who reminds me of Poppy because she has a box of colored pencils shoved into her pocket. And a little boy who reminds me of my brother with his curly hair and long eyelashes. I wonder if he likes dragons as much as Sequoia. When our food shift is over, my grandparents and I walk around, stopping at tables to say hello and passing out bottled waters. Some want to chat, while others want to be left alone. I listen to those who want to share stories.

In the evening, after we've cleaned up and locked the doors behind us, we drive back to join my mom, Poppy, and Sequoia for Thanksgiving dinner at home.

The house smells delicious when we walk in, like pungent garlic and the sharp bite of onion. Like spicy cinnamon and nutmeg. Like real butter and cream. The kitchen is warm from the oven, and I'm so glad to be back.

Because I have here.

I have home.

For now.

My whole family sits at the table, passing dishes, sharing what makes them thankful.

My dad is thankful for family.

My mom is thankful for love.

Poppy is thankful for books.

Sequoia is thankful for nature.

Mimi is thankful to be here.

Bumpa is thankful there wasn't too much traffic on the drive down.

I'm thankful Nico is okay after his beesting.

I tell my family about him asking me to the Snow Ball. Mimi claps excitedly and bounces in her chair.

"Oh, please let me take you shopping for your dress." She turns to my mom. "May I, Melinda? My treat."

"That would be lovely and generous. Thank you, Mimi."

"Tomorrow," Mimi says. "This is going to be so much fun!"

THIRTY-SEVEN

As it nears sunset on Saturday, about two weeks later, I'm all done up for the Snow Ball dance. Hair. Nails. Jewelry. Makeup. Poppy and my mom fussed over me like a beauty pageant contestant—minus the sash—all afternoon, knowing just the look I was going for.

I knew the sleeveless long black sheath dress was the right one as soon as I stepped out of the fitting room and Mimi pressed her hands to her cheeks and gasped, "Oh, my goodness, you look like Audrey Hepburn in *Breakfast at Tiffany's*. Classic and sophisticated."

Even though I'd never seen the movie, I knew who Holly Golightly was and what Audrey Hepburn looked like playing her. I was sure Nico would, too. Her look was polished. Chic. Iconic. I couldn't imagine getting anywhere near that. But when Mimi twisted my hair up and fastened it with a clip from her purse, then unhooked the pearls from her own neck to wrap them around mine, I saw it. The gloves we added pulled the whole look together.

"I think you have a new talent," I told my sister when she twisted my hair up to look like Audrey's again today. She even managed to make it stay in place. Coconut oil might've played a part. I didn't ask.

When the doorbell rings, my whole family rushes to the living room. Even Sequoia. My dad snaps a photo of me opening the door to Mrs. Noble and Nico, who's wearing a fitted charcoal-gray suit and a tie. I wait for him to fidget with his collar to remind me of how much he hates dressing up, but he doesn't. Instead he stands there, looking tall and sleek and gorgeous, clutching a plastic box containing a corsage of ivory roses.

"Oh no! I don't have a flower for you." I turn to my mom. "Aren't I supposed to have one of those things to pin to his suit?"

"A boutonniere." She smiles. "Your sister has it covered."

She nods at Poppy, who pulls her hand out from behind her back and hands me a handmade red origami rose, complete with safety pin.

My heart swells.

"You're the best." I gather her into a hug.

I look at my family, pride and joy radiating off each and every one of them as they look back at me. Like my dance is their dance. My life is their life. And I wonder if all families have this. I kind of think they don't.

I introduce Nico's mom to my dad and siblings and we all traipse outside to take photos before the sun fades.

"You both look stunning," Mrs. Noble says as she beams at us making our way down the front walk, then suddenly snaps a photo I wasn't expecting. "It's called journalistic photography," she explains. "It's about being in the moment instead of posing."

My dad doesn't take the same approach, and instead poses and props us in front of the tree in our yard "because the greenery is such a pretty backdrop."

As dual cameras battle, and we're not sure where to look, the mail carrier walks up with a stack of letters and bills. Instead of going to the front door to shove them through the slot, he hands everything to my mom.

My dad keeps taking photos and insists that Poppy and Sequoia join in. From the corner of my eye, I see my mom sifting silently through the mail.

Then she stops sifting.

Her forehead crinkles at the return address on one of the envelopes.

She opens it.

Reads.

Looks at me.

Looks at the letter.

Her smile drops.

"Over here, Junebug," my dad says, but I'm too distracted by my mom to look at his camera.

He stops taking photos when my mom shoves the letter into his hand and turns her back to me.

Her shoulders shake.

"Mom?" I step forward.

She pivots. Points. "Don't."

Nico and his mom look confusedly at each other.

"Juniper," my dad says, skimming the letter. "How could you?" His voice isn't angry. It's full of disbelief. Like I told him flaxseed causes cancer.

And then I know exactly what he's reading. Laurel told me this letter would come. And while I tried to prepare the words in my head, I didn't want to have to use them yet. Not tonight of all nights.

"What is it?" Sequoia says.

My dad clears his throat. "Your sister has apparently taken it upon herself to petition the court to get her vaccines. Apparently we can come if we want. It's not an order. Just a suggestion."

Nico's mom stiffens.

"How gracious," my mom snaps.

"Mr. and Mrs. Jade—" Nico attempts, but my dad interrupts him to address me.

"How long have you been planning this?" my dad asks.

"Since I got sick."

"How did you even . . . Who's helping you?"

I look at Mrs. Noble. "Nobody. It's just me."

"I find that hard to believe," my dad says. "You can't

exactly just walk into court on your own when you're sixteen."

"I helped her," Mrs. Noble blurts. "I have a friend. Her name is Laurel Ward. She's an attorney, and she's working pro bono for Juniper."

"*You* helped our daughter?" my mom sputters. "We sat and drank tea together while your son was in the hospital." She walks back and forth in our front yard. "There I was, trying to comfort you, mother to mother, and you knew all about this."

"It's not as if we were plotting against you," Mrs. Noble says. "Juniper simply needed professional assistance, and I put her in touch with someone."

"Well, you should mind your own business," my dad says. "This town is unbelievable. Can't anyone just let people live their lives?"

My mom steps forward to address Nico's mom. "You played me for a fool, knowing all along what was going to happen to me. To us. To our family."

"It's not like that," Nico says. "I asked my mom to help."

"Well, isn't that the nicest!" my mom shouts. "What a nice, supportive boyfriend you have, Juniper."

"Hey," Mrs. Noble says. "That's enough."

Nico looks at his feet.

"Don't talk to him like that," I say to my mom. I grab Nico's hand to reassure him.

Poppy and Sequoia stand straight and still. Eyes wide.

"We will talk to the people who visit our home under false pretenses any way we damn well please," my dad says through gritted teeth. And then directly to Mrs. Noble, "I think you should go."

He wraps my mom in his arms, trying to comfort her.

I stand there, watching it all, in my dress and my shoes with my hair and my jewelry. On the outside, I probably look the most beautiful I've ever looked, but on the inside, I've never felt uglier.

I was expecting that letter to feel gross when it happened, but I'd forgotten about my mom meeting Nico's mom. About tea and talking. Mom to mom. No wonder this moment feels deceptive.

"I feel so foolish," my mom says, shaking her head and burying her face into my dad's chest, letting out a dramatic sob.

"Melinda, please don't feel that way," Mrs. Noble says. "Maybe we can all talk about this together."

"No," my dad says. "We have nothing to say to you."

"So foolish," my mom says again.

"Mom, you're not." I put my hand to her back, but she won't look at me.

Nico slumps in his dark suit, that little red paper flower the only spot of color. This has to feel as bad for him as it does for me. His mom is being made to take the fall here, and she shouldn't. She did what she did because I asked Nico to ask her to help me. She introduced me to Laurel because I wanted her to.

"Mom," I try again.

Nothing.

"Go to your dance, Juniper," my dad finally says. "Just . . . go."

THIRTY-EIGHT

I sit in stunned silence while we drop Nico's mom at home and continue on to the Snow Ball. I don't know what to say. I don't know where to start. My face heats with shame. It was supposed to be a perfect night. Something I've wanted forever. And now it's ruined.

"You okay?" Nico asks after we've driven a couple of blocks alone in the quiet car.

"No. Are you?" He shrugs. I twist my corsage around my wrist. "I'm sorry my mom said those things about your mom."

"She was mad."

"That doesn't make it all right."

"No. It doesn't." He looks at me. "But I get it. People say shitty things when they're mad."

"I think it makes them feel better to make someone else hurt, too."

"Your mom made my mom sound like a mustache-twirling villain in a silent film."

"Which film?"

"All of them."

"I'm sorry."

"You don't have to apologize for your parents."

We pull into a parking space in the lot of the old Victorian resort hotel in town where the dance is being held. Nico shuts off the car. Rests his hands on the steering wheel. I look at him, so handsome in his charcoal jacket. His tie has tiny dots on it, barely a shade darker than the pale gray underneath them.

"I know it feels like everything sucks right now," he says. "But I hope we can still have fun tonight." He smiles, but it's not one of those smiles that lights up his whole face. I want to be happy like that. I want to forget about everything that happened back at my house. "We don't have to go straight in. We could walk around. Check things out."

"Be fashionably late?"

"Exactly." He points up at the bright red turrets standing out against the night sky. "There's supposedly a ghost that hangs out on that balcony up there."

"Do you think we can find it?"

"We can try." Nico opens his door and I reach for my own door handle. "Wait. Stay there."

"Why?"

"Just wait." He gets out and walks around and opens my door for me. "I'm trying to be chivalrous."

I take his hand and let him help me out. "Better?"

"Yeah." He shuts the door and clicks the lock as he stands back to look at me, really taking me in from head to toe. "I didn't get to say it before, but you look really beautiful tonight. You're Audrey-esque."

"You recognized it." I love making his celluloid world come to life.

"How could I not?"

We stroll through the massive courtyard, where Adirondack chairs are lined up like soldiers and perfectly trimmed topiary bushes are dotted with holiday lights. We squint our eyes at the turrets, trying to spy a ghost. But we only see the moon and stars. I shiver against the cold, and Nico pulls me closer. Rubs my bare arms to warm me.

"Let's go inside."

We continue into the lobby, where other Playa students wander around and the tallest Christmas tree I've ever seen takes up the entire center of the room, the top of it reaching a whole floor above us.

"It's real," I say, inhaling the crisp scent of pine. "I can smell the needles."

"The sign says it's twenty-five feet."

"Can you imagine having that in your living room?"

"Only if I carve a hole in the roof."

We stand at the base of the tree and look up to the sparkling golden star on top. Hotel guests and other Playa students in formal clothes collect along the railings of the wraparound balcony on the floor above us, taking photos against the backdrop of the top of the tree.

"We should take a picture," I say.

Nico pulls his phone out, and I snuggle closer to him for a selfie. "We should get a *real* photo," he says. "Let's ask someone."

I instantly remember the pumpkin patch and how nobody wanted to take our photo with my dad's camera. "No, this is fine." I reach for Nico's phone to hold it out for us.

He pulls it away. "Juniper, it's not a big deal."

He stops a woman passing by, and I wait for her to refuse. But she doesn't. Maybe because she's a tourist who couldn't possibly know who I am. She counts to three while we stand in front of the tree, our arms wrapped around each other like Christmas ribbon. We both thank her as she hands the phone back. Nico scrolls through the photos.

"Damn, we're a good-looking couple," he says, and I laugh. "Should we keep walking?"

"Yeah."

We pass through a door on the other side of the lobby, which takes us to the beach side of the hotel and down a corridor where the sweet smell of freshly baked waffle cones drifts through the air from the ice-cream parlor. At the end of the corridor, a pathway weaves its way down to the beach, where there's a seasonal outdoor ice-skating rink mere steps from the sand.

"Whoa," I say.

"Pretty cool, huh? My mom used to bring Matteo and me here every Christmas Eve when we were kids. We'd skate. See Santa. It was a whole thing."

We pass a cart selling hot cocoa with candy cane garnishes and burrow our way into an empty spot along the outside of the rink, where we can stand and watch the skaters. Some are seasoned pros, while others hold tightly to the side railing, taking tentative baby steps around the ice.

"I want to bring Poppy and Sequoia here."

"Oh, they'd love it."

"Yeah. But will they love it with *me*?"

"It'll get better. Your mom and dad just have to get over their own shit."

"I just don't want it to suck forever."

"It won't."

"Promise?"

"If it does, you can come live in my tree house."

I laugh. "Okay. Deal."

He kisses my temple. "So what do you think? Should we go to the dance now?"

"Yeah. We should."

"Then we shall."

We wander back through the hotel, passing other students as we go. Nico never lets go of my hand. When we finally enter the double doors into the dance, I can't believe what I see.

The ballroom is beautiful, with ornate chandeliers dripping from the mile-high ceiling. Everything else sparkles in winter white. There are starched table linens and pale blue crystal goblets that look like glaciers. There are hand-cut snowflakes and intricate ice sculptures decorating a long banquet table down the center of the room, while twinkle lights adorn the outer columns. And the entire back wall is floor-to-ceiling windows that look out to the beach and the ice-skating rink. I feel like I've walked into another world.

"Everything looks too pretty to be real," I say. "I'm afraid to touch it."

"It's something," Nico says, practically turning circles to see everything, like he's setting up shots for a movie. "I guess school dances aren't as bad as I thought they were."

"Thank you for bringing me," I say.

"Thanks for coming."

Someone calls out Nico's name, and we turn to see an excited girl in a long royal-blue dress, with hair to match, waving us over to her table.

"Do you want to sit at the film club table?" he asks me.

"Sure. It'll be like sitting together in the cafeteria."

"Right." He shakes his head, laughing. "You're in for some real disappointment if you think the cafeteria is anything like this."

When we get to the table, he tells his friends my name.

I already know Jared, but Nico introduces me to everyone else by going around and pairing each name with that person's favorite film. Tess—*Lady Bird*—Nakamura, the one who waved us over, insists I sit next to her.

"I need to meet the girl who saved Nico's life," she says as we take our seats and her blue hair falls over her shoulders.

"I didn't . . . it wasn't like that."

"Part of me wants to make you tell me all the gory details, because it sounds like it was all very cinematic and I should put it in a screenplay, but the other part of me can't handle hearing it because I know him. So can I just say thank you instead?"

"I did what anyone would do."

She props her elbow up on the table and leans against her hand, studying me. "I don't know. I'm pretty sure I would've passed out from fear. The paramedics would've thought I was the one in anaphylactic shock."

I set my clutch down. "No, you wouldn't have. You would've done what you had to do because there was no other choice. But I hope you never have to find that out in person."

"Right?" She takes a sip from her crystal goblet, and I notice every finger on her hand has a ring on it, some more than one. They clink against the glass as she clutches it, and then she looks at Nico. "We give him a hard time, but we all know there'd be no film club without him." She looks back at me. "I'm so glad you were there."

"Me too," I say.

"Okay. So on to other things. Did your parents name you after a My Little Pony on purpose? Because that's amazing."

"Um, no? What?"

"Your name. It's the same as a My Little Pony character."

"It is?" How are my parents so out of it? How am I? "That's kind of embarrassing."

"Actually, I think it's really cool." She waves her hand in the air, and her rings sparkle as they catch the light. "So don't worry about it."

"Okay. I won't."

"Good. So anyway. Your whole look is drop-dead Audrey, and I think we need to go dance right now so you can show it off." She stands up and holds her hand out to me. "Right?"

"Um, yeah, okay."

"I'm stealing your girlfriend," she says to Nico. "You can come if you want."

Nico stands up. "I'm ready."

Tess, Nico, and I walk to the dance floor, and our whole table follows. We form a big film-club circle, and everyone dances together instead of pairing off. I love that. It feels dependable. Protective. Real.

I don't actually know all the songs the DJ plays, but everyone else seems to, because they're singing along at the top of their lungs. Others jump with their hands in the air, pumping their fists. The wooden dance floor literally sinks down and springs back up with the movement of two hundred teenagers dancing. I can feel the vibration of the music come up through the floor, into my feet, until it hits every nerve ending in my body. Between that and the music and the lights and Nico, I can't help but jump up and down, too. It's impossible to hold on to anything other than what's happening right here.

THIRTY-NINE

The whole house smells like butter and cinnamon the next morning. Warm. Cozy. Home. Everyone was asleep when I got back from the dance, so I tiptoed upstairs, hung up my dress, pulled on pajamas, and crawled into bed.

As I head downstairs, I hear the low murmur of voices. Poppy's giggle. Sequoia humming to himself. The gentle scrape of forks against dishes. I enter the kitchen, the corners of my mouth turning up hesitantly.

But my parents don't greet me.

There isn't a place set for me at the table.

There isn't a juice cup or silverware or a napkin or a plate.

Poppy slides her eyes to me as she gulps down her OJ. She watches as I take a step forward, then turns her head to watch my parents.

Waiting.

I wait, too. I wait to see if they'll say anything.

But they don't.

Not even hello.

I walk to the cupboard and pull out a plate for myself. But the dish that usually holds a pile of pancakes for all of us is nothing but crumbs and a few smashed blueberries. Fine. I'll make toast instead. I rummage through the bread basket and pull out a slice of homemade honey wheat. I slide it into the toaster, lean against the counter, and wait.

"Hi," I say, my voice an echo. Distant.

"Hey," Sequoia says without looking up.

Nobody else responds.

"Hi," I say again.

My dad looks at my mom. "As I was saying, that's the deadline, so I'll need to work today even though it's Sunday."

"Um, hello," I say. "I'm here. I exist. You could've left me some pancakes."

"Oh," my mom says, looking up at me like she just realized I exist. "We thought you might rather go to Starbucks. You don't seem to want to be a part of this family or our ways anymore, so we just figured we'd let you do you."

My dad nods. "Yep. Starbucks. You have birthday money, right? Knock yourself out."

"I don't want Starbucks. I want to sit down and have pancakes with my family."

My dad harrumphs. "Hindsight is twenty-twenty, as they say."

"What's that supposed to mean?"

Poppy rolls her eyes. Sighs. "It means you should've thought of what you were doing before you did it."

I turn to her. "And what exactly is it that you think I did?"

She shrugs matter-of-factly. "Ruined our family."

My mom winces. But she only spends a split second with that expression on her face before she goes back to her juice and the conversation she was having with my dad. "Might as well work through today and get it done. Refill?" She holds the juice pitcher up to my dad. He nods, and she pours OJ all the way to the top, emptying the pitcher so there's none left for me.

Poppy chews on her pancakes. Sequoia stabs at blueberries with his fork. My mom and dad look at each other and smile their unspoken smile.

I'm on the outside looking in.

Like I'm in one of those stories where a person has come back as a ghost and wants to make enough noise to let the people they care about know they're there, but no matter how much they scream and shout, nobody hears them.

The toaster dings as my toast springs out. I plunk it onto my plate, grab a glass from the drying rack next to the sink and fill it with water, and take a seat next to Poppy.

"So this is how it's going to be? Everyone is going to ignore me?"

"I don't know what you expect us to do," my mom says. "You've chosen to spit in the face of everything we stand for. Everything we've fought for and believe to our core. How do you expect us to feel?"

"I tried talking to you about it. I tried everything to avoid it going this far. I had no other choice."

"No other choice?" My dad's face goes red and bulgy. He reminds me of Teddy at the party after the football game. "You do realize you can't come back from this, right? You take us to court, you get your vaccinations, and things will never be the same in this family. I promise you that."

Poppy sits there opening and closing her mouth like she's debating whether or not to chime in.

"Maybe I don't want to come back from it!" I yell. "Maybe I want everything to change."

Sequoia puts his hands over his ears to block out my shouting.

"Well, you've certainly done a good job of it," my mom says.

"Do you not want to live here anymore?" my dad says. "Do you not want us to be your parents anymore?"

"No." My bottom lip wobbles. I try not to cry. "I want to live in this house. I want to live with my parents and my family."

"Well, you can't have it both ways," my dad says.

"You can't actively decide to go against everything we believe in and expect us to throw you a party at the same time. These choices you've made, they change everything. They change the dynamic of this house. You and your mom and me. Poppy and Sequoia. Everything's different now. And excuse me if I'm not going to high-five you for making it happen."

"I can't do this anymore," my mom sputters tearfully.

"I'm done, too," my dad says, scooting away from the table.

Poppy clears the plates, sets them in the sink, and leaves, too.

Sequoia and I are left sitting at the table together. He chomps on his last bite of pancake. I watch him until he looks at me. Grins a gummy grin that comes from missing his top two front teeth. He wriggles in his seat, leaning his chair back and almost losing his balance. He rights himself quickly and pushes away from the table.

I reach for his hand. Pull him back to me.

"What?" he says, sitting down again.

"Don't go."

"Why?"

"Do I have to have a reason?"

"Guess not." He picks at a blueberry. Tosses it into his mouth. Studies me. "But why?"

"Do you hate me?"

"You're my sister."

"So?"

"So how could I hate you if you're my sister? I'm supposed to love you."

"But do you actually love me or do you just think you're supposed to love me?"

He props his elbow on the table, rests his chin in the palm of his hand like he really has to think about it. "I actually love you."

My eyes mist. My vision blurs. "Thanks."

His eyes crinkle. "Why are you crying?"

I swipe at my face. "I just am."

He studies me. Shrugs. "Okay."

I spend the rest of the day continuing to feel like a ghost in my own house, shuffling down hallways and tiptoeing down stairs. Pouring a glass of water. Taking a shower. Brushing my hair. Reading my books.

My Snow Ball dress hangs from a hanger on the back of my door. Sometimes, when I walk past it, I create enough of a breeze to make it flutter. Last night already feels like a lifetime ago. My dress is a memory. A ghost, too.

I spend my day alone.

Nobody comes to check on me.

Nobody cares.

FORTY

On Christmas Eve a week later, my whole family piles into Bessie to make the trek up to Sacramento to stay with Mimi and Bumpa. As if my parents aren't embarrassing enough, they insist on dressing Bessie like a reindeer at Christmastime, with antlers on the windows and a red nose on the front bumper. I'm always positive people in other cars on the freeway are rolling their eyes at us. So I'm not sad when the rain picks up and Bessie loses an antler and her red nose to the downpour. The traffic gets more horrendous, but I'm grateful for the reprieve it brings because it means my mom and dad will be too busy focusing on taking turns driving to bother arguing with me. I nestle into the cocoon of a blanket in the back of the van, leaning my bed pillow against the window until I fall asleep to the sound of the rain on the roof.

We make a few bathroom stops and take a lunch

break. Because of the pouring rain, we have to eat the picnic my mom packed inside the van in the parking lot of a gas station. When we finally arrive in Sacramento, we're all swept up in hugs and Duke barking and nipping at our legs. I pick him up and nuzzle him.

"Aw, he missed you," Mimi says. "He's been so excited all day, almost like he knew you were coming back to him. Bet he can't wait for you to take him for a walk."

When I stayed last summer, Duke slept on my bed every night. I scratch him under his chin and he licks my wrist. "I missed him, too."

"Bad traffic?" Bumpa asks, because traffic is his favorite subject. He lives for stories about harrowing travel conditions.

My dad puffs up his chest like he just survived the Indy 500. "What should've been a six-hour drive took nine."

"Wowza. How many accidents did you pass?"

"At least five," Poppy brags.

"Thank goodness you survived," Mimi says, scratching Duke's scruffy neck. Some strands get caught on the big, fat diamond of her wedding ring and she has to untangle herself.

"Mimi, where do you want us?" my mom asks.

"Russell's old room. I've got Juniper in the guest room. And Poppy and Sequoia can take the sofa bed in the rec room." She looks at them, grinning. "There's a second Christmas tree up there."

Poppy squeals in excitement. I have to hold back from doing the same because the truth is, I want to do a happy dance, too. The guest room is downstairs, away from all the other bedrooms, and it has its own TV and bathroom. It's where I stayed this past summer, but I thought Mimi might give the room to my parents since it's more private.

"Both trees have twinkle lights," Bumpa informs us, like they're some fancy new technology.

"Cool," I say to humor him.

My dad grabs the suitcases, leaving my duffel bag on the floor by the piano, and heads upstairs. My mom goes to the kitchen to unpack her reusable grocery bags of food, because she doesn't trust Mimi's refrigerator or pantry.

Mimi whispers to me, "How many superfoods will she have us consuming this week?"

"Tons."

Bumpa lands in his La-Z-Boy with a grunt and points the remote at the TV. Sequoia rushes to the couch, eager to watch whatever he puts on.

Mimi pokes at the logs in the fireplace as their flames rise and crackle, the reflection catching in the big silver bulbs decorating the Christmas tree. Duke curls up on the rug in front of Mimi's feet, rests his head on his paw, and closes his eyes.

It'd be the perfect day-before-Christmas setting if there wasn't that anger from my parents bubbling underneath the surface.

286

"One hour of TV. And only something educational," my mom mumbles to us as she passes again. She turns to Mimi. "I'm going to lie down for a bit. It was a long drive."

"Do you need me to do anything?" I ask.

"Nope," my mom says. "You make up your own rules now anyway."

"Mom—"

"What's that about?" Mimi says as the door shuts upstairs and my dad shuffles back into the living room.

"Oh, you didn't hear, Mom?" My dad flops down on the couch, pushing the decorative holiday pillows into a pile to the right of him. "Juniper is taking us to court. Apparently she can take care of herself now."

"That's not the whole story." I turn to Mimi. "I just want to get my vaccinations."

"Ah." Mimi nods her head knowingly. "I could've told you something like this would happen eventually." She looks at my dad. "Your kids are going to grow up and realize your ways are too extreme, Russell."

My dad tosses a glare at his mom that isn't unlike one I'd give my own mom. "I didn't come here to be lectured about the way I'm raising my kids."

Mimi shrugs. "Very well. Snacks, anyone?"

"Mom," my dad warns. "Melinda brought food for them. They should eat that."

"Fine. I'll have a look. Come on, kids."

Sequoia pops up from the couch immediately, but

Poppy chooses to stay by my dad's side when he hands her the remote for the TV.

Bumpa snuffles out a snore.

"Looks like we already put him to sleep," Mimi says.

"Think I'll do the same," my dad says, closing his eyes and crossing his arms over his chest. "Remember, Poppy, only something educational."

Mimi rolls her eyes and heads to the kitchen, with Sequoia hopping behind her. She pulls a package of Oreos out from the pantry and puts her finger to her lips. "Shhhh," she says, and Sequoia looks at me uneasily.

"They're good," I tell him. "You eat the insides first. Here, I'll show you."

Mimi plunks the package onto the middle of the table, and we all settle into our chairs. I twist the top off an Oreo and lick at the white goo in the middle. Sequoia untwists his own cookie and tentatively touches the tip of his tongue to the filling. He screws up his face in disgust and bites into the chocolate wafer instead. He grabs a napkin from the holder on the table and wipes the white residue off the other half so he can toss that wafer in his mouth, too.

Mimi laughs. "I guess your mom still wins this one."

"Not entirely," I say as I lick up more filling and push the wafers I didn't lick over to my brother.

"So tell me what this court thing is about," Mimi says, tapping her Christmas-red nails against the table.

I fill her in as she tuts and groans, finally shaking her head in exasperation as I finish.

"They don't want to even try to listen," I say.

"I've certainly tried to talk to them myself," Mimi says. "As a parent, I support their right to raise their children as they see fit. But for crying out loud, they've got to get out of their own heads. Your dad tries so hard, but sometimes it's too hard. He doesn't realize how he ends up pushing people away."

"He's very stubborn," I say.

"Ha!" Mimi guffaws. "Stubborn is an understatement. Did you know he got booted from the Boy Scouts for refusing to wear the uniform?" She can't help but smile at the memory, the same way my mom gets all choked up when she tells me about something I used to do when I was little. "And he never played sports, because he didn't like the idea of looking like everyone else." She waves her hand. "Thank goodness I didn't send him to Catholic school. He would've led a revolt."

"Yep. Classic Dad."

"He means well, I know that, but he's a stubborn one, isn't he? Skipping sports because of uniforms. My goodness."

"Yeah. Sometimes it's not so bad to be on a team."

"Exactly." She pats my hand. "I'll try to talk to them for you. Again."

"Thanks for offering, but I wouldn't expect them to listen," I say.

"I can be calm and rational when I want to be."

"I'm sure *you* can. But I'm not sure they can."

I stand up and wet a paper towel to wipe off the chocolate crumbs that have collected all around Sequoia's mouth. He jerks away and rushes to the living room when I'm done.

Two seconds later, my dad bursts into the kitchen.

"Oreos, Mom? Seriously?"

"He only had a few. And he didn't even eat the filling."

My dad pulls at his hair in frustration. "What do I have to do to get you to respect our rules?"

"This is my house. I have rules, too. And they include spoiling my grandchildren."

"Your rules do not apply to my children when it puts them at risk."

"From a cookie?" Mimi says. "Please."

He looks at me. "I'm sure you encouraged this, right?"

Mimi stands up. "She had nothing to do with it. I pulled the cookies from the pantry and Sequoia didn't even like them. I doubt he'll ever try another one as long as he lives, so calm down."

My dad talks through gritted teeth. "Do not tell me to calm down."

"Oh, go take your nap," Mimi says, shoving the Oreo package back into the pantry. "You need it. That long drive made you grumpy."

My dad groans and stomps out of the kitchen.

I stifle a laugh in my hand. "Is it weird to say that's the most I've related to him in the last year?"

Mimi laughs. "Nope. That was definitely a flashback to his teen years. Next thing you know, he'll tell me I need to relax because piercing his ears with a safety pin he pulled from my sewing kit was no big deal."

"He did that?"

"Oh, he did. And I have the trip to the doctor and the antibiotics to prove it."

FORTY-ONE

Later that evening, when the rain has let up, Mimi asks Poppy and me to take Duke for a walk around the block. He gets all excited as soon as he sees me grab the leash, rushing for the door and yipping. I clip the leash to his collar, and my sister and I head out to the sidewalk.

It's dark now and various houses are lit up with colorful Christmas lights. The air is crisp and clean, like the rain washed everything dirty away.

Duke pokes his nose into the wet grass and mossy tree trunks of every house we pass.

Poppy's quiet for the first block or two. And then she turns to me, her face serious. "Am I supposed to choose a side?" She holds tight to Duke's leash. "Between you and Mom and Dad?"

"No. You can do whatever you want."

"It doesn't feel like that. You can basically taste the tension in our house. My insides hurt when we're all in a room together. I swear I'm going to throw up one of these days."

"But it's not about you."

"Yes, it is. It's about our whole family. And I'm a part of this family, too."

Duke happily bounces along at my side, completely oblivious to Poppy's annoyance. I envy him.

"You don't have to choose a side," I say.

We stop to let Duke do his business and Poppy hands me a plastic baggie to scoop it when he's done.

We walk another block in silence. When we arrive back at Mimi and Bumpa's, Duke has a spring in his step and I have a pit in my stomach. I don't want my sister to feel sick because of me. I only ever wanted this to be a thing between my parents and me.

I can hear Mimi laughing through the front door when we walk up to it. The Christmas tree lights glow through the window, and white twinkle lights crisscross the eaves of the house. It all seems so festive and fun. Maybe being with Mimi and Bumpa is just what our family needs.

Poppy opens the front door and I unclip Duke from his leash. But when a car pulls into the driveway next door, Duke takes off running, tearing across the front yard and into the neighbors' driveway, all barks and bounces.

"Duke!" I yell as he jumps up and down at the driver's side of the car.

The door opens and I recognize Noah, the boy from

college with the tattoo and the lawn mower and the boring-sounding internship. I wonder if he's literally just getting home from school, his duffel bag full of dirty laundry in the trunk. I shouldn't care. I like Nico way more than I ever liked Noah. But I can't help but be curious after all those weeks I spent wondering about him last summer.

Noah stomps his foot and shoos Duke away.

Duke barks back.

"Get out of here," Noah says.

"Sorry," I say, rushing over to scoop up Duke.

When my eyes move from Duke to Noah, I notice he's wearing a North Face jacket, the long sleeves covering his tattoo, and a baseball hat. He doesn't look like the same guy who headed to his fancy financial internship last summer. He just looks like a regular kid home from college.

"That dog is always so out of control," he says.

"Duke?" I scratch at Duke's head and he leans into my hand, licking my face. "No, he's not. Maybe he just missed you."

Noah slams his door shut. "Doubt it. I hate dogs. That one's always just been too dumb to figure it out."

His tone is harsh. Like a slap in the face. I take a step back. In a split second, any fantasy I ever had about Noah is destroyed.

I'm holding a plastic baggie full of dog shit in my hand, but Noah's attitude is way more disgusting.

"I'll try to keep him away from your house," I say.

"Right. I'll believe it when I see it."

My mom has always said you can tell a lot about a person by the way they act around animals. Now I see what she means. I grunt, turn on my heel, and walk back to my grandparents' house as fast as I can.

And maybe that's life. Maybe we go through it, imagining things will always be better if we do this one thing or we have this one thing or we go to this one place or we know this one person. But a lot of the time, the reality doesn't live up to the expectation at all.

Is it the same with my vaccines? I thought everything would be better if I could get my shots, but now my parents barely talk to me and my sister feels like she has to choose sides, and she'll probably choose theirs because she always does.

Is it worth it? At the end of the day, does it really matter, if it means I could lose everything? Maybe the fantasy of taking my parents to court is better than the reality. Maybe I've been so caught up in the fight that I didn't stop long enough to think of the consequences.

FORTY-TWO

I claw my way out of a dream, only to realize the shouting I'm hearing isn't something I made up in my head. It's coming from the living room. I scramble out of bed to see what's going on.

Mimi shouts, "I've bitten my tongue for sixteen years, but this is ridiculous. What you're doing to your kids isn't right." Duke barks when she raises her voice. "Hush," she tells him.

"Everyone calm down," Bumpa says, standing in the middle of the chaos. "It's Christmas morning. Mimi has hot cocoa and biscuits. There are gifts under the tree. Let's enjoy ourselves."

"I refuse to spend Christmas morning with my mother making snide comments," my dad hisses.

My mom puts her hand on my dad's arm. "Russ. Your dad's right. Not now."

"When then, Melinda? We might as well get it all

out in the open. Why are we pretending everything's fine?"

"Maybe you should let Juniper live with us," Mimi says. Her tone is very matter-of-fact. Like it's the solution to everything.

"Stop it!" I shout.

The room goes silent. Poppy looks at me, then my dad. My mom looks at my dad, then Mimi. Sequoia looks at me. Bumpa looks at the Christmas tree lights, avoiding eye contact altogether.

"Is that what you want?" my dad asks me. "Do you want to stay here with your grandparents?"

"What? No!"

"It's something to consider," Mimi says, looking at me seriously. "You don't have to decide right this very second."

"You know what?" my dad says, standing up and pointing his finger in the air. "Here's what we're deciding right this very second. We're going home. Get your stuff, everyone."

"Russ," my mom says. "It's Christmas."

"Nope. I'm done." My dad turns on his heel and pounds up the stairs, taking them two at a time.

I can hear him yanking things around, shoving clothes and toothbrushes into suitcases.

"What do I do?" my mom says, wringing her hands. She looks at Mimi for answers.

"What can you do?" Mimi shakes her head. "He's as stubborn as always."

Poppy edges closer to the Christmas tree, like the gifts might disappear if she doesn't guard them with her life. "We can't leave. We haven't even unwrapped our presents."

Sequoia joins her, practically flinging his body across the presents to protect them.

Christmas gift rules say that my brother, sister, and I can only give each other something we make ourselves, so I made a kaleidoscope for Sequoia and repurposed an antique tin box into an art supply center for Poppy. I polished it until it shone again, then added dividers, some long and skinny enough for her colored pencils, others small and square for stamps and sequins.

My dad stomps down the stairs juggling two suitcases—one belonging to my parents and one belonging to Poppy and Sequoia.

"Get in the car," he says to us.

Sequoia rushes into my mom's arms, crying.

"Oh, sit down," Bumpa says.

"Poppy, Sequoia, car. Now," my dad says, brushing past Bumpa.

Sequoia grabs a gift from under the tree. Clutches it. "Can we bring our presents?"

My dad ignores him. "Melinda, are you ready?"

My mom stands there, looking stunned.

Mimi stands up. "This is absurd. You can't make the kids spend Christmas Day driving in a car."

"I think I've made it clear that I don't appreciate you

telling me what I can and can't make my kids do." He turns to me. "Juniper, you're coming home, too."

I cross my arms. "No."

"Get. In. The. Car."

My dad has never, not once, hit me. He never would. But the look on his face scares me enough to do what he tells me.

"She needs to get her things," my mom says.

"You have two minutes," my dad says, yanking open the front door.

"The presents!" Sequoia shouts.

"I've got them," Mimi says, bending down to quickly gather the gifts. "I'll put them in the car. You can open everything when you get home."

I rush to the guest room and shove my dirty clothes from yesterday and my homemade deodorant into my duffel bag as Sequoia's sobs echo from the living room.

When I get to Bessie, Poppy turns to me with rage in her eyes.

"You ruined Christmas!" she screams. "You're not the only one in this family. Today isn't just about you. Today is Christmas for all of us, and you ruined it!"

"I guess you chose a side," I say.

I fling my duffel bag into Bessie, knowing she's right.

I ruined Christmas.

I ruined everything.

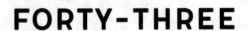

FORTY-THREE

Nico stops by on New Year's Eve to tell me Tess invited us over to her house for a get-together.

"It won't be like the football party," he says.

"Promise?"

"Promise."

I agree to go because I might as well make myself as scarce as possible until my court date next week. Things have been excruciating since getting back from Mimi and Bumpa's. The days have been long. Quiet. Lonely. I check in with Mimi every day, but I have to sneak calls when my mom and dad are working or running errands because they're still not speaking to my grandparents.

"We're not angry, we're hurt," my mom says. "There's a difference."

What they still don't get is that I'm hurt, too. So I mostly keep to myself. I make my own meals. Go for rides on my skateboard. Do my chores. Hang out with Nico at the library or his house.

My parents don't ask me much about where I'm going during the day. But a New Year's Eve party at night is different, so I ask if it's okay if I go to Tess's house.

"As long as you're home by your regular curfew of eleven o'clock," my dad says.

"It's a New Year's Eve party. I'd like to stay until midnight."

He glances at my mom.

She shrugs. "That makes sense," she says to him.

"Right. And she makes her own rules now anyway."

This is how it is in my house now. My parents talk about me like I'm not even here.

Sequoia is indifferent. Poppy has disowned me.

So when I walk into Tess's beach cottage, my whole body decompresses. Nobody ignores me or glares at me or harrumphs in my direction. Instead, Tess sweeps me into a warm hug and asks what I want to drink. And by that, she means lemonade or soda.

Her parents are home.

Tess introduces us as we pass through the kitchen to get to the backyard, but our introductions are brief, as Mr. and Mrs. Nakamura are busy preparing *toshikoshi* soba for everyone. It smells amazing, and I can't wait to try it.

"It's a Japanese New Year's Eve tradition," Tess says

as she shrugs into her coat to head outside. "The noodles break easily, and each break symbolizes moving on
from the past year, leaving regrets behind us so we'll
have good fortune in the next year."

"I could use more than one bowl of that," I say.

"I know, right?" She opens the sliding glass door, and
half the film club greets us with cheers.

Nico's correct. This isn't like the football party.

It's way better.

Comfortable. Familiar.

It's like his house two days ago when it was raining,
and Tess and Jared came over to watch the first season
of *Stranger Things* with Nico and me. In between epi-
sodes I told them all about my vaccines and my court
date next week, and Tess looked at me in awe.

"Wow! You're like our very own Ruth Bader Gins-
burg right here in the flesh." She high-fived me. "Keep
fighting for what you believe in, Juniper."

Jared is here again tonight, and he waves to me as Nico
and I walk over to scan the elaborate s'mores station,
complete with ten different chocolate choices. After taking our picks, we snuggle into a corner of the wraparound
couch built into the patio wall and roast our marshmallows while mellow music oozes softly from the nearby
speakers.

Nico spins a marshmallow into the flames, and it
catches fire. He lets it burn for a split second, then blows
out the blaze.

"I like the outside extra crispy," he says.

"You would, weirdo," Tess says as she settles in next to me.

I deposit my marshmallow between two graham crackers and set it aside so I can help Nico slide his charred marshmallow onto another graham cracker. We skipped the chocolate, since most of the candy bar selection had warnings about how they might've comingled with peanuts in the factory.

"Thanks for inviting me," I say, turning to Tess. I take a bite of my s'more. It's sticky and gooey even without the chocolate.

"Sorry if you were expecting a total rager. I'm not into stuff like that," she says.

"Totally fine by me."

"Good. I knew I liked you."

Jared and a few others shuffle back into the house.

Nico reaches for his s'more, and his shoulder brushes mine. I'm instantly transported to that night watching *Stand By Me* with the film club. When I wasn't sure what was going on between us, but every time he took a breath, and his shoulder pressed against mine, I was hopeful it was something good.

And it was.

It is.

It doesn't seem fair to have something so good when the rest of my life seems so bad.

"Mine's cooled down enough," Nico says, angling

the s'more toward me. I take a bite. "Well?" he asks hopefully as I chew.

"It's a little overdone," I say, and Tess laughs.

"Oh, shit," she says, suddenly scrambling up. "Jared's already hauling in that karaoke machine he rented." She eyes him through the sliding glass doors. "It's too early." She looks at us. "Right?"

I shrug.

"Is it ever too early for karaoke with Jared?" Nico asks around a bite of s'more.

"Well, you're no help." Tess puts her hands on her hips. "Come join, okay?"

I nod at the same time Nico shakes his head and says, "No way."

Tess rubs her hands together. "Ooh, this is excellent. One of you is in and one is out. The only solution is to find the perfect duet for the two of you to sing." She sits down again and taps her finger to her chin, thinking. "Maybe 'Summer Nights'?"

Nico cringes.

"Do I know that one?" I ask him.

He looks at me like *really?* "*Grease?*" he asks. "You seriously haven't seen it?" He sinks his fingers into my knee. "I guess it'll have to be our next movie. Mostly because I want to know if you find Sandy's transformation sexist or feminist."

"What's he talking about?" I look to Tess for an explanation. "Who's Sandy?"

"She's this high school girl in the 1950s who basically changes everything about herself to get this guy, who's kind of a bonehead, to like her."

"It's a musical classic," Nico says.

Tess sets her s'more on the edge of the fire pit, crosses her legs, and leans forward. "Some people think Sandy is actually a feminist hero. They insist that when she transforms, she's embracing her true self. I personally don't see it. Rizzo? Okay, sure, let's talk. But Sandy?" She shakes her head. "No."

I turn my focus to Nico. "Which version do you believe?"

"The sexist one. I think Sandy changes who she is to be what Danny wants. Although it can be argued," Nico says, grinning, "that Danny made some changes of his own in order to be what Sandy wants. He's even wearing the letterman's sweater he earned in track by the end of the movie."

"Which he ditches immediately when the new Sandy shows up," Tess says.

"Your point being?"

"Everything?" Tess huffs. "Okay, we definitely need to do a deeper dive on this." She makes a move to settle back and enjoy her s'more until there's a screech of feedback from the karaoke machine. All three of us automatically press our hands to our ears to block it. "Not right now, obviously, because I have to go save the night." She strides toward the house. "Jared, you better not blow a fuse!" she shouts at him through the open sliding glass door.

Jared looks at her, confused, microphone in hand. He looks like Sequoia the time I caught him drawing with a bright blue crayon all over his bedroom wall when he was four years old, and I can't help but laugh.

Nico tips his s'more like he's tipping his hat in farewell. "Have fun, everyone."

I rearrange myself, and Nico drapes his arm across my shoulder. I settle, content, into the crook of his arm. We sit still, peacefully watching the flames of the fire spit sparks into the dark night air. It reminds me of camping on the beach with my family a couple of summers ago. Sitting around a bonfire while my dad strummed a guitar. Sleeping in tents. Listening to waves crash. All of us together and happy. So different from the past weeks at my house now.

"Are you okay?" Nico asks after a few minutes of not talking. "You're quiet."

"I'm just tired."

"Are you sure that's all it is? I'll do karaoke if you really want. You wouldn't be forcing me."

"I'd love to see you do karaoke." I laugh. "But that's not what I'm thinking about."

"What's on your mind?"

"The fire pit, the night, the music, it all reminds me of camping with my family . . . when things were good with us."

He rubs my shoulder. "And?"

I focus on the flames crackling, almost dancing. "I'm wondering if going to court is worth it. Maybe I *should* just wait until I'm eighteen. What if I lose them over this?"

"You're not going to lose them."

"You don't know how bad it's been at home. It's like they wish I didn't exist."

"The reason they're mad is *because* they care that you exist."

I thread my fingers with Nico's. Run my other hand across his knuckles. "I think maybe I've been so laser focused on this one thing—getting my shots—that I lost sight of everything else. Like I never thought about what I could actually lose in the process." I look at him. "My parents are really mad. Even worse, they're really hurt. I've morally wounded them."

"But you're standing up for something you truly believe in. Do you realize how many people would be too afraid to do that?"

"But is it worth it?"

"It's worth it."

"Convince me. Because I'm having a hard time seeing it right now."

He turns sideways to face me. Pulls my hands into his lap. "Okay. I've got it." He smiles. "You'll like this one."

"Let's hear it."

"It's like you're the opposite of Sandy in *Grease*. You're fighting for this because it's who you are to the core. If you didn't do it, you wouldn't be you. You're the anti-Sandy."

I laugh. "That's quite an analogy. I think I really need to see this movie."

He laughs. "You do." He holds my hands in his, looking at me more seriously. "We're all going to grow up and make choices that might not be the same ones our parents would make for us. And they're not always going to be happy about our choices. But we can't let our parents stop us from being who we are. And living our own lives. Right?"

"Yeah, I guess."

"And I really do think it'll get better. Court just needs to be over first."

"I hope you're right."

"I am." He tucks one of my curls behind my ear. "So for now, let's just celebrate New Year's Eve. It's a new beginning and all that."

"With off-key karaoke and burnt s'mores."

He laughs. "What could be better?"

"Kisses at midnight."

"Yeah, there's always that."

"Do we have to wait until then?"

"I'd rather not."

He leans in and presses his mouth to mine just as Jared launches into an impassioned rendition of Journey's

"Don't Stop Believin'." I know all the lyrics because my mom insists on blasting it to sing along when it comes on the radio in Bessie.

And somehow, in this moment, I'm able to forget and remember and forgive all at the same time.

FORTY-FOUR

I have this version of court in my head. Of a judge and twelve jurors in a box and rows and rows of onlookers. But my case isn't like that at all. There's only Judge Elizabeth Coffman on the bench and a table where Laurel and I are supposed to sit.

Nico and his mom are here, too. I drove with them. Nico left school after third period and picked me up midmorning. I felt bad about him leaving early, since it was only the first Monday back after winter break, but he insisted. And in the end, I liked having the moral support. I'd spent up until Nico's arrival avoiding my parents, which wasn't hard to do, since we hadn't done much talking since New Year's Eve a week ago. During one of our phone chats, Mimi offered to come down for court today. I told her I thought it would be better if she didn't come. That it would be easier to figure out next steps after I have a judge's official decision.

If it's a yes, maybe I really will have to move in with my grandparents.

I hope not. I don't want to leave Nico and the life I've made here in Playa Bonita just when I feel like I finally have a shot at normal.

"There's still time to change your mind," Poppy said to me when I woke up yesterday morning. She'd tiptoed into my room, letting my door snick shut behind her. "Everything could go back to the way it was before you started all of this."

"I don't want to go back. I'm sorry."

"It doesn't seem like you're sorry." She gripped the edge of her pajama top in frustration. "It's pretty obvious you don't care about anyone but yourself."

"That's not true."

"You should just wait until you're eighteen."

"Do you really think that would make a difference? Mom and Dad are going to be mad no matter when I do it. It's not about age. It's about the thing itself."

"Why do you want to make them mad in the first place?"

"I don't." I looked outside my window at the school across the street. I could smell the hallway. I could see the football field. I could feel the vibration of drums from the school band. "And I don't only care about myself. I'm doing this for you and Sequoia, too." I looked at her hopefully. "You might want something different someday."

"I'm not like you," she said.

After I met with Laurel last night to go over things one last time, Nico suggested we watch *A Few Good Men* and *Legally Blonde* to prepare for today. That might be why I expected more drama in this courtroom where we huddle together, talking, before it's time to get started.

But just when I'm feeling good about everything, like I've really got this, Laurel pulls me aside.

"We have a last-minute change," she says. "Your parents have asked to make a statement."

"What? Can they even do that?"

"They can."

"Crap."

"We're just going to do this the same way we planned. Your parents can say whatever they want, but it won't make your argument any less compelling. Okay?"

I nod. "Okay."

Just then, the doors to the courtroom open and my mom and dad walk in with some guy I've never seen before. He's wearing a navy-blue suit and carrying a messenger bag. My mom has flat-ironed her hair and my dad is wearing a tie. They almost don't look like my parents.

They walk through the galley, past Nico and his mom, and sit down at a table on the other side of me. My mom looks at me with sad eyes, like she's holding back tears, but my dad is all business, looking straight ahead, leaning toward his attorney as he speaks into his ear.

Judge Coffman indicates it's time to begin by asking Laurel, "Do we have any preliminary matters?"

Laurel answers, "No, Your Honor."

She asks the same of my parents' attorney, and my heart thumps in my chest, faster than it should. My palms sweat. I knot my hands together in my lap to keep from shaking.

"No, Your Honor," the other attorney says.

After some general introductions, where Laurel explains who I am and why I'm here, she says, "Ms. Jade has prepared a statement she would like to read aloud."

Judge Coffman nods to me. "Very well. Ms. Jade, you may approach the stand."

Laurel leans closer so only I can hear. "You're going to get up and read, just like we practiced last night." She smiles at me. "You've got this."

I look at Nico. He gives me a thumbs-up.

I take a sip of water. Swallow. I can hear the gulp echo in my ears as I approach the stand.

The bailiff swears me in, asking, "Do you promise to tell the truth, the whole truth, and nothing but the truth, so help you God?"

"Yes."

Laurel approaches me. "Ms. Jade, you may read your statement now."

I wrote what I wanted to say on paper from a spiral notebook, and the torn pages crinkle in my shaky hands as I sit. I glance quickly at my parents sitting in front of me.

They look ready.

I gaze back at my pages. The words blur. But I concentrate and focus.

"Thank you, Your Honor." I try not to fidget. "I'm Juniper Jade, and I'm sixteen years old. I am seeking the right to consent to be vaccinated in order to protect myself and others from devastating, life-threatening viruses and diseases. A lot of people might say I'm too young to have a say about something like this, but I don't think that's true."

My voice wobbles. It feels like my whole body is shaking with nerves.

"There are a few things I could do confidentially. I could seek out mental health treatment. I could be tested for STDs or get a prescription for birth control. I could have an abortion. But for some reason, I have not been able to find a doctor willing to give me a meningitis shot or a tetanus shot or a whooping cough shot. I blame my parents for that. It's because of their deliberate choice to not get me vaccinated that I contracted the measles last fall and ended up in the hospital. It was a very scary and trying experience."

I can *feel* my mom and dad watching. Their eyes burning into me. I can't look.

"There was a quarantine sign on the door of my hospital room, and back at home, my younger sister and brother got the measles, too. Since then my family has been continuously harassed by our community. We've been threatened in public and our house has been vandalized. And because of me, or really because of my parents, a baby in town contracted the measles and died tragically."

I clear my throat.

"I respect my parents and everything they've taught me. Because of them, I know how to spot a rip current in the ocean and how to swim out of one if I get caught. I know how to identify poisonous mushrooms in the wild, and I know how to forage for the ones that are edible. I know how to eat and live healthily. I know how to create less waste by composting and recycling and growing my own food. I know how to respect the world and the people in it. The truth is, my parents have taught me a lot of important things." I look right at my mom and dad so they'll hear the words. "We just disagree on this one thing."

And then I turn back to Judge Coffman and look at her.

"The irony is that it's because of my parents, and what they've taught me, that I disagree with them. When my dad teaches me in school, he tells me to weigh all the arguments. I've done that. I've thoroughly considered all the angles and heard the reasons why my parents don't want me to be vaccinated. And after doing all that, I can say with full certainty that on this particular thing, I think they're wrong. Yes, I'm sixteen years old, but I also think I'm clear-minded enough and thoughtful enough to make this choice for myself."

I grip my papers tighter.

"One attorney in town told me the only way to proceed would be by emancipation, which would mean leaving my parents and my family. I'd have to move out and get a job and make a life for myself without my mom and dad and brother and sister." I turn to my parents. "But I don't want to do that. I don't want to live my life without my family. I love them. They love me."

Judge Coffman listens intently.

"I simply want to have the right to take control of my own health. I'm the only one who has to live in this body, and I want to do everything I can to protect it and the people around me. So I'm here today, with my counsel, petition in hand, asking for the right to be vaccinated. Thank you."

I leave the stand and sit down next to Laurel, setting my crinkled papers on the table. My heart races and my hands shake. I look at Nico. His smile is huge.

"So good," he mouths.

I look at Judge Coffman, anxiously awaiting her response. I hope she heard what I meant for her to hear: a young woman fighting for autonomy over her own body.

The same thing happens all over again with my dad.

He approaches the stand, gets sworn in, and sits down with his prepared statement in his hands. He straightens his tie.

"Mr. Jade, you may read your statement," his attorney directs.

"Thank you. I do have something I'd like to say." He looks at my mom, who gives him an encouraging nod.

"I guess it starts with the literal beginning. I want to tell you about the day my daughter Juniper was born." My dad looks at me, his expression soft and full of love. "It was raining. Not just a sprinkle but a torrential storm that flooded the Pacific Coast Highway and blocked off roads due to mudslides. Because my wife was a week past her due date, she and I had mapped out three different routes to the hospital just in case of road closures. We were as prepared as we could be. But wouldn't you know it? My wife's water broke at rush-hour traffic time in the middle of a downpour. The drive was so harrowing that it's one of the reasons we opted for home births for our second two children."

My dad looks at my mom and they smile at each other, a shared memory passed between them of a time Poppy, Sequoia, and I don't know in the same way they do.

"Juniper was our first baby. The whole time my wife was pregnant, we worried over everything. She'd had two miscarriages before Juniper, so perhaps we were hypersensitive."

My jaw drops. I had no idea my mom had ever had a miscarriage before I was born, let alone two.

"I thought I couldn't possibly worry more than I did in those nine months my wife was pregnant, but when I held Juniper for the first time, looking down at her pink, round face, after waiting for her for so long, worry was all I felt. Looking at her and knowing her life was literally in my hands, my fear only grew. My love for her was so profound, I don't think I can adequately put it into words." His chin quivers with emotion, and it looks like he's holding back tears. "But I'll try.

"We brought Juniper home from the hospital, where we fretted over everything as new parents do. We worried about whether she was getting enough to eat. Whether she was sleeping too long or not long enough. Whether the sounds she made were typical or a sign of distress. Each day, we got better at deciphering her cries and knowing which ones meant she was hungry and which ones meant she needed to be changed. Most of all, I knew which cries meant she needed to be held and comforted. I sat countless hours with her in a rocking chair in the middle of the night, fully committed to my job of protecting her.

"And maybe I took my job too seriously at times. Maybe I became obsessed or extreme. Maybe my love for Juniper, and putting her life above anyone else's, made me selfish. And maybe it still does. Because I cannot sit here in front of you today and say I've changed my mind. I cannot say it doesn't cause me literal physical pain to think of my child putting something into her body to which I am so vehemently opposed. So I would like it to go on record that I do not want Juniper to be vaccinated. Perhaps it's emotion that brought me here. And I feel terrible"—his voice cracks—"terrible about what happened to the baby in town, to Katherine St. Pierre, because I know her parents loved her and wanted to protect her just like I love and want to protect my own daughter. But I still wouldn't change my decision. Because I believe in what I know, and I believe I, as the parent, should have the right to make this decision for my daughter. It's my job to protect my own child above all else and I feel, very strongly, that's exactly what I'm doing." He turns to me. "I love you, Junebug. I'm doing this because I love you."

"Thank you, Mr. Jade," Judge Coffman says. She turns to Laurel and asks, "Do you have an argument?"

"We waive," Laurel says.

My dad leaves the stand and sits down next to his attorney.

I feel a tear fall down my cheek. I look at my parents and see my mom dabbing her own eyes. My dad looks ahead, his chin still quivering. All this time, he's been ruling with an iron fist, adamant about his supposed scientific reports and statistics, but it isn't until today, this very moment, that I finally understand his convictions are about so much more than numbers and articles on the internet.

Still. What he said doesn't change my mind. I want my vaccinations.

"Ms. Jade," Judge Coffman says, looking at me, "I commend you. I can tell you've given this a lot of thought and you're taking the circumstances very seriously."

"I am, Your Honor."

She nods. Looks to my parents.

"Mr. and Mrs. Jade, while I appreciate that you've made decisions on your daughter's behalf, decisions you've ostensibly made in good faith and out of love for your child, I do see the important and valid point Ms. Jade is making." She leans forward, addresses all of us. "We have laws in California that are in place to protect the best interests of our citizens." She looks at me. "But in this case, as evidenced by your contraction of the measles and your subsequent harassment, I can see clearly that not being vaccinated has not been in your best interest, even if it was a decision made by your parents, who only felt they were doing what was best. It is for this reason that I am ruling in your favor and granting you the right to be vaccinated."

My dad gasps.

My mom sputters.

Their attorney shakes his head.

I try to steady my hands.

I turn to Laurel. She's smiling so big.

"She just . . . Oh my god . . . We did it," I say.

"Juniper," Laurel says, beaming at me. "*You* did it."

I sit for a moment. Quiet. Taking it in. My parents get up. Shuffle closer.

"Well," my dad says quietly. "You got what you wanted."

"It didn't have to be like this," I say. "It didn't have to get this ugly."

"It did have to get this ugly. You never would've gotten it any other way. But I respect this courtroom, and we'll speak outside instead of in here."

My mom can't get any words out through her tears. She just holds tight to my dad's hand as they go.

Nico rushes over and pulls me into a hug when the doors to the courtroom shut behind them.

"You were so good," he says.

I reach for my notebook pages. My words. I want to hold them to my chest. Remember them forever. At the same time, I want to chase after my parents and hug them, too. I want to know they'll still hug me if I try.

"She was brilliant," Laurel says as all four of us walk out. My eyes are focused on what's in front of me.

My shoes clack against the shiny marble floor of the courthouse as we pass security guards and the doors of adjacent courtrooms. We walk down the stairs and into the lobby. I feel numb. Like it isn't real.

"Did she really say it was okay?" I ask. "I can get my shots?"

"She really did," Nico says. "You really can."

We walk through the courthouse doors into the fresh, clean air outside. Nico holds my hand. Laurel and Nico's mom chat excitedly. I can hardly feel my feet. It doesn't seem true.

I scan the steps out front, looking for my parents, but I don't see them.

The next thing I know, a microphone is shoved in my face. A news camera. A reporter.

"Ms. Jade. What do you have to say to your parents?"

"What?" I turn to Nico. I turn to Laurel. "How does she know?"

"Sometimes local news teams check to see what's on the dockets," Laurel says. "They must've found your case intriguing."

"Ms. Jade," the reporter says, "what message would you like other teens your age to hear?"

I look at her, clutching the microphone with the logo of the station she works for on it. I look at the cameraman standing beside her, lens still focused on my face.

And then my parents approach fast and furious. My dad tries to shoo the reporter away. But she's persistent, shoving the microphone in his face instead. "Mr. Jade, how do you feel knowing your daughter will be able to get her vaccinations?"

"I feel sick," he says. "I respect the law, and I have no choice but to accept the decision made here today, but this is a monumentally sad day for our family."

"It doesn't have to be," I say to him.

He turns to me. "You know, Juniper, you keep saying we just disagree on this one thing. Like one thing is simple. But it's not. This one thing is about everything we are." He shakes his head in defeat. "It's as if you took who we are and completely rejected it."

The camera keeps rolling. This will be everywhere by five o'clock tonight.

"Ms. Jade?" the reporter says. "Do you have a response?"

I can't move. Can't speak.

I don't know what I was thinking. Today didn't push everything behind us and make it all better. My parents have to accept the judge's ruling, but that's it. They still don't have to accept me.

"What about you, Mrs. Jade?" the reporter says.

My mom juts her chin forward, and I know she's trying to appear confident. But her voice wavers when she says, "Juniper is my daughter. That will never change. And that's all I have to say." She holds her arms tight at her sides and pushes past the reporter.

My dad follows, and all I can do is watch them go.

"Ms. Jade, where do you go from here? Home? Capitol Hill?"

I try to step away. Dip my head. Ask Laurel, "What does she mean?"

The news reporter presses forward. Wind in her hair. Makeup two layers thick on her face. Her microphone practically pressing into my nose. *Go away*, I think.

Laurel leans into me. Her voice is a hushed whisper in my ear. "What you did . . . it's contained in our little town of fifteen thousand right now. But if you want to make this bigger . . . louder . . . if you really want people to know . . . I'm telling you, you could really change things. You could make a difference, Juniper. For other kids like you with parents like yours. Kids who want to be heard and parents who don't want to listen."

"I'm only sixteen."

"And look at what you've already done."

I turn to Nico. "It's true," he says.

"Ms. Jade?" the reporter prompts. "Do you have anything to say?"

I push my hair behind my ears. Then stand tall and proud. "I want to say that I really believe in what I did. And when you really believe in something, it's worth fighting for. It's worth . . . everything."

"Even losing your family?"

"I believe my family is worth fighting for, too."

Nico takes my hand and we push past the reporter as she signs off from her story.

The sun is warm on my shoulders, bouncing off the cars in the parking lot, shooting sparks at my feet. I roll up my shirtsleeves. I want to feel the sun's heat on my skin. On my face. Like a pinch to my elbow to remind me I'm really here. That today really happened. I want to relish this. But then I turn back and look at my parents one last time. They're walking together toward the parking lot, holding hands, shoulders slumped. My mom takes her free hand and swipes at her eyes to catch her tears.

I consider running to them. But I don't know what more I could say. The only thing that will make this better is time.

"Are you okay?" Nico asks.

"I don't know." I give my parents another glance. My mom's dress flutters out behind her. My fingers reach forward as if to grab it. To hold on to some part of something even though she's too far away.

Why does winning feel so much like losing?

FORTY-FIVE

It's two o'clock in the afternoon by the time we leave the courthouse. Nico's mom said she'd get a ride with Laurel so Nico could keep the car. Today is a special occasion. We drive through town, past the library, around the cliffs, and down to the beach. The morning was overcast and chilly, but the clouds have parted now. It's funny how you can wake up expecting one thing but it can all change by the end of the day.

School's out now and Nico's phone has been blowing up with texts ever since sixth period ended. Jared and Tess. His friends—our friends—wanting to know how things went today. When we get back to my street, Nico parks in front of the school instead of my house.

"Come with me real quick. I just need to grab something from my locker."

I follow him up the steps and down the hallway. Past the lockers and the posters and the smelly walls.

We end up in front of the cafeteria door. He opens it wide, ushering me inside, where the scent of grease and fried food lingers.

"What are we doing?" I ask.

"Look closer."

The whole film club is at a table in the corner. Now I know each of them by their favorite movie *and* their favorite karaoke song.

"You've always wanted to go to the cafeteria." Nico tosses me a satisfied smile. "So here we are." We move closer and I see there's a carton of Neapolitan ice cream, bowls, and spoons. Plus confetti stars sprinkled across the table. Everyone stands and claps when Nico and I walk up.

"You're the shit," Tess says. "Seriously." She locks her pinkie finger with mine, then pulls me into a hug. "Congratulations, Juniper."

"You're like my hero," Jared says. "For real. Someone needs to make a movie about you."

I manage to mumble, "Thanks," as I'm torn between focusing on this celebration here and what awaits me at home.

Tess hands me a spoon. "We didn't know what flavor you liked best, so we got all three."

"Strawberry," I say, sitting down.

Jared puts his arms out like he's a bouncer assigned to crowd control. "The strawberry section belongs to Juniper, so back off."

"Dude, we're good," Nico says. "Nobody's gonna fight her over it."

"Everyone fights over the strawberry ice cream at my house," I say. "My dad makes it from scratch."

"That's so cool," Tess says. "I love homemade ice cream."

"Yeah, it's pretty cool," I say. I dig my spoon into the ice cream and take a bite. It's not even close to as good as my dad's, but I didn't expect it to be.

Tess says, "We figured you should get to celebrate your victory at the best table with the coolest people. Really, it's the only table you need to know when you start school here."

"After you get your shots, you can eat lunch with us every day," Jared says.

"Probably not," I say.

"What do you mean?" Tess asks.

I take another bite of ice cream. "My parents don't believe in public school any more than they believe in vaccinations. And even after I get my shots, I won't be able to enroll without their permission, because I'm a minor."

Nico huffs. "Sounds like another battle for Laurel."

"Right? Do you think she'd work pro bono for me again?"

"Wait," Tess says, her spoon frozen in midair. "You did everything you did to get your vaccines and you still can't even go to school like you want to?"

I shrug. "Pretty much."

"Well, that sucks."

"Yeah."

"You've got time to figure it out," Nico says, bumping my shoulder with his. "Maybe try for next year."

"You're better off coming in as a senior anyway," Jared says around a mouthful of chocolate ice cream. "Sophomore and junior years are like the middle-child years of high school. You're not a shiny new freshman and you're not a senior getting ready to graduate. Sophomores and juniors are just kind of . . . there."

"Good to know," I say, smiling.

I spend the next hour trying not to think about what's waiting for me at home. I try to eat and talk about court and movies, but I can't help but worry about what Poppy will say to me when I walk through the front door. Or if my parents will say anything at all.

It's probably better that everyone eventually decides it's time to head out. For homework and family dinners and guitar lessons. Nico holds my hand as we stroll down the hallway, past the lockers, and through the school. I want to be able to imagine being here next year. Saying good-bye at separate classrooms, then meeting up again for lunch, where we'll sit with the film club. But I know there's a lot more work to be done to make that a reality.

Outside, the sun is setting, bruising the sky in bursts of pink and purple.

The JROTC wears fatigues and stands in salute as the flag is lowered at the end of what has been a long and momentous day. For me, at least.

Nico and I linger at the bottom of the steps of the school.

"I'm proud of you," he says.

"I'm proud of me, too."

He wraps me in a hug. And when he kisses me, everything else falls away. He tastes like vanilla ice cream and smells like winter. When he stops to come up for air, I pull him back to me so we can kiss some more.

As much as I don't want to, I know I have to go home. So I do.

Nico walks me across the street and asks if I want him to come inside.

"No," I say, because I know it isn't the right thing right now. Not for him. Not for me.

So I kiss him one last time and watch as he drives away.

I stand on the sidewalk for a moment after he's gone. I wait and watch the shadows of my family inside my house. Until Poppy suddenly bursts from the front door, startling me from my stupor. She talks over her shoulder, then shuts the door behind her. I watch as she sits on the front porch, book in hand, opening to where she left off reading.

"Hey," I say, from the end of the front walk.

She purses her lips. "Hey."

I walk forward. Sink down next to her. "Am I still allowed inside?"

"Possibly," she says. "Mom made dinner and actually set a place for you."

"Okay." I pull my jacket tighter, protecting myself from the cold bite of winter air. "That's something at least." Poppy feigns reading, but I can feel her watching me. I eventually stand up and brush off the back of my skirt. "I might as well go see what's waiting for me."

Poppy stands up, too. Shuts her book. "Do you want me to come in with you?"

I'm deeply touched by her offer. It gives me hope. "Only if you want."

She moves forward, standing closer to me. "Let's go."

I nod and brace myself.

Poppy twists the knob. Opens the door. Goes inside.

I hover on the threshold. I can see my mom and dad in the living room. They turn when they see me, their faces mixed with emotions. But also relief. Like they were afraid I might not come back at all and they're glad I actually did.

I can smell dinner simmering on the stove.

I can see through the living room to the kitchen. To the table set for all five of us. For my whole family.

I take one step and then another, until I'm through the front door, too.

Until I'm home.

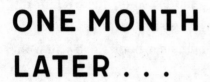

ONE MONTH LATER . . .

The urgent care clinic isn't crowded.

I sign in at the front desk and hand over my insurance card.

Nico stands by my side. Mrs. Noble is here, just in case, but she's confident I have all I need, so she takes a seat in a chair in the waiting room and lets me do the talking.

"I'd like to see Dr. Villapando," I say. "I'm here for my vaccinations. He told me he'd see me if I had my legal paperwork." I hold up a folder and pat it.

The young woman behind the front desk studies my card. Studies me. "Have a seat and we'll call you in. It shouldn't be long. It's been a slow day."

"Thank you."

Nico and I sit in two empty seats next to his mom.

I'm too anxious to thumb through any of the celebrity magazines on the table next to me. I simply sit. And wait. Nico puts his hand on my knee to keep it from bouncing.

I'm on sensory overload. There are voices behind the door to the hallway. The sharp smell of antiseptic. Soft shoes shuffling. Pens clicking. Keyboards tapping. Bright fluorescent lights buzzing and flickering.

A patient with his arm in a sling enters and walks to the counter to sign in. And then the nurse opens the door to the hallway and calls my name.

"Well," I say, standing up and looking at Nico and his mom. "Here I go."

"Would you like us to come back with you?" Mrs. Noble asks.

"Nope. I need to do this on my own."

Nico hooks his pinkie finger with mine. "See you on the other side."

I laugh. "Way to make it not sound scary."

"Ready?" the nurse asks.

I stand up straight. Smooth out my cardigan. "You have no idea."

I follow her to the nurses' station in the hallway behind the door, where she takes my vitals. She weighs and measures me, then shuffles me off to one of the exam rooms, where I sit on the oh-so-familiar paper-covered table and wait for Dr. Villapando.

He isn't at all surprised to see me.

"You did it," he says, holding his hand up for a high five.

I slap his hand. "I did. Where do we start? I can pull up a makeup vaccine schedule." I thumb through my folder.

He gently pushes it away. "I've already researched everything. I got curious when you came in demanding your shots the first time." He shrugs. Smiles. "I guess I had a pretty good feeling you'd be back with everything we needed." He rubs his hands together. "We should start with the Tdap vaccination today. That's tetanus, diphtheria, and pertussis, also known as whooping cough. It'll be two doses. One today and the next one four weeks from now. How does that sound?"

"It sounds good. I trust you."

He stands up and the stool slides back behind him. "Let me just prep the shot."

He heads out the door and I sit and wait. My eyes dart to posters and ibuprofen dosage charts and a glass jar of otoscope specula next to the sink until Dr. Villapando returns with a small black tray like you'd get your bill on at a restaurant.

"Okay," he says, putting on latex gloves. He wipes the top of my arm clean with rubbing alcohol, holds up the syringe, and flicks it once like he's swatting a mosquito. "You ready?"

"Will it hurt?"

"A little."

"Okay." I drag in a breath. Squinch my eyes shut. "Go."

"It'll feel like a little pinch, but it'll be over before you know it."

He stabs my arm with the needle, and I hiss through my teeth. It hurts more than a pinch. I remember plunging the EpiPen into Nico's thigh and counting.

One.

Two.

Three.

And then my shot is over. So quick. Like Nico's EpiPen, something so important, so vital, takes literal seconds.

"All done." I open my eyes as Dr. Villapando fastens a small circular Band-Aid to my arm. "I usually pass out lollipops." He raises his eyebrows at me. "Want one?"

"I'll take a lollipop."

He pulls a yellow one from the front pocket of his lab coat. "Lemon okay?"

I rip off the plastic cover. "Lemon is perfect."

"Okay, then." Dr. Villapando shoves the used syringe and latex gloves into an orange hazardous waste receptacle attached to the wall and gathers his little restaurant waiter tray. "See you again in four weeks. I'll have a lollipop waiting."

"See you then, Dr. Villapando. And thank you."

He shakes my hand. "My pleasure, Juniper."

I follow him out of the exam room. He heads to

another patient in another room, and I head back to Nico and his mom. I don't *feel* any different, but I also know I'm not the same person who walked in here. I can't help but smile.

Nico stands up, excited, when he sees me.

"All good?" he asks.

"All great."

AUTHOR'S NOTE

While *A Shot at Normal* is a work of fiction, it was inspired by reality. In reality, the World Health Organization (WHO) declared the measles to be eliminated in the United States in 2000. At the writing of this book, that eliminated status is threatened due to more and more diagnosed cases of measles every year.

The anti-vax movement is largely responsible for this resurgence, gaining momentum from a now debunked study in 1998 that linked the MMR vaccine to autism. Sadly, this movement, by continuing to spread misinformation about the safety of vaccines, puts the most vulnerable populations—babies, the elderly, and those with compromised immune systems—at the highest risk.

While 95 percent of kindergartners in the US are up-to-date on their vaccinations, an article published by *The Washington Post* noted that the percentage of unvaccinated children in the United States "has quadru-pled since 2001" ("Percentage of Young U.S. Kids Who Don't Get Vaccinated Has Quadrupled since 2001," Lena H. Sun, October 11, 2018).

I came to Juniper's story when I began to envision what the teen years of children whose parents chose not to vaccinate them as babies might look like. Once they were old enough to understand, would they agree with their parents' choices or question them? What if those choices kept them from something they really wanted, like attending public school or participating in extra-curricular activities? At what point does a person have the right to make their own medical choices? Is it eigh-teen years old? Or should someone younger, like Juni-per, have that right? And if so, what might the journey to earning that right look like? What could be gained? What could be lost? These are just a few of the questions I wanted to try to answer in *A Shot at Normal*.

Certainly, as we learn and grow, it's important to question things. I hope Juniper's story will inspire read-ers to examine some of the tough questions in their own lives.

May they be lucky enough to find the answers.

ACKNOWLEDGMENTS

Sometimes characters jump in front of you, grabbing you by the shoulders and begging you to tell their story. That's what Juniper Jade did to me. I'm so thankful for everyone who helped me bring her words to the page.

To Joy Peskin, my brilliant editor. Thank you for having faith that we would find our next story and for sticking by me and cheering me on through the ups and downs of the journey. Your steadfast support means more to me than you could ever know, and it's truly an honor to work with you.

To Kate Testerman, my equally brilliant agent. Thank you for always believing in me and for being tirelessly optimistic throughout every step of the publishing process. I am forever grateful to you and so honored to be part of the KT Literary family.

To Aurora Parlagreco, the talented designer of the wonderful cover of *A Shot at Normal*. Thank you for perfectly capturing so much of Juniper's story. To Elizabeth Lee, thank you for being extraordinarily patient, kind, and reassuring during edits. And to the entire team at Macmillan/FSG, thank you for your endless support of my books and me. I'm a very lucky author.

To Elise Robins and Stacy Wise, my first readers. Thank you for finding what needed to be fixed and loving what worked. This book is better because of you.

To Jeff Zentner, the person I definitely needed on the other end of a panicked email one afternoon. Thank you for your valuable insight into some of the legal bits of Juniper's story and for your continued support over the years.

To the incredible community of young adult authors, especially Marci Lyn Curtis, Shea Ernshaw, Laurie Elizabeth Flynn, Jeff Garvin, Kerry Kletter, Shannon Parker, Amber Smith, Amy Spalding, Kali Wallace, and Darcy Woods: thank you for supporting and inspiring me. To the passionate YA book bloggers and librarians and booksellers, thank you for the amazing work you do and for sharing my books with readers. And to the best cheering section ever, Carol Adler, Elise Adler, Brooke Barnum, Lori Carter, Louisa Cushman, Laura DePetra, Jenny Fix, Brooke Hodess, Julie Laing, Gus Mastrapa, Kat Monk, Jenny Moore, Lisa Pak, Carli Parker, Gwynn Parker, Michelle Phillips, Missy Robertson, Mike Shore, Amy Slack, Molly Sampson (an extra hug to you for walking me through some of the legal parts of Juniper's story), Geri Shapiro, Melody Stanger, Dina Stern, Mariano Svidler, Jane Tate, Aliza Zarcoff, and Stacey Zarcoff, thank you so much!

To my mom, my biggest fan, thank you for always being excited about every little thing. You remind me to celebrate it all, too. And to my brother, Michael, thank you for being almost as excited as Mom.

And lastly, to Jon and Kai. You two are my everything, and I couldn't pursue this writing dream without your patience and support. Thank you. I love you forever and ever. And ever.